# The
# Midwives

# The Midwives

## ANNA SCHOFIELD

Harper
North

HarperNorth
Windmill Green
24 Mount Street
Manchester M2 3NX

A division of
HarperCollins*Publishers*
1 London Bridge Street
London SE1 9GF

www.harpercollins.co.uk

HarperCollins*Publishers*
Macken House, 39/40 Mayor Street Upper
Dublin 1, D01 C9W8, Ireland

First published by HarperNorth in 2024

1 3 5 7 9 10 8 6 4 2

PB ISBN: 978-0-00-871385-0

Printed and bound in the UK using 100% renewable electricity at CPI
Group (UK) Ltd, Croydon

This novel is entirely a work of fiction.
The names, characters and incidents portrayed in it are the work
of the author's imagination. Any resemblance to actual persons,
living or dead, events or localities is entirely coincidental.

*To women like Sue, who just carry*
*on through it all…*

# Chapter One

## Sue

I stare out at my colleagues in the audience. Each year, Darkford General Hospital holds an award ceremony. This year is different from other years for me, when it's always been a real celebration. I have to present an award, but one of us isn't here. I lean into the microphone and read the announcement from the card on the lectern in front of me.

'And the winner of the Darkford General Rising Star Award is Erica Davies, for services to midwifery.'

Erica, one third of my team, walks towards me. She looks as lost as I am.

The audience stands and cheers. I pick up the fake brass trophy and hand it to Erica. She deserves it after what she has been through. After what she had to do. One minute, all three of us were in the break room with a cup of tea and some jammy dodgers. Next minute, there's just us two, and our best friend, Katie, is behind bars.

Erica holds the trophy to her chest. She adjusts the microphone with her free hand.

'Thank you. Thank you so much. Although I feel like a bit of a fraud. Most people here, including Sue, have delivered far more babies than me.' She smiles at me, then turns back to the assembly of nurses and doctors. 'It's an absolute privilege to help children into this world. I love my job and I am only sorry that the events of the last months have happened. I just played my part. Anyone would have done the same.'

She holds the trophy high above her. A camera flashes and she turns and hurries into the wings. She played her part. That is true. My stomach flips as I think about it. *Anyone would have done the same.* She's right. But I didn't. These past seven months, the shame of not noticing what was going on has driven me to exhaustion.

The clapping and cheering subside, and I follow her off the stage. We return to our seats as the introduction is made for the next award – another Rising Star but this time for paediatrics. I sit down heavily, grateful I only had to present one award as there's only one midwifery Rising Star. Today's been a busy one. Premature twins and a lady with an adverse reaction to an epidural. After all that, I didn't feel like coming tonight. But I couldn't let Erica, or the rest of the team from the maternity department who came to support, down.

I kick off my chunky-heeled sandals under the table, and pour a glass of bubbly each for myself and Erica. She is a hero. Someone who did the right thing. But she's looking unsure now, pulling up the straps of her soft, satin evening dress. I wonder if, like me, she's afraid of what will happen next. I take her hand.

'It's OK,' I say. 'It's not long until the trial. Then we'll have answers.' She smiles and nods. My stomach is still in knots. 'I can't believe we were all sitting here last year. She was laughing with us. Drinking. I just don't understand why she did it.'

Erica shrugs. 'We'll probably never know. She'll get what she deserves.' She reconsiders her words. 'I only hope she gets the help she needs.'

So do I. These women are my life. I would even go as far as to say I love them. I've worked with Katie for almost ten years, and Erica for two. To operate the way we do to take care of mothers and their babies, we need complete trust in each other. Our team of three worked. Other members of the department would often comment on how tight-knit and organised we were.

Now I feel lost. Katie was my wing-woman. She even has a badge saying that pinned to her scrubs: *wing-woman*. We're both married, but we made time for each other. We went out at least once a month for a meal and a catch-up. Since Erica joined the department, she's come along, too. She's younger than us, but that didn't stop us getting close. She's always happy to fetch and carry and do the – often literally – shitty tasks involved in midwifery. And her sunny attitude to life has got us all through some hard times, both at work and outside.

But this sorry situation has tainted Erica too. I often wonder how she summoned up the courage to whistleblow. Despite all her optimism, she must have been sure. Unlike me. I was completely in denial.

On the ward, Katie was always at the business end. Completely skilled at every aspect of obstetrics. She was better than most of the doctors. Erica is at the mum-end. Reassuring and calming. Taking them through antenatal and making sure they knew what to expect. And me? I'm at the baby-end.

I make sure the babies have the best possible treatment and I have a qualification in special care of poorly infants. Of course, some don't make it, and those little mites still haunt me in my low moments.

But I didn't have a clue about all this. I've gone over and over it in my mind. How Katie could have duped me. How she could have lied to Adam, her husband. They don't have children, but she always said it was by choice after their first round of IVF was unsuccessful. They could have adopted, but they chose not to. Now I wonder if there's something else. Something deep inside her that went wrong.

The fifth of many awards of the night is presented and then there is an interlude. Music blasts out and there is a rush for the dancefloor. Pat Styles, a nurse from the gynae ward Erica is friendly with at work, grabs her out of her seat and drags her into the party. I stay at our table, watching as she smiles and spins to Kylie Minogue. At least I've still got her. But the rest of it feels like a divorce, where you were so sure your partner loved you and then you find out it has all been a lie.

I recall that January day, as I have so many times. Erica and Katie were with Mrs Bolton when the police arrived at the locked department door. Ian Bowers, the senior ward clerk, wore a dark grimace as he spoke to them. I lingered longer than I needed to in the linen room, hoping to catch a snippet of their conversation. I could see them through the window, pointing urgently at our department. I thought they must be after one of the patients. Never for one moment did I think it would be one of us.

Once, we had a woman who was arrested on leaving the hospital with her newborn. She'd been involved in a robbery and her waters broke on the job, so to speak. I even laughed and told myself I'd seen everything.

But I hadn't. They strode in from reception. Two male officers and one female. I followed them up the corridor as Ian led the way.

There had been extra security on the ward lately, because several women had complained they had been 'drugged'. The Practice Committee had been looking into the complaints for months. But when we looked at the patients' files and medication lists, there was nothing to suggest anything abnormal had happened. Then, four days before the police came, one of the care assistants who was serving breakfast had been unable to wake one lady. She had pressed the alarm, and everyone had rushed in. Even Katie.

I can see it now. Katie's face, full of concern. Quiet, competent Katie. Her mannerisms urgent as we helped to transfer the woman into the ICU. What did I miss?

But this police visit was unexpected. This was serious. I remember feeling a tingle of anxiety that they were here to accost a lady who was pregnant or, worse, in labour. I hurried my step until I was beside them.

'Can I ask what your business is here, please?' I said. 'It's just that we don't want to distress the ladies who are in labour.'

Ian's expression told me everything and nothing. His eyes pleading, telling me this was something else, but I couldn't process what it was. We continued into the labour ward and the police stopped. Ian went into Mrs Bolton's room. Calm, compliant Mrs Bolton. *What on earth could they want with her?* I wondered. I really was deluded.

Because, as it turned out, they didn't want Mrs Bolton. They wanted Katie. My kind, lovely friend. I stood at the door as Ian tapped her on the shoulder. She half turned towards us.

'In a minute, love. Our lady is six centimetres now.' She leaned over Mrs Bolton. 'Won't be long, love. Then you will meet your baby.'

I remember Erica made a *squee* face at that. She was always as excited as the mothers. But then Katie looked up and saw the police standing in the hallway. The colour drained from her face and her eyes found mine, questioning. Ian spoke softly.

'Just come with me, Katie. We'd like to ask you a few questions.'

I shrugged and mouthed to her the *what-the-fuck?* we usually reserve for much less serious situations. They were

6

gone. Into the meeting room at the end of the corridor. Erica was beside me. I realised I was shaking.

'Do you think it's Adam? They don't come to your place of work for nothing.'

She shook her head, blinking back tears.

We stood and waited as long as we could. But Mrs Bolton needed us, so I asked the care assistant, Julie, to tell us when Katie came out of the meeting room. It was more than an hour. Then the assistant appeared.

'They're out. But she's not happy.'

I hurried to the end of the corridor and there Katie was. Flanked on either side by a police officer. She was crying her eyes out, glasses off, mascara everywhere and her face blotchy. Her long blonde hair, usually straight as a die and tied in a ponytail, was now loose and over her shoulders. She saw me and tried to move towards me, but the police officer held her back. Then she shouted it.

'Sue! Love. Tell them. Tell them I haven't done anything. It wasn't me. I swear. I wouldn't do something like that. Tell them!'

Ian stood watching after them. He was shaking his head, rubbing his face with both hands.

'It was her,' he muttered. 'Bloody hell. It was her. You never really know someone, do you?'

I moved closer to him and spoke in a calm low voice that did not reflect the anxiety rumbling in my soul.

'What was her? What has she done?' But he went into his office and shut the door. He must have felt as shocked as we did. He was on the ward as often as we were, filling in forms and discharge sheets. Giving patients their prescriptions and physio instructions. That afternoon, the police came back to take statements. I told them it couldn't be her, that she was an angel.

But they showed me the CCTV footage. Black and white and grainy from the ancient camera at the end of the department. Katie here when she shouldn't be. Off-shift. Her long blonde hair tied back and her thick-framed glasses. Her trademark leggings under a skirt and her plain black trainers. The camera showed her back as she walked up the corridor. And a momentary side view of her glasses. Into a side ward. Ten minutes later, she left by the door at the other end.

I'd blinked at the footage as my world shattered.

And that's why Erica was presented with the award tonight. Erica was the one who caught her. She had been on shift five nights before the police came, and Katie had popped in. They hadn't spoken, but she'd seen her. The incident with the mum who couldn't wake up was the following morning. It was only after the mum had been resuscitated in the ICU – luckily, both mum and baby were fine in the end – that Erica started to suspect Katie had tampered with the bloods.

She told Ian, and he checked the CCTV. The following night, Katie was also captured on camera, off-shift and sneaking into a laundry room. When the room was checked, hidden medication was found.

I haven't seen Katie since her arrest. I asked the police if I could go to the prison where she is being held and ask her what happened. I reasoned she might tell me the truth. But they advised against it. And besides, the police didn't need my help. The cold, hard facts were already there. Amid this glitzy party, I have to face the reality. My friend and colleague was over-medicating the mums-to-be.

My mind couldn't yet fast-forward to the end-game, but the media did. They spoke to some of the expectant mums and put two and two together, and soon pressed that particular button.

She wanted a child. She drugged those women to take a baby.

## Chapter Two

This morning I arrive at work more tired than ever. Which isn't ideal, because Karen Slater, the Team Leader, has asked to see me and Erica first thing. I spot Erica going through the swinging front doors of the hospital just ahead of me, and rush to catch up with her. She looks fresher than me, although she drank more at the awards ceremony.

'What time did you get home last night, then?' I say, linking arms with her. I'd slipped out while she was still dancing.

She laughs. 'I left just after you,' she says, snuggling into me. 'I needed my beauty sleep.'

*As if.* I scoff and elbow her playfully. I always have bags under my eyes, but she never looks haggard. The ward is a stressful place at the best of times, and she's thrived under that pressure. But I'd be lying if I hadn't noticed her looking troubled since Katie's arrest. She clearly misses her as much as I do. In some ways, this has been hardest on her.

We reach the door to Karen's office. I can see her through the glass panel. She's only been in post about eighteen months, but I've known her longer. She's good company when she wants to be, but I am sometimes guarded with her because it's clear she doesn't fully understand what being a midwife involves. She knows about the practicalities. But I'm not sure she understands the deep connection we have with our patients. And, more than once, I've heard her gossiping about a colleague, which means she probably talks about all of us.

This morning, I hope she'll talk about Katie. I can't imagine her in prison. Trapped in a cell. I'm hungry for any scrap of new information about her, but scared at the same time. My god. How could I not have seen her? How could I not have known?

I've spent all my time since her arrest divided. One minute I think, *she couldn't have. Not Katie. She's lovely*. And then I think that she must have. But there's no time for that now. I feel my mouth go dry and my stomach flips. But I go into Karen's office, anyway. Because that's what we do here. Carry on.

Erica follows me in. Karen gestures for us to help ourselves to tea or coffee from the thermos pump pots in the corner. Erica opts for milky coffee and I stick to tea that I sip slowly – I have a slight headache coming on from last night's bubbly. When we're both seated opposite her desk, Karen looks up from her papers.

'Erica. Sue. Thank you for coming.'

Erica looks at her. 'Before we start, I'd like to say thank you for last night. I was so thrilled to get the award.'

I feel a warmth between us, so comforting in the current situation. I speak up.

'Is there any news about Katie? I'd like us to be kept as up-to-date as possible. So we can reassure the patients.'

*Like* is a misleading word. I'm certain I'm not going to like any news Karen can give us.

She nods and shuffles through some papers. 'I'm afraid there is. The thing is, there have been two more accusations. Two more ladies have come forward.' She passes us a report each. 'It's all in there.'

I feel darkness descend. Two more patients. Two poor pregnant women who had been abused without me realising. I try to read it, but I can hardly focus. Though I see the dates. The same month as the other ones. And only weeks apart.

My voice trembles. 'I'm so sorry, Karen. I should have…'

She slips out of her formal manager role and into the friend who has sat in countless bars with us after work.

'No. No, love. None of this is your fault. It was hidden from everyone.'

Erica shakes her head. 'This is terrible. I don't know what to say.'

Karen gets up to pour herself a coffee.

'I can't thank you two enough,' she says. 'The information you have both given made sure we could stop all this. But the media are all over it now. As you know, they've reported most of the public case details, and interviewed some of the mums-to-be. But they've started to approach staff now.'

I do know. I can't open the internet without seeing an article about Katie or her marriage. Or an account from one of the ladies we looked after about how terrified she was. Karen is right, I concede. It's just a matter of time until they are trying to speak to us.

'I've seen this sort of thing before. Hounding people for comments and disrupting the department. Things are going to have to change. It wouldn't be fair of me to keep you in the spotlight, working as staff midwives. Not after all you have done.'

I freeze. They're taking our jobs away? For a moment, I want to retort that *I* wasn't the one who reported Katie. I didn't do it. And the truth is that all I want, deep down, is for things to be back as they were.

But Karen is telling me that things will never be as they were again. Because *things as they were* would mean women suffering. And their babies in danger.

'So,' Karen goes on, 'I want to offer you both a promotion. Sue, you will become my deputy. It's a role the hospital has been looking to create for a while. You can still be hands-on when needs be, but it will give you a chance to move into management and, more importantly, policy.'

I stare at her. Management. It's been a goal of mine, for later in my career. Maybe this *is* later. Yet it feels like a consolation prize now.

She continues. 'You'll be office-based with some remote days. And you'll have some responsibility for budgets and procedure.'

I reel. I've dreamed about this, but now it feels like it's too much.

Karen hasn't finished. 'And Erica will move to Head of Outreach. We have some very scared ladies out there. Ladies who were Katie's outreach. Women she saw at ante-natal and went out to visit. We are finding there is a high attendance refusal rate, unsurprisingly, and we need Erica's skills to reassure them.'

I shudder. Attendance refusal. That means much more risk for mums and babies. And risk is something we need to reduce, especially now.

Karen turns to Erica and leans in. 'I need you to go out and do an initial assessment of all the ladies whose due dates are within six weeks. Check everything. We can't afford for anything else to go wrong now.' I stare at the frown lines gathering on her brow. We can't afford. I get a familiar feeling. One I've had about Karen before. That she likes to cover her tracks. She sees my look and qualifies her statement. 'For the ladies' sakes, primarily. Of course. And Erica is the obvious choice for this role.'

Erica's cheeks have gone pink. She's never been comfort-able accepting compliments, and it takes her a moment to collect herself. 'Thank you so much,' she says. 'It's an opportunity I can't turn down. But I'll be sad to not be working with Sue. We're a team.'

I nod. Yes. We were a team. But now all that is changing. I take her hand. 'You'll be perfect.'

She grins. 'So will you.'

Karen laughs. 'Congratulations, ladies. I know it's a difficult time. And I have to stress that this will be a time of transition. You'll probably have to step up and cover the maternity ward in your old roles as well as learning your new jobs. But it will be better for you in the long run. We'll move some staff midwives over and recruit. And, as always, the mums come first.'

She leans forward. She is very pale, and her face has thinned out since the winter. She opens her mouth to speak but thinks better of it and gets up to shut her office door. She sits back down heavily. When she speaks again, her voice is lower. 'Look. I know I can trust you two. I wanted to let you know something else. We've had the bloods back from the incident. It's very strange. I had to read it twice, but it looks like a mix of morphine and scopolamine.'

She looks at us, eyebrows raised.

I beat Erica to it. 'Twilight Sleep? Are you kidding me?'

It seems very strange that a super-competent nurse like Katie would resort to such an old, and risky, method. But everything about this situation is strange and unnerving. I don't even want to consider what she could have used – the very thought makes me feel sick – but she knew all about medications.

I know all about Twilight Sleep. When I was doing my Nursing and Midwifery degree, there was a nurse who was into everything gothic Victorian. She talked about Twilight Sleep as one of the tenets of feminism. It was the first widely used anaesthetic for childbirth and, as well as removing pain, it helped women forget about the experience.

I will Karen not to ask me if Katie had ever talked about Twilight Sleep. My heart sinks as I remember her laughing about it.

*Bloody hell. I bet they thought they'd died and gone to heaven.* That's what she said about it.

She was right. And, if Katie's plan had succeeded, the mum would have been completely out of it, from the stages of labour to delivery. What I can't fully accept is exactly how she planned to kidnap the child. What when the baby was born? *What then, Katie?*

But Karen doesn't ask me about Katie. Instead, she hands some buff folders to Erica. 'These are the ladies who are very worried about coming in. They all live out of town, and our risk assessment tells us they need the most reassurance.'

'Thank you,' says Erica, taking the folders. My heart warms as she looks humble and proud. 'I won't let you down.'

Karen smiles at her. Then meets our eyes. 'One last thing,' she says. 'I'd like you to try to avoid the reporters. A staff member has already reported being offered a substantial amount of money to sell their story. If anyone accepts such an offer, it will be another nightmare for the legal team.'

I feel fire rise inside me. This situation is a nightmare for everyone. For the patients, and everyone who trusted Katie. But something about Karen's body language – the way she's rubbing the back of her neck and suddenly avoiding my gaze – tells me the hospital's *reputation* is what this whole conversation has really been about. I've seen it before. Not with Karen, but with senior managers offering jobs in return for silence.

'So, are these promotions a bribe, then?' I blurt out, before I can stop myself. 'To stop us talking?'

Erica's eyes widen. 'They're not, are they, Karen?' she says, a reproachful edge creeping into her voice. Neither of us would ever sell our story. But we deserve to know if we're being manipulated.

Karen stands up and leans over the desk. 'No, Sue. It's not a bribe. You both deserve these roles, and you would have got them anyway in time. But we also need to keep you and Erica safe. The whole department is under investigation and media scrutiny, and I have to consider what is best for all involved. As I said, you will still have to go on the wards until a full hand-over, but your new jobs mean you will be there as little as possible and you have the roles you deserve and would get in time, in any case. So, it's a win-win, isn't it?'

I try to breathe deeply. I tell myself I will not let my temper get the better of me, even as I raise my suspicions about jobs for silence. I will know soon enough what happened. I turn to Erica and see she is almost in tears. She stands. Her legs shake a little.

'Can I go now?' she says.

Karen nods. 'Yeah. Since you've accepted the post, it's effective immediately. And, again, thanks.'

Erica looks at me and tries to smile. I choke up. None of this feels right. Karen is thanking her for grassing Katie up. And these new jobs will change everything for us. I'll miss us being on the rota together. But better pay and better hours are hard to argue with. I can just see Tom's face when I tell him there'll eventually be no more night shifts.

Karen waits until Erica has gone, then she flops in the chair.

'Good one, that. She'll do well.' She sips her coffee. 'Are you up for the job, then? I was worried you might leave.'

I scoff. 'Leave? Me? Never.' A memory flashes into my mind of me, Katie and Erica huddling in the corridor outside the ward. We're pretending we're a girl band about to go onstage at a gig, then we open the doors with a roar, and laugh until we cry. 'I guess I'll just have to get used to it, won't I?'

Karen nods. Her barriers come down and she sags. 'It's a fucking mess. I have to admit, it's got to me.'

I know how she feels. We barely discuss the case with anyone. It's too awful. And I'm sure we're all afraid that, if we say too much, people will think we were involved in some way.

She pauses, then looks straight at me. 'And to make it worse, she's denying it all.'

I freeze. *Denying it?* 'What? But I thought…'

'No. She's pleaded not guilty. Says she won't admit to something she didn't do.'

I can't believe it. This is not the Katie I know. She's straight down the line, she is. Or so I thought. 'But the CCTV?'

She shrugs. 'I know. And all the other times were when she was on-shift.' She stops and thinks. 'I probably shouldn't be telling you all this. But with the trial looming, you'll find out, anyway.'

We'd been expecting it to happen quickly, but not this quickly. Even at the start of the investigation, it was rumoured to be an open-and-shut case. Then several of the women who had been drugged formed a pressure group, and their demands for an early court date went viral on social media. There was a flurry of posts demanding Katie be banged up and worse. Shortly afterwards, a big case in Manchester fell through, leaving a gap in the court calendar. And so the date was set.

'The other thing that's been nagging at me is,' says Karen, 'well... There's a pattern emerging.'

'What pattern?' I ask, bracing myself. A sinking feeling floods me. I didn't think it could get any worse.

Karen grimaces. 'It's the victims. They're all from a certain demographic.'

I think about the final victim. Around twenty. Beautiful blonde hair. Almost childlike herself. 'Go on.'

'They were all under twenty-one. Some of them were just out of college. All first pregnancy.'

I sigh. How *could* she? I stare at the report Karen has slammed on the desk, trying to read it upside down. She sees me and puts her hand over it.

'Sorry. But I can't let you see it. The police have warned us that we have to keep details to ourselves until trial. As head of department, I had to check it over. Sign it. You know, the details I gave. But I can't share it with you.'

Since this began, I've devoured every piece of information about the case. It doesn't seem fair that Karen can see the report and I can't. Nothing about this seems fair. But I have to know what happened. Exactly what happened. 'Are they all OK still? The mums and the babies?'

She nods. 'They are. All the mums have been offered counselling, just like us.'

Karen, Erica and several of the other midwives took up the hospital's offer of free talking therapy after Katie's arrest. But I didn't. Not because I didn't need it. More because, with Katie missing from our team, we were busier than ever. I wonder now if I should have.

'In Katie's favour,' Karen continues, 'she asked if they were OK, too.' She pauses. 'I went to visit her at the weekend.'

I summon the words I've been desperate to ask someone for months. 'Is she... how is she?'

Karen pales. 'She's not good. She keeps repeating that she didn't do it. Over and over. We've shown her the CCTV, and she can't explain it. She says she was somewhere else that night but can't corroborate it.' My eyes are welling up now. She continues in a strained but measured tone, flicking through the pages of the report between us. 'But one thing's for sure. She's facing a custodial sentence. A long one. And no matter what we think and how much we liked her, she deserves what she gets.'

# Chapter Three

## Leila

I don't want to be here.

The clock's ticking down to my appointment, and I'm alone in the waiting room at Darkford. I nearly didn't come, but the woman on the phone made not showing up feel scarier. *You've developed placenta previa, Leila. We need to scan you urgently.*

I don't know how I can trust anything now. It's all been too much. First Mum, and the funeral. Then that Katie Withers getting arrested. I didn't believe it when I heard it. She'd been my midwife right from my first appointment. She'd been so nice then, offering to come out to see me, to save me the long journey to the hospital.

Now, I can't even think about that woman in my house. In my baby's nursery. Touching me.

I lift myself out of the hard plastic seat and walk over to the vending machine. I've been getting these panicky feelings whenever I think about this place. Dry mouth and a dodgy tummy. The fact that Ben's still not here isn't helping.

I take out my phone. No messages. I know he calls in on Deano on Wednesdays. He must be on his way, though. He promised.

I'll make sure, anyway. My fingers hover over the buttons – I'm unsure how to phrase it without sounding clingy.

*Are you nearly here, love? The appointment's at ten x*

I scan the rows of crisps and chocolate bars, then decide I'm not hungry and, reluctantly, return to my seat. The seconds pass, and I watch the other expectant mothers sitting in silence. This isn't the cheery, chatty place it used to be. I bet the others are thinking the same as me. *Was it my baby she wanted? Was she acting alone? Am I still in danger?* I wonder how many people in this room are like me – 'the women affected'. That's what the hospital called us in the letter they sent out, claiming it was all fine now.

As we wait quietly, the nurses move around doing their job. Carrying files and leading people into tiny cubicles. I can feel my heart beating fast. This isn't at all how I imagined my final weeks of pregnancy. I thought it would be all choosing baby clothes and chatting about breastfeeding with other mums-to-be. Ben with me at antenatal classes, holding my hand. I swallow hard. Mum getting ready to be a grandma. She was really looking forward to it.

I miss her so much. She was straightforward. Honest, but kind. When I first told her I was expecting, she said twenty years old was young to have a baby, but it was a good thing Ben was older because, at twenty-three, he had a good job, and was more likely to settle down. She promised she would be there for me too. But she hasn't been. For almost six months now. I'm just glad it was quick, and she didn't suffer.

My phone beeps. I fumble to see Ben's message, but it isn't him. It's my alarm telling me there's five minutes to go until the appointment. I look at the board on the wall. Staff midwives today are Sue Springer and Erica Davies. There is a space underneath their slide-in name holders, and I go cold as the realisation hits me – that's where Katie's name would be.

She told me everything would be fine. I explained all about Mum and how Ben and I had moved into her house when we got together. Katie was so happy for me. She arranged everything for me, even helping me set up these alerts on my phone.

Whenever she came over, though, I got the feeling she never wanted to leave. Sometimes she'd bring some doughnuts or buns, and we'd sit for hours, drinking tea and chatting. About my job at the hairdresser's, what would happen at the birth, and what my plans were for my family's future.

Ben and I had decided that we wouldn't find out the gender. I'd seen gender reveal parties on Instagram and read about them in more detail, and I expect the girls from the salon would have arranged one for me, but Ben didn't want any fuss. I didn't mind, but I sometimes got the sense Katie did. It was like she wanted me to argue with him about it, or even go behind his back. *Don't you want to know? I would, if it was my baby.*

Like I said to her, I don't care if it's a girl or a boy. Either way, my child will have my mum's maiden name as their middle name. A precious part of her and me. Baby Carlton Summers. Or Clarke, if Ben and I had got married. Which we never have because of all this. No gender reveal party. No engagement party, because I was organising a funeral. And no wedding, because my midwife was arrested for attempted murder.

Ben says there will be plenty of time for us to get married when the baby's here, then all three of us can go on honeymoon. It isn't how I'd imagined it but, when I told Katie, she thought it was a great idea. I remember her going gooey-eyed, talking about tiny flower-girl dresses and pageboy suits as she took my blood pressure.

When she was arrested, the liaison officer asked me if she had acted strangely or done anything suspicious. I told her I didn't think she had, but how would I know? I always see the best in people. Mum often told me to be more careful, but even she would've agreed that we have to put our trust in people like Katie. They are trained and we aren't, and we are at their mercy. So, if Katie was trying to harm me, I didn't see any signs of it. Once she made a comment about Ben being flaky, and asked if I was sure I could cope if he didn't help more with the baby. Another time, I thought I heard her crying in the bathroom when she went for a wee. But none of it made me doubt her. Then again, neither did anyone else doubt her. Until she was caught.

I look at my phone again. My hands are shaking, and I try to make them stop. No message. I wanted my pregnancy to be perfect, but so much has gone wrong. I have to push the upset down because I need to get through this, but it's pressing against my chest, and I wipe away a tear.

Then a midwife walks in. She looks different from Katie – younger and prettier, with dark brown hair and blue eyes. She smiles at me. I feel better for a moment as she looks kind, but then I remember what the other one did with a nice smile on her face.

'Leila Summers?'

As she calls my name, everything goes into slow motion. My hands cover my stomach and I hold myself tight. Somehow, I am nodding, and my mouth forms a smile. But I don't feel like smiling. I feel like running out of here and never coming back.

The midwife comes over to me. 'Leila. Hi. I'm Erica Davies. I'm going to take you for your scan, but first I want to have a word with you to make sure you feel safe.'

Her eyes are warm, and I feel my body relax a little. I heave myself up and suddenly my baby kicks. My hand goes back to my belly and my gaze meets Erica's.

'Oh,' she says with a laugh. 'Baby's excited too? Not long now.'

*Not long.* I've been given a due date but read on the internet it goes from your last period, which would make it two weeks longer. I counted back so many times, marking various dates on a calendar. Then I read an article saying baby can come any time. I want to ask Erica, but my sensible, non-panicky self tells me to just stick to their due date. I feel like asking again will make me look young and stupid.

She walks towards a cubicle, and I follow her. I check the corridor outside in case Ben is waiting there, but there is still no sign of him. We go into the cubicle, and she shuts the door. I feel short of breath and I want to ask her to leave the door open, but I can't speak. She taps on a keyboard, and I pass her my Mum and Baby Book. I can't bear to see all the notes that evil woman made in there. Erica opens it and scans the pages, then turns to me.

'Are you OK? The past months must have been difficult for you. Do you have anyone here with you?'

I sigh. Am I OK? A question I have asked myself a lot recently. 'Yes. Well, still getting over the loss of my mum. She had a heart attack. And my boyfriend… partner was going to be here, but he's late.'

She nods and looks at her computer screen.

'Well, when he arrives, someone will show him through. And for this appointment, I'll be here throughout to support you.' She scrolls down on my file. 'So, I see you live in Dobcross. Which is quite a distance. Have you planned how you'll get here when Baby is coming?'

I nod.

'Yes. Ben will bring me.'

My heart speeds up again. Will he bring me? He doesn't drive and taxis take ages to get to my house. What if he's not there and I have to wait to even phone a taxi? He's not here when he said he would be today. What if I'm on my own in labour? But the midwife, Erica, has already typed in that he will, and she's speaking again.

'And it says here you had outreach visits from your previous midwife.'

I stare at her. 'Katie? Yes. She came to my home. I've already spoken to one of your liaison people about it when I came to my appointment last month.'

She nods and looks steadily back at me. 'Look, I know this is difficult. But I can assure you, you're in safe hands with me. I've been specially tasked with helping all the ladies who have been affected. If you ever have questions, you can speak to my team leader. We want you to be as comfortable as possible and, most of all, to keep appointments. We want you and your baby to be safe.'

'Did you know her?' I suddenly feel like I can trust Erica. Like she really is on my side. Like I can ask her anything. 'I want to know if I was in any danger.'

She pauses and breathes in deeply. 'Yes, I worked with Katie. But I don't know very much about what happened or how. I think, for now, it's better if we let the authorities do their work and focus on you and Baby. It will be dealt with. You are all right now, love. If anything, this is the safest the hospital has ever been, because everything is being constantly checked.'

I relax a little. She's right. 'Did you trust her, too?'

She turns back to the screen. 'I can't talk anymore about it. I'm so sorry. And I know you must be very scared. But I'm on your side. Do you want to check if your partner is here before we go down to the scan room?'

I nod. *Scared* is an understatement. I think about asking her if she can prescribe me something to stop me being worried, but she has closed my file. I can ask later on. I open the door and step outside. The room is half-full of pregnant women and most of them have people with them. Ben isn't here. I look at my phone. No messages. I step back into the cubicle.

'No. he must have been delayed.'

She smiles. 'Don't worry, I'll be there for this one. Shall we go?'

# Chapter Four

## Sue

In the car after work, I still don't know how to feel about the promotion. Instead, Karen's painful words about Katie hit me again and again. They ricochet off everything I thought I knew. *She deserves what she gets.*

I start the engine and grip the steering wheel. I should go home. The police have told us not to contact anyone in Katie's life, besides the witnesses at the hospital.

But as I turn left out the carpark – the opposite direction to my house – I've made up my mind. I've known I would do this at some point. There's someone I need to visit.

I drive through the nearby estate and onto the back roads. I'm not sure if I'll ever see Katie again, but what I can do is the next best thing. I'm not the closest person to her. Adam is. As I drive through the tree-lined avenues towards their house, I don't know exactly what I am looking for, but I know Adam will tell me his side of the story. I need another soul who is feeling this like I am. Tom and I used to go out with her and Adam. We'd go for a curry, then to a bar. Tom and Adam would drink beer and talk work; Katie and I would sip cocktails and talk shit. And all the while she was planning this.

Of course, the press had got hold of all the details of their marriage and their struggles to conceive. Each time I'd read a new article about it, factual and stark on my phone screen, I'd felt terrible for Adam. We were all friends after all, and I can't imagine what he's going through.

Once I'm parked outside their house, I get out of the car and walk up the path. I expect to hear Polly, Katie's dog, barking, but it is completely silent. I ring the doorbell, and, after a pause, Adam opens the door. He's lost weight since I last saw him, on my birthday night out before Katie was arrested. It flickers through my mind that she was a bit sullen then. Katie was never a dancer, but she shrugged Adam away when he tried to get her on the dancefloor. He stares at me, unsmiling.

'You took your time.'

I follow him into the lounge.

'They told me I couldn't come.'

He sits. 'Yet here you are, anyway.'

He is silent for a moment then. I can sense his grief. His loss.

'Our Lisa's got Polly,' he says. 'It wasn't working with Katie not being here. I can't work thirteen-hour shifts and look after the dog.' He looks around. 'They took her laptop and some of her stuff. Her workbag. Shoes. And a phone I didn't know she had.' His voice trembles. Is Katie's big, tough, paramedic bloke about to cry? 'Hidden behind a bath panel, it was. Not very original.'

I blink at him. 'So, someone else was in on it?'

I realise in that moment I was still holding onto the fraying thread of hope that someone else is responsible for this. I look round Katie's lounge at the family photos. I'm in some of them. There's one of her, Erica and me at the previous year's prizegiving ceremony, when our department got an award. We are smiling, arms around each other. Adam wipes his eyes.

'No. No, there isn't. Just her.' He sobs, gulping air. 'Just her keeping tabs on things secretly. I heard one of the police say people use burner phones to keep track of victims.'

I feel my face burn. *Victims*. I am trying to process this as he continues.

'One of the women in the ambulance control room asked if I was her accomplice. She asked me straight out. As if I was waiting in a fucking getaway car while she drugged someone and took their baby.'

I am shocked into silence. Adam has always said it how it is. Everyone else has danced around the issue, and not a single person has said it like that before. *She tried to drug someone and take their baby.* I go over it again. The evidence that she was planning to do this. The women who struggled to wake. Their stories about a blonde nurse with a surgical mask on. The CCTV. The hidden medication. It's run through my own mind that they have no evidence she would take a baby. But why else would she do it? *Why else?* Somewhere in the blur of my confusion, I remember the accusations are attempted murder. Of the mums. But every-one has jumped to the same conclusion. She did it to take a baby.

'I'm moving out this week,' he says. 'I'm going to stay with our Lisa until the trial is over. My solicitor says it'll be like a media circus here.' He composes himself. 'I don't even know if I'll come back.'

*Poor guy,* I think. Forced out of his own home. But, as painful as this must be for him to talk about, there's more I need to know. I broach my next question carefully. 'Have you… seen her?'

He shakes his head. 'No. They offered, but I can't.' He straightens. 'You're still not sure she did it, are you? I was like that. I couldn't believe it. But it's true. I know this isn't what you want to hear. But she'd been all quiet for a while. Acting strange, being secretive. I couldn't work it out. We had a few arguments about it.' He pauses to take a deep breath. 'And now it's all over the internet. Some woman at the clinic telling tales. Making two and two make five and suggesting I knew. The press have picked it up and now it's all over the internet.' He holds his phone up and shows me an article I have already scoured dozens of times. 'They're saying I must have known. But I swear I didn't. That night, when she was caught on the CCTV, I woke up and she wasn't in our bed. Then, on the other times it happened, she said she was with you. Or Erica. But they checked the shift patterns, and she was lying.' He runs his hand over the fabric of the sofa. 'She's still lying. Saying it wasn't her. But she can't explain where she was on any of those nights.

I asked my solicitor what she said. No comment. She had no fucking comment on where she was.'

I can't speak. So, she used *me* as an excuse. And she used Erica. Lovely, bright Erica who trusted her.

'They're all saying it's because I couldn't give her a baby,' Adam says. 'Do you know how that makes me feel? After the IVF, she seemed to be accepting we couldn't have kids. She never once told me how desperate she was.'

I take a deep breath.

'She never told me either,' I say. 'I had no clue. It wasn't just you, love.'

He's nodding. But I can see that he doesn't feel any better. And why would he? Their future together disappeared overnight.

'Yeah, well, if I'm honest, it hadn't been right for a long time. But, yeah. What the fuck did she think was going to happen?'

I've been asking myself the same question over and over. I suppose, if she ever saw her plan through to its grim conclusion, she would have run away with her victim's baby. And that means I – we – would have lost either way. She didn't care about me or Adam or anyone except herself.

I shake my head. 'I honestly don't know. But it must have been hell for her. Working all that time with babies when…'

He snorts. His face is beetroot red. 'Hard for *her*? What about those women? She almost scared them to death. And what about me? And you? And Erica? She'd had you both round here the week before, playing happy families. All the while, she was scheming behind our backs.'

I shudder at the memory of that evening. It had seemed so normal. She'd made us spag bol, opened a bottle of wine. We'd laughed about one of the patients who'd wanted her dog there at the birth. But she knew then what she was going to do. She'd already had who-knows-how-many practice runs.

I run my hands through my hair. 'Adam, I'm sorry. It must be horrendous for you.'

He nods. 'Yeah. I've gone over it thousands of times. How I didn't know. How she could have even thought about it. I bet you have, too? But we've just got to remember that it's not our fault. The only thing that's wrong with this is Katie.'

## Chapter Five

### Leila

As I round the corner onto Mum's road – *my* road, now – I can see we have company.

Ben's friend Dean's car is parked outside the house, and the garden gate is left open and banging in the breeze. As I walk up the pathway, I can hear the dull thud of bass.

I need to remember what Erica said this morning. That the past is gone and now I just need to think about my baby. Our baby. But it's so hard for me to be focused when Ben clearly isn't.

It wasn't always like this. When I first met Ben, he treated me like a princess. I was fresh out of school – he'd just graduated and landed his fancy job. I knew it was serious when, after only six months, he asked me to move in with him. I thought that high-rise in Manchester was so glamorous and grown-up. We'd spend long evenings with a bottle of wine in our seventh-floor flat, looking out over the glittering cityscape below us, talking about all our plans for the future. We wanted to travel overseas, throw parties for our friends, climb the career ladder together.

It didn't matter to me that the flat was tiny, or that all our furniture was second-hand. I thought it made us trendy and quirky. It took me weeks to notice that the lift was always broken, and the stairwell smelled like pee. But back then, none of it mattered, because Ben was my world. He brought me flowers and those cakes I loved from the bakers in the Arndale. We only had eyes for each other and I fell deeply in love with him.

Then Ben stopped enjoying his job and got a new one – an administrative office role that didn't pay as well, and had shorter hours. When I got pregnant, he said it would mean he'd have more time to help with the childcare. I had some cash put away from my hairdressing job, and we were just about managing. But there's no way I'd have coped there with a baby, lugging a pram up all those flights of stairs. I sometimes wonder what we would have done, if Mum hadn't left us so suddenly.

The sickly stink of weed hits me as I turn my key in the unlocked door. Walking down the hallway, past the lounge, I see them sitting around an XBox. Two grown men playing games. Before I pull the door closed, I catch Ben glancing at me, then turning back to the screen.

The whole house smells of them. I shut myself in the kitchen, opening the back door to let air in. There are dirty cups in the sink and plates with toast crumbs on the work-top. I can't work out what I'm more upset by – the fact that *this* is what he was doing while I was in hospital, or the thought of Mum's face if she could see the state of her kitchen.

But, as I keep reminding myself, this is *our* house now. I've been painting, making it all nice for when our baby is here. As nice as I can make it, anyway, with the little money we have. I can barely afford the bills without breaking into my tiny savings or the money Mum left. And Ben's putting away any spare cash he can find for the wedding.

I hear voices in the hallway and the front door slamming. The kitchen door opens in synchronisation with a boy racer boom as Dean's customised car races away down the country lanes. Ben appears and smiles at me.

'All right? Where've you been?'

I stare at him. 'Antenatal. It was the scan. Remember?' I see a flash of a frown as he searches his memory, past the hours he's spent inhaling toast, booze and weed. 'You know how scared I was, after all that with the midwife. Where the hell were you?'

I know where he was, of course. He was here with his mates, like always.

He moves towards me. 'Sorry. It was a mix-up. Deano needed to talk to me about Sammy. She's thinking about moving her brother in and he's upset.'

I blink at him. A terrible image returns to my mind, of being stuck here alone when the baby comes. It pricks at me, making me feel sick.

'*He* was upset?' I hear myself shouting. 'What about me?'

It's coming out all wrong. I meant to be completely calm, to reason with him so he understands how I feel.

He tenses. 'That woman's in prison. You're stressing about nothing again.'

He touches my arm, but I pull away. 'I don't want your mates here anymore, smoking. It's only weeks until the baby's here and...'

He holds his head. We've had this conversation so many times. I've seen what happens to his friends' girlfriends when they have kids. One minute they're in a club, drinking shots, the next they're chained to their one-bedroom flats, while the boys carry on as they were. Lazing around here all day, as if nothing's happened. I don't want that for our family.

'I told you,' he says after a pause. 'Deano was only here because Amanda's doing his head in. She keeps complaining and stressing, and her mum's being a right battle-axe, so he just needs someone to talk to. You said it yourself. He needs to get his act together. So I'm helping him.' He gives me the puppy-dog eyes. 'I'm sorry, right? I thought you were OK going on your own. Strong woman, yeah? And everything was OK, wasn't it? Just like I said.'

I nod at him. Yes, it was OK. It turns out the placenta has moved, and the birth will be straightforward. *Straightforward!* I almost laughed when Erica said that. I know she was trying to put me at ease, but she has no idea how worried I am about just getting to the hospital.

'Everything was OK, except you weren't there. We're supposed to be a team. And what about when I go into labour? What then?'

He stares at me blankly. I know it's a bug-bear of his that he's never learned to drive and he hates me mentioning it.

'We'll call an ambulance like everyone else. Or Dean can take us, if he's around.'

I go to the sink and run some warm water. I soak my hands in it, like I did as a child when I needed soothing, and wash the cups as he stands behind me.

The brittle silence between us breaks when another engine rumbles outside. *Please,* I pray silently, *not another one of the lads*.

'That'll be Tommy,' says Ben. 'We've got a surprise for you, love.'

I put down the cup on the drying rack and turn back to him, my heart lifting. 'You haven't?'

He grins. 'Come see for yourself.'

Two months ago, I told him I was upset because Mum's sofa was falling to bits. He kissed my tears away and told me he'd get a new one.

I got excited. It was a while since I'd had anything new that wasn't baby related. I'd looked online and shown Ben sofas I liked. He nodded and smiled and told me he'd work overtime so we could afford it.

But then the weeks ticked by, and no sofa appeared. I was beginning to lose hope that he'd deliver on his promise.

We go to the front door together. Tommy's squeezed his van onto our little driveway. The elderly couple who live opposite are peering through their curtains to watch – large vehicles are an oddity on our quiet lane. Tommy emerges with a wave and opens the back doors of the van, asks me to stick the kettle on. I glimpse one arm of the sofa – brown and made of roughly woven fabric – before I step out of their way into the kitchen.

With the kettle boiling, I peer over Ben's shoulder as he and Tommy struggle to get the three-seater over the threshold. They set it down in the middle of the lounge, and I squeeze past Mum's tatty old one to stand beside them and look at it. Ben is grinning like he's overjoyed.

'Look at it,' he says. 'A real bargain.'

I scan the puckered material, and the faded fire label. I'm horrified, and I feel ungrateful. I'm always talking about sustainability, but this time, I wanted something new. Just one thing to start our new life with. Something I could relax on and feed our baby. Instead, this one's hardly in better condition than Mum's.

Ben sees my frown, and shrugs. 'It'll clean up. It's sturdy.'

To prove his point, he pushes the back of the frame and it creaks loudly. Tommy laughs, and they edge past me to fetch the seat cushions from the van.

*This is how we've always lived*, I argue with myself, standing between the two ragged settees. *Don't act spoilt*.

But when they come back in with the cushions, I watch a half-empty crisp packet fall out from between them. And as someone else's crumbs shower the carpet, something inside me snaps. I run up the stairs into our bedroom and burst into tears.

I know this has to change. Something has to give before the baby is born. Ben has to step up.

He used to keep his promises. The terrifying question is: will he start again, before it's too late?

## Chapter Six

### Sue

I hardly slept last night. Adam's words played round and round in my head as I dozed in and out of restlessness. Tom was up and down all night, and around three I went downstairs to check he was OK. He was sitting at his desk, laptop glowing.

I wanted to go to him. I wanted to run my hand over the worn dressing gown I bought him for Christmas three years ago. But, if he wanted that, he'd still be in bed, holding me and letting me stroke his hair. So I went back to bed. He's just trying to get through this in his own way.

After two decades of marriage and three kids, I know all his little foibles and habits. What he wants and doesn't want. Lately, I've wondered if he's the only person I truly, completely understand. Before this year, I always prided myself on understanding people, and sensing where their line is. I thought I could read any situation.

This morning I went downstairs and it was a normal Wednesday. Well, as normal as it can be. Liam was eating cornflakes at a million miles per hour and Dan and David were staring at their tablets as they munched toast. Tom smiled at me as I passed them and ran my hand over his shoulder. I shouted, 'Come on, you lot. Shape up.'

Liam laughed. 'I've got cross country today. Jibbin' out halfway, we are.'

I had to smile. A bolt of deep love for my kids hit home.

'Ey. No.' I wagged my finger at him and he laughed and smoothed back his brand-new floppy haircut. I turned my attention to Dan and David. 'Don't forget your lunch boxes.'

Normal everyday stuff that overlays my mounting stress. It brightened my morning and I was relieved that Tom was OK. For a moment, everything was right again.

Now, though, I am riddled with doubt. I didn't know Katie at all. All I knew was what she let me see. And now Adam says she had a secret second phone? In all the times I've been to that house, I never saw a hint that she was hiding something like that. I dread to think what she was using it for.

I really don't know what to think. Was she working with someone else? Using it to contact that someone? I don't know, and neither does Adam, by the sounds of it.

A series of sharp wails punctuate the air. It's the emergency buzzer. I jump up and dash to the door. The ward sister is already sprinting down the corridor and into the farthest cubicle on the left. A flimsy, dark hope flits through my mind – if another woman has been drugged, could that mean it wasn't Katie after all? – but then I remember that room is where the patient who came in with extremely high blood pressure is staying. Leah's her name. She was in early labour, and we kept her in for monitoring. Just as well.

I am running and spot Erica emerging from another direction. She sees my speed and falls in behind me. I see a red flashing light reflected on the white wall before I even get to the cubicle. The cardio monitor is showing an irregular heartbeat.

'Call crash!' I shout to no one in particular. 'We can't take any chances.'

The junior clerk dashes out to do as I say, while Erica reassures Leah. She goes into a contraction, and I grab her chart. They're five minutes apart. I don't know if she'll be able to sustain this. The anaesthetist arrives and I know someone has to make a decision now.

'Erica. Can you check how dilated Leah is, please?'

But Erica is busy recording Leah's vitals, telling her all the while that everything is going to be all right. Checking the dilation was Katie's job. For a moment I feel unmoored, then I roll my sleeves up. If you want something doing, do it yourself. She's seven centimetres. Almost there, but not enough.

I glance at Erica, head down, writing all the notes up. Poor Leah is starting yet another contraction, and the cardiograph is going crazy.

I strap in a baby heartbeat monitor and quickly find the *bump, bump, bump* of the tiny heart. It is fast. Too fast. I press the emergency buzzer again.

'OK, Leah,' I say. 'We need to get you to theatre. We are going to do a C-section. With your permission, of course.'

She shrinks away from me.

'No. No. I want a natural birth. I had it all planned…'

Her words tail off into a screech of pain and I signal to the anaesthetist to come over and insert a canula.

'Call theatre. Let them know Leah will be on her way soon. We need to move fast.'

Erica runs to the phone. We both know the emergency buzzer will bring the crash team to us. But that isn't enough now. The surgeon in theatre needs to be warned. I see her talking urgently and read a *thank you* on her lips. She hurries back with a clipboard and a permission slip for Leah. The baby's heartbeat is echoing chaos on the monitor and the cardiograph is almost flickering onto red – the danger zone.

Leah shakes her head.

'No. No. I can't. I wanted it all to be perfect.'

I force a smile. So did I want everything to be perfect. But life isn't like that, is it? Leah and I have both let ourselves believe a lot of things. Painted ourselves a picture that glossed over a frightening truth. But the reality of childbirth is messy, bloody and dirty, and in this case, it might be deadly unless she signs that paper Erica's holding. I want to scream at Leah to listen to us and stop this nonsense. To think about her baby and not the best possible scenario for Instagram.

But I don't. Because I am a professional. Instead, I placate her.

'I know, love, but this way will be safer for you and Baby.'

I can hear the edge of fear in my singsong voice, because this is not going well. The crash team arrives and takes over. Leah signs the form and lets them prep her for theatre, and in minutes she is being wheeled up the corridor towards the lift. Erica stands at the door and signs her out on the clipboard. She hands it to me.

'All done. Nothing to write up.'

It's a relief. It's cases like this, where multiple issues crop up, that are so hard to capture in our notes, but so easy to prosecute. It's never our fault when something goes wrong, but if we miss out any details of how we have worked to put it right, we are heading for a malpractice case.

I put my arm round her.

'Where are the other ladies up to?'

She nods and consults her notebook.

'Mrs Burrows is progressing. Mrs Brown is sleeping. Her contractions have stopped, and I was thinking about sending her home. And the others are no change.'

I hug her to me, relieved that she's so on the ball.

'Let's get a coffee,' I say. I'm gasping, and there's something I've been meaning to ask her about.

'It's a good job we were there,' she says with a sigh, when we reach the break room. 'No one else is. Janet from the management team told me she is pulling in some staff midwives from the Royal, but they'll need to finish shifts and write up first. I guess we'll see them when they get here.'

'So,' I say, as she gets us both a black coffee from the machine. 'Have you had a summons? To appear as a witness?'

She nods and picks out a packet of ginger nuts.

'They're sending me a confirmation with further details this week.'

'How do you feel about it?'

'About the trial?' She stops mid-rip of the packet. 'I'll just tell the truth. About what happened. About what I know. And saw. But I'll be honest. I'm a bit scared. I've never been to court before.'

I lean back. Poor Erica. This is so hard for her. I see her hand is shaking as she sets our mugs down on our usual table, sits with me, and offers me the first biscuit. I always think a problem shared is a problem halved.

'Yeah. Me neither. And I'm scared, too. But I still think something isn't right about all this. That Twilight Sleep. I can't believe she'd have used something so... I don't know... so basic. It goes right back to the beginning of maternity pain relief. I mean, she knew bloody everything about procedure. About anaesthetic. She wouldn't have picked something so...'

Erica puts the biscuits down. She reaches over and takes my hand I and I almost break down.

'It doesn't make sense, does it?'

I nod. 'No, but…'

She squeezes my hand and whispers, 'She was clearly very troubled.'

I stare at her. She is suddenly very serious, and so am I. 'I could never imagine anyone doing that to one of the patients. Never.'

She sighs. Her lip is shaking. 'Me neither. I just think she must have had her reasons.'

My temper, still hovering from my interaction with Leah, rises. 'Reasons for drugging ladies or reasons for taking a baby? Or what?'

Her voice shakes as she speaks. 'I don't know. Reasons for choosing Twilight Sleep. But I guess we'll never know, because, whatever she says now, no one will believe her.'

She's right. This isn't going to be a trial. It's more like going through the motions until the final verdict that has already been decided. Life has rearranged itself and closed up the spaces where Katie used to be. Her home, with Adam leaving. Here, with new staff stepping into the air we have shared for a decade. Even this room, where the chairs are all arranged in twos – we were the only ones who ever sat together as a trio. Her mug is gone from the cupboard, and the space in the fridge where she kept her peach yoghurts is filled with someone else's lunch box.

'Have you?' Erica says through a mouthful of ginger nut. 'Got a summons, I mean?'

'No. I'm not giving evidence. My statement was enough. And I... didn't see anything. So, there's nothing to testify.' I take a fortifying gulp of coffee. 'But I'm going to be there. I need to know everything.'

She looks at the table and fiddles with her cup. 'I would come with you, but I'm not allowed. I'm only allowed in court to give my evidence.' Her features soften. 'Will you be OK on your own? Or is Tom going?'

I shake my head. He won't be coming. He will be at home, with the kids. We haven't discussed the case in weeks – whenever we're watching the news and it's mentioned, he changes the channel. He's trying hard to make our home a safe space, where we can forget all about Katie. But we both know that's not possible – not really. All the signs are telling me that Tom has his own feelings on this. Something he'll eventually tell me, like usual. Something boiling up inside him that, no doubt at some critical point for me when I'm really busy, he will release full pelt. But that's us, I suppose. What we're like.

Erica scrapes her chair out from under the table and stands. She washes her cup, a delicate china one with red roses and a gold rim that is one of twelve she brought in for the staff room because she thought we deserved something refined, as well as the set she brought in for the ward. When she turns around again, her face is a study of sadness, and it looks like she might cry.

I hurry over and hug her. She squeezes me tightly and sniffs. I let her go, and she wipes her eyes.

'Right,' she says, with a pained smile. 'I'll go and check on Leah's progress and see how long until she is back.'

'Better make the most of it, our new jobs might not involve so much running,' I joke, touching her arm once more before she leaves. This could be our last full day on the ward, and then everything will change. Everything.

## Chapter Seven

### Leila

I turn over in bed and open my eyes. Ben isn't there, and the sheets are cool to the touch. The alarm clock on his bedside table reads 07:52. It's not the first time he's stayed out all night.

I roll over again and cradle my belly, wishing the little one good morning. My baby still seems like a distant thing that I know nothing about, even as it grows inside me. I wish I had found out if it's a boy or a girl. Every time I had a scan, I wanted to ask, but it was Ben who shrugged. I thought he just wanted to leave it to chance, but now I wonder if he even cared. If I had known, I could have started to buy baby clothes that weren't just white. I still have so much to do. It's so close now. I wish I knew exactly how long. Not months, but weeks, I know that much. An avalanche of dread washes through me that I will have to do it alone.

I feel tears coming and I panic a little. It's Friday. Weekend. He's started to go out more at weekends. But then the baby kicks and I pull myself together. I can't get upset. I've been stressed enough over the past months and everything I read tells me it's bad for the child.

I ease myself out of bed and get dressed, so I'm presentable for when Erica arrives. Her first home visit is at 9 o'clock. Ben knows about it – I pinned the date and time to the fridge – so maybe he'll be back in time.

When I go downstairs to the kitchen, there is a note on the table.

*Gone to Bailey's for a bit as I couldn't sleep. Love you… X*

One kiss. And he loves me. I sit down heavily at the table. I've no doubt that he does, in his own way. But where would I go if I couldn't sleep? I can't just leave and go to a friend's. And what's going to happen when there is a baby crying in the night? Will he go to Bailey's when he can't sleep then?

Before I was pregnant, I was sure he loved me. That he was committed to me. He asked me to get engaged. We were a proper couple.

Then I missed my period. I told him and we decided to take a test together. I wanted to make a TikTok of us doing it, but in the moment it seemed too precious to share. We both stood in the bathroom, silent. Then the second line appeared on the screen. When I looked at him, he was pale. His hand was shaking as he picked up the stick and checked it again.

No cuddles and whoops of happiness. No excited phone calls to our relatives. Just a silence. I took the initiative and hugged him. His body was hard, and he didn't bend to kiss me or pat my stomach. I instantly made excuses for him, and I've been making them ever since. *He's shocked. He's overwhelmed. He'll be happy, once he's had time to process it.*

And he was. In the first few weeks, he spent hours online looking up facts about pregnancy, and asked lots of questions about how I was feeling. He talked about decorating the small bedroom and buying nursery furniture. And, even when he was scared, he never suggested I have a termination, and he didn't leave. I know in my heart I shouldn't be grateful for that, but I am. Or I was, until I realised that for him, *not leaving* wasn't the same as *being here.*

See, I am crying now. I just need to get through these next couple of weeks and put me and the baby first, then I can worry about Ben.

My tea is ready, and I fetch it to Mum's easy chair in the lounge and snuggle into it. Since we got rid of her old sofa, I've taken to sitting here instead of on the replacement settee – it feels almost like a hug from her. I relax a little and switch on the TV while I sip my tea. The place on the screen looks familiar, and I lean forward. It's Darkford General. A photograph flashes onto the screen and it's Katie. I jolt and spill tea on my legs. The newsreader is talking about the upcoming trial.

… *and in an earlier plea hearing Katie Withers pleaded not guilty to seven sample charges of attempted murder and intended abduction of a child. The trial will start on Monday at Manchester Crown Court.*

My stomach flips. I try to rewind the footage, but I can't get it to work. Seven women. Seven women who were drugged. Seven babies who could have been taken. And I was going to let that woman deliver my baby too. It could have so easily been me.

It's almost 9 o'clock, and Erica will be here any minute. But having someone here, in the place where that Katie was, doing all the same things without Ben here to hold my hand, makes me feel weak. I think I might be sick.

Bile rises in my throat, and I am halfway to the bathroom when the doorbell rings. I see a shape through the glass, a blue uniform, and I tell myself to get a grip. It's not Katie. She doesn't work at the hospital anymore. But what if she's on bail? I check myself. I have no reason to think she's on bail. I'm just panicking. I say it out loud.

'Get. A. Grip.'

It's just Erica. She rings the doorbell again and I hurry to the door and open it. She is smiling and I stand down a little.

'Leila. How are you? Oh. You look…'

I open the door wide.

'Come in. I'll put the kettle on.' She follows me into the kitchen and looks around. 'I was just a bit scared. I saw something on the TV about the trial.'

She puts her bag down on a kitchen chair and sits.

'Oh, I'm so sorry. But you have absolutely no need to worry. That's in the hands of the authorities now, and all we need to focus on is you and your baby.'

My hands are still shaking. I try to control them, but it's all too much. I slam the kettle down and slump forwards, my body heaving with sobs. Erica is beside me.

'Oh, Leila. Is everything all right?'

I shake my head. My tears drop onto the counter, wetting Mum's stripy tea towel.

'No. He went out in the middle of the night. And I don't know how I'm going to get to the hospital when the baby comes, if he's not here. I'm too scared to go there on the bus, on my own. I don't know how I'm going to do this. I feel so stupid.'

I'm too embarrassed to meet her eye. But she puts her arms around me and offers me a packet of tissues from her pocket.

'Oh, don't worry, love,' she says, without a hint of judgment. 'I'm here now. And I'll make sure you're looked after. Partners are sometimes a bit unsettled around the birth. I'm sure he'll be here soon.'

She's saying all the right things to make me feel better, but I can't stop crying. I can't even tell what exactly I'm feeling – anger, exhaustion, or just mourning for my failed expectations.

'It's not just now. He's always out, or having his mates around smoking.' I see her sniff the air and tense. I shouldn't have said that. The last thing I need is her tipping off the health visitor, getting us in even more bother. 'I'm probably exaggerating. But it's confusing. I don't know why I feel so...'

She nods deeply. She guides me to sit back down, and touches my hand across the table.

'Look, you're young and pregnant. Hormones play havoc at the best of times. But right now, your body is full of them. And it's natural to feel scared. Especially with the trial happening…' She coughs and lowers her gaze. 'So. I have some options for you. You could access some counselling at the hospital.'

'No,' I say, dabbing at my eyes. There's no way spending more time in that place would make me feel any better. 'I don't want to go there.'

She gets her laptop out of her bag and opens it. I wait quietly as she powers it up, wondering how this could have all gone so wrong. Then she presses a few keys, types something in and nods.

'OK,' she says. 'I've checked, and because the placenta has rectified, and it looks like you are on track for a normal birth, you can choose a home birth, if that would be better for you.'

'Really?' I take in a deep breath, already relieved at the thought of never going to that hospital again. 'How would that work?'

She laughs, glad to see me perk up. 'Well. When you go into labour, you'd call me and I'd come straight here to deliver the baby. I can arrange for any equipment and medication we would need to be delivered in advance. And the hospital would be on alert in case of complications. And if you changed your mind, even at the last minute, you could still go to the hospital. I could ferry you there in my trusty car. It's all up to you. All options are open for you.'

I frown at her. 'It would definitely be you? Only I don't want someone I haven't met before here.'

She taps into the laptop again. 'Yes. Barring illness or accident, it will be me. And perhaps another midwife who'll be there to assist us. But I'd introduce you first. Because your due date is so close, I'd need to start the equipment requisition as soon as possible, so everything was here in time. I really don't want to push you, but I would need a decision today.' She smiles at me with kind eyes, fishes a card out of her bag, and hands it to me. 'Like I said, whether you decide to give birth at the hospital or at home, I'll be there to look after you. But, if you want confirmation of anything, you can reach my boss, Karen, at the number on here.' She touches my arm. 'I just want you to feel reassured.'

And I do. I turn the card over in my hands and think about it. No more worrying about getting to the hospital. No more relying on Ben. It feels risky, but somehow right.

'Yes,' I say, fully composed now. 'Yes, I want a home birth.'

She smiles, and I feel lighter already.

'Home it is,' she says. 'I'll order the equipment today, and when it's delivered I'll come along and set everything up. Then as your due date approaches, I'll be here every day, I'll pop in to see you are all right. Does that sound OK?'

I nod. It does sound OK. Someone will be here. Someone will *definitely* be here.

'Don't worry,' she says, shutting her laptop. 'It's my job, love. It's my job.'

# Chapter Eight

## Sue

It's as if I can't stay away. I was en route to some training when Karen messaged me to tell me the bank staff she had asked to fill in for me and Erica didn't start until next week. It's Saturday and no one is available from any other maternity unit, so I have to go in. She said she was very sorry. Not as sorry as me, though.

This is all taking its toll. Another night of tossing and turning. Another morning of getting up to Tom sitting at his laptop working. He turned and smiled when he heard me flick the kettle on. But we've barely spoken this past week. I haven't even told him exactly what I'll be doing in this new job yet, because I'm still not certain of when it will start or the job description. All our time is taken up with our children, cooking, eating and then collapsing into bed, exhausted. In normal times, this domestic routine is just what it is, but now it seems like this whole thing is a big barrier to something bigger we need to discuss, but don't get the space.

But here I am. I've just checked on the ward, and no one is imminently delivering, so I've left the care assistants to carry on with their tasks. Now I'm in the break room, staring at the space where Katie's mug was again. I open the cupboard. Someone's tucked it away, right at the back.

She will have to give evidence. Quiet, humble Katie will be grilled in court. Every detail of her life exposed to the world. Even more than it has already through the drip, drip, drip, then explosion of media articles. She will hate that. She's always been an intensely private person. Although she was one of my best friends, if she didn't want to talk about something, she could be more tight-lipped than a monk after a vow of silence.

For a moment, I feel sorry for her. A shiver runs through my soul at the thought of a judge and jury finding out about *my* darkest secrets. I'd die of humiliation if I had to publicly air the things that keep me up at night – my days of underage drinking, of stealing another girl's boyfriend when I was fourteen, of the few bad decisions *I've* made at work. But then I remember. Quiet, humble Katie's secrets are so much darker. And who's to say if she even feels remorse in the same way I do? For all I know, she was never my friend at all.

The sound of the door opening jolts me back to the present. 'Here we are again!' Erica says, bustling in and hanging her coat on the back of the door. 'I was supposed to be on outreach, but Karen rang me in.'

'Join the club,' I sigh. I get up to make us both a drink.

'Tea for me, ta.' She sits at the table and pulls her laptop out. 'Do you mind if I work while we're in here? I need to get a home birth booked in as soon as possible.'

'Oh?' I ask, flicking on the kettle. 'Which lady is this?'

She tells me all about Leila Summers while I find two of her nice china cups and sniff the milk from the fridge to check that it's not gone sour. It sounds like the poor girl's going through hell – living miles away from hospital with a negligent boyfriend and a recent bereavement, not to mention the trauma of what Katie did. And at her age, she's just the type of patient Katie was targeting.

'She's lucky to have you on her team now,' I say, stirring the tea while Erica types away. 'And are you going to lead on the delivery? Only you haven't…'

The look on her face is so diligent. Bless her. I wish I still had all that energy, that optimism.

'No, I haven't led before,' she says, 'but there has to be a first time for everything. And with this new job, I want to prove myself. I never really had the chance before, with Katie taking charge all the time.'

I stare at her. I hadn't realised she felt like we were holding her back. I thought the three of us worked like clockwork, but in retrospect, I can understand why Katie's methods might have frustrated her. Always dominating the delivery, leaving Erica on the sidelines.

'Erica, I'm so sorry,' I say, handing her a cup and sitting beside her. 'You should have said something earlier. You know how capable we both thought you were, right?'

She bats my arm playfully. 'Don't worry. It wasn't you, and I know it wasn't personal. I'm just keen to progress, now that I can.'

She absolutely can – I'm sure of it. I've seen her cope in all kinds of challenging situations – premature births, haemorrhages, and more. She loves the job and the care she provides is impeccable. And, if I remember correctly, she had more than five years' experience on another unit before she joined us.

'Do you want me to come along? Just to assist, I mean. And to give you moral support.'

'Thanks,' she says, flashing me one of her megawatt smiles. 'I might take you up on that. But with the patient being so nervous about hospital staff, I'm wary of bringing anyone else in unless it's completely necessary. Can I get back to you nearer the time?'

'Of course,' I say. 'You'll know what's best.'

She squeezes my arm and goes back to her work for a few minutes while I sip my tea. Then she gets up to check her pigeonhole. I watch her pale as she pulls out a white envelope and read the contents.

'It's the final summons,' she says. 'I'm on the second day.'

She tosses the letter on the table, and gestures for me to read it. She sits back down while I do, but her knee bounces under the table. She looks anxious now – nothing like the cold detachment she displayed on Wednesday. My heart beats fast at the thought of her there on the witness stand, under all that pressure. I don't envy her one bit.

'Don't worry,' I say. 'I'll be there to support you. And, like you said, all you have to do is tell the truth.'

Neither of us notice Karen walk in. She clears her throat behind us and when we turn, she shakes her head. Her expression tells me that Erica's summons is not the worst thing that's happened today.

'So,' she says after a pause, 'I need to let you know that there's been a development in the press. Unfortunately, the *Mail* have run a story that takes some liberties, and I thought you should be informed immediately.'

This is official, serious Karen. Her tone is hard. She grabs Erica's laptop, minimising the equipment requisition and loading an internet browser. I stare as a familiar picture loads. It's me, Katie and Erica at the awards ceremony last year. Arms around each other and smiling. This picture says we're all in it together. The headline is:

*Midwives from crime-ridden maternity department on the lash as mums-to-be are drugged*

I am shocked at the angle. I know the press will do all they can to sensationalise stories, like they did with Katie and Adam's fertility issues, but this implies that Katie is not the only guilty party. That *we* were her accomplices. Before I can begin to process it, Erica jumps up from her seat.

'Tell them to take that picture down,' she says to Karen. 'We didn't give permission. That needs to come down.'

Karen reddens. 'The hospital has issued their position on this matter. The picture didn't come from us.' She sits down heavily. 'This is just the start of it. As I said the other day, they were always going to come down hard. But we're doing everything we can.'

Erica's face clouds, her eyes glassy. She looks like this is more than she can take. Just when I think she might break down, she shuts her laptop and strides from the room. Karen and I let her go – she needs space, and right now I don't have a clue how to comfort her. Instead, I google the article on my phone. It's on most of the national media websites. It doesn't say it directly, but there is a strong insinuation that Erica and I are somehow involved. I google my own name and the article appears at the top of the listing. What the fuck does this mean for me – for my career? My reputation? My family?

'It's bad, I know,' says Karen, as if she can read my thoughts. 'I'm so sorry, love. On top of everything else, you didn't need this.'

I look out of the break room window, onto the department. 'What do we do now?'

She swallows. 'After today, the new staff will be here. I've got extra security coming in, and we're diverting as many patients as we can to the Royal, until the investigation is complete. As for you and Erica, I'm sorry, but I think the best thing for you will be to take some time off starting tomorrow. You'll be paid in full, and your jobs will be waiting for you after the trial. But for now, you need to keep a low profile. Keep in touch with each other, and with us. We're here to support you.'

I manage to nod. Karen keeps talking, but I'm numb to everything she's saying. The hurt has run such a deep trench through my heart that I'm past tears. All I can do now is hope that Erica and I can pull together to get through this. For all our sakes.

---

At twenty past six, I drive past my house. I can't park outside, because there is already line of strange cars stationed outside with people sitting in them. I know people are interested in this story. And, in many ways, it's right it is reported. But I can't let this interfere with my family life. I hope they haven't seen me as I turn onto the next street. There's a cut-through to my house from there and I hurry along the copper-beech-lined pathway and into my back garden.

No need to get my keys out, as I can see Tom sitting at the kitchen table. He spots me and his face hardens. I hesitate. Surely he doesn't think this is my fault?

I open the door and he holds his phone up on a news page showing the article and the picture. 'And it's been on TV. The kids saw it. Why didn't you warn me?'

I sigh. 'You think they told me in advance? You're not a fucking child, Tom. You know that's not how this works. And we agreed not to let the kids watch the news.'

He stands up, roughly scraping his chair from under the table. He shouts his anger. 'Are you saying this is *my* fault? Are you?'

I put my head in my hands. I don't want to fight. 'No. No, I'm not. But it's not mine, either. I didn't post that story and I didn't put it on the news. And I didn't nick drugs and dope women to steal babies, either. I've got nothing to do with this. This is Katie's fault. Not mine. Hers.'

For a moment, I think he's going to apologise.

But then panic flares in his eyes again. 'You think that makes me feel better? This will be nonstop until the trial ends now. The kids have to go to school. We have to go to work. The house is going to feel like a fucking prison, Sue.'

I imagine our lovely boys and Tom on our front doorstep, being harassed by journalists and photographers. Me, trapped in here and only leaving to go to court next week. I can't stand it. Even though none of this was my doing, the words spill out before I can stop them. 'I'm sorry, Tom.'

I wait for him to say something. Anything. Reassurance that he doesn't blame me, or even a sarcastic comment. Instead, he just goes upstairs and shuts the bedroom door.

# Chapter Nine

## Leila

'So, what did Katie Withers do while she was at your house?'

I've agreed to talk to someone from the hospital on the phone. Erica set it up and told me it would lead to counselling or therapy. She promised I wouldn't suffer like this forever, and, even though it's Sunday, she said she's popping round this morning – she wants to check we are ready for the equipment to be delivered, which reassured me she is on the case. I thought Ben would be back, but I haven't heard anything from him. It's been days. Every time I think about the time he has been gone I get cold shivers. He's never been gone so long before. I glance at my phone as Vicky speaks on speakerphone, hoping there is a message or a text.

'She just did the usual things. Blood pressure. Writing notes. Telling me what would happen. Listening to the baby's heartbeat. She stayed quite a long time. I always made tea and biscuits.'

I hear the tapping as she enters the information. Erica explained that Vicky was gathering information about the women who had suffered, as part of an internal investigation. That the hospital was determined to help, and that some of the women who had been drugged had set up a support group. That anything I could tell her would help.

'Thank you. So, was there anything you thought was unusual at the time, or have thought so since?'

'No. Well, yes. A couple of times she went to the loo, and I could hear her talking on her phone in the bathroom. And a few times in the back garden.'

She taps again. 'And what kind of conversation was it?'

I think. She would rush to answer her phone. *I have to get this.* Right in the middle of a blood pressure test or telling me about something. And she always had her back to me or spoke in the bathroom.

'Hard to say. I couldn't hear her properly or see her. She turned away to speak. I thought you would have asked me about this earlier.'

'It's a terrible business. They're only just scratching the surface, by all accounts. They're prosecuting her for sample offences. Then, when the rest come out, they can charge her with those as well.' I feel a wave of fear again. Erica had made me feel much better about all this. Safer, like it was nearly over. But there could be more women. Vicky goes on. 'They simply don't know how many women were attacked.'

My mouth is dry, but I manage to speak the word. 'Attacked?'

'Yes. Well, better to say it how it is. She didn't kill anyone, but she wanted to.'

My heart is racing. I've had a killer in my home. She sat here and ate my biscuits. She touched me.

I feel like I'm going to faint. But Vicky is still speaking. 'You have to wonder what checks happened. On her. But we'll all find out in the end. It's those women I feel sorry for. And you, love. I hope you are OK? You were lucky.'

I don't feel lucky. My head is swimming with what could have happened. And everything that is happening now. I want to scream at her that I am scared to death and the only things holding me together right now are Erica and the thought of my baby.

'Yes. I expect I was.'

She flips back into professional mode. 'Thank you so much for answering my questions today. These will be recorded in your hospital record and passed on to the relevant authorities. Have a nice day.'

I sit down heavily. It's not long until my due date and I have to keep calm. Things are bad enough with Ben and his randomness without this hanging over me. I shut my eyes and start some deep breathing exercises I found on YouTube. I'm less than a minute in when the doorbell rings.

I knew it. Something's happened to Ben. No one ever comes here, and he has a key. I peep through the curtain expecting the police, but it's Erica. She smiles and I feel much better. I hurry to the door.

'Hello! I wasn't expecting you yet.'

She hurries in. 'One of my other ladies cancelled, so I'm a bit early for our appointment. I should have phoned. Is it convenient?'

I nod. Somewhere inside me, a little bit of normality returns. Something regular and planned. 'Yeah. I just spoke to Vicky from the hospital enquiry team. She asked me about Katie.'

'Thank you for doing that. They need as much information as possible. What did you tell her?'

Her eyes are on me, hungry for my words. I know she worked with her. I saw them on the internet. On Twitter. Erica, Katie and another woman, all laughing together in a photo. But that was before that Katie was arrested. Erica must feel terrible about it.

'It must have been a shock for you. I saw you knew her. I just told Vicky what I told you. That she was here a lot and always talking on her phone outside.'

She looks at her shoes. 'Thanks. It was. And yes, we worked together. But you have to know I'm fully committed to getting justice done.' She reaches into her bag. 'Anyway, on to more positive things. Here's a list of what will arrive in the next couple of days. Ladies can deliver at any time from now, so it's best to be prepared.'

She hands me a printed sheet with a lot of things I don't recognise. Her phone is ringing, but she ignores it. I see the screen flashing through her uniform pocket.

'I'm still not sure…'

I'm not. I thought I was sure before, but I keep going backwards and forwards. I'd assumed I would be in hospital. In fact, I'd looked forward to it. I was dreading not knowing how to care for my little one, and the nurses and midwives would show me. No mum now to help me. And everyone I know who has had a baby has been in hospital. Everything I know about childbirth involves a maternity ward. But, with Ben still not here, it does make sense.

'I'm scared something will go wrong.'

'And if it does, we will have the hospital on standby. It's routine procedure. I've got another lady in a similar position. Don't worry. I discussed it with my colleague, Sue. The other midwife who worked with Kat… us.' I remember the picture from the internet. Three of them. 'She's just been promoted to deputy team leader. She agrees it's the safest way. What with you being so far from the hospital. Would you like to talk it through with her?'

I shake my head. 'No. If you all think it's the best thing, then it is.'

I hear a key in the door and voices in the hallway. Erica turns and I hurry out. Ben and Deano stand there grinning. The smell of cannabis fills the hallway. I look back at Erica. And Ben looks past me.

'What's she doing here?'

It's weekend and he clearly didn't expect anyone to be here.

Erica pulls her phone out of her pocket. 'I'll take this outside.'

She leaves and pulls the front door closed behind her. I am suddenly tense.

'In case you hadn't noticed, I'm pregnant. And my baby is due any time. She's my midwife. And you'll be seeing a lot more of her.'

I am clinical. This is how it has to be now. But he moves closer to me. I can smell whisky on his breath. It's only now I realise how wearing his drinking and drug-taking has been on me. On us. With the chaos of the arrest and the trial. And my grief, which he has conveniently waved to one side. I hadn't had any stability. Until now. I feel a familiar sinking in my stomach that comes with his mood swings.

He sneers at me. 'Get rid of her. Now. And about our baby. And it's not due for weeks.'

I stand my ground. This is an escalation. He hasn't been so aggressive before. But I stand up to him.

'No. I won't get rid of her. She's helped me when you were… out. When you weren't here.'

Deano laughs. 'This is too heavy for me, man. I'm outta here.'

I suddenly realise Deano speaks in a ridiculous gangster voice, even though he was born round the corner from Ben. They are both acting like teenagers.

Ben flings his hands in the air, a sure sign that he's going to have a tantrum. 'Look what you've done now. I'm just as entitled to have friends here as you are.'

I face him off. 'She's not a friend. She's a midwife. She'll be here when I have my… our baby. I don't want to go to the hospital after all that business with that Katie. And you're never here, so I can't rely on you.'

He erupts. 'You don't know what happened. You have no fucking idea what I have just been through.'

I don't know how I remain calm, because fear bolts through me. A triggering memory of my mum and dad shouting before she left him. 'No, I don't. But I'm sure you're going to tell me. Was Deano's cat ill? Someone forgot to top up their gas meter? Please tell me what's kept you out for two full nights and had you coming home smelling of weed and booze. Do tell.'

He grabs my arm and pulls at me. His mouth is close to my ear, and I am hot with fear. He speaks low and slow. 'You think you're smart, don't you? Now you've got this place, you think you're it. But you'd better be careful.'

He squeezes my wrist so hard I feel a crack. I hear the door open, and Erica appears. As I turn, she is leaning on the doorframe, arms folded.

'Everything OK here?'

He laughs in her face. 'She's not having the baby here, so you might as well shoot off.'

She looks at me. 'Is that what you want, Leila?'

I look from one to the other. I need to make the right decision, but I'm scared of both. Ben stands, hands in pockets now. Just like my dad did when he was stopping himself from hitting my mum. Again.

'I want it all to go well. I only want to have my baby safely.' I turn to Ben. 'What'll happen if you're not here? And I can't get hold of you?'

He steps forward and holds my shoulders gently. But I still feel the sting of my injured wrist. 'But I will be, bae. The birth isn't for ages yet. Weeks. I told you. I'll be here twenty-four-seven.'

He's adopted Deano's gangster twang and I cringe at the word *bae*. That's a new one.

Erica makes a face and sniffs. 'OK. You two have time to think about it. But I'll be round here on my appointments in any case as I'm the outreach lead for ladies who have come into contact with Katie Withers and are traumatised.' She accentuates the word 'traumatised' and stares at Ben. 'And because Leila has come into contact with someone under arrest, they will likely want to come and search this property as Katie spent so much time here.' They both look down at the sports bag at Ben's feet. 'So, I'll get that arranged.'

For once, he is lost for words. I rub my wrist and Erica gets her bag. Her phone rings again and she ignores it.

'OK. I'll be off then, so you two can have a chat. I'll be back tomorrow to check your blood pressure. As arranged.'

She stares at Ben as she leaves.

As the door shuts behind her, he backs off. 'Very clever.'

I shrug. 'I don't know what you mean.'

'Her. Getting someone on your side.'

I think about when we met. How much he chased me and bought me gifts. How he messaged me and posted photos of us on his Facebook page. How he took me out to dinner and promised we would be together forever. I wanted to finish college and go to university, but he was adamant he would look after me. He wanted me. He wanted a baby. He wanted us.

Now I am the enemy. He's defensive and angry. I look at him. All indie and unemployed and acting like an overgrown teenager.

'I thought we were on the same side, Ben? I thought we were a team?'

# Chapter Ten

## Sue

It's only just sinking in. The devastation caused by Katie, and how far it has reached. Even into my own home. It's like Groundhog Day, but it has to change when the trial is over. It has to. It's been months now since she was arrested, but every day brings something new and worse. The trial has to be the peak, but I have heard the police are continuing their investigation, and we might all be interviewed again.

And to make it worse, I have to sort through all the files from the past year and organise them to train someone new. Which, inevitably, will include the incidents that Katie was involved with. I checked with Karen after what she said yesterday about staying away until after the trial. This is what it's like. A hot mess of being told one thing one day and another the next.

I told her the new staff would need training. I'm worried. This hospital has been my life and I can't simply let go.

From Erica's face yesterday, neither can she. Karen said it was fine to come into the ward office on a Sunday to do this, but to use the back entrance and to keep off the wards as much as possible, as patients and partners would have seen the picture in the paper.

She told me there had already been two complaints that ladies didn't want me as their midwife. She told me not to worry. It was a short-lived occurrence as the trial would solve it. Katie would be prosecuted, and it would be made clear the hospital and its staff were not to blame. We are all victims. That's what she said.

But I'm not so sure. I look at the photo of us on my phone. It's from exactly a year ago. Just before she started her stint of over-medicating. Although, for all I know, she could have been doing it then. And in the months before. But I cannot think of a single time I thought there was anything odd. The only times were when the first ladies complained. Katie was outraged. She examined every single record and every chart. Nothing was recorded wrongly.

We triple-checked the medication cabinet records and, again, nothing was wrong. I pull out the records now and see her initials next to mine and Erica's. So she falsified records as well, when all the time she knew what had happened.

Karen is right. She duped us all. My brain makes a connection with something I don't want to think about. Was her whole practice leading to this? Was she always going to take a baby? She was meticulous about CPD.

Continuing Professional Development. So much so that she gave a presentation about it. She loved her job, but did she only love it because it gave her access to commit her crime?

It hits me like a brick. Her practice logs. She took great pride in keeping a private diary of her practice, just like me. Erica didn't, she recorded on the hospital system. But we are old-school. We write it down. I pull out the reports Karen gave us and flick through to the evidence pages. I run my finger down the lists of records the police had copied or removed and then referred to. It isn't there.

I know they jemmied open her locker and took her change-of-clothes bag. But she didn't keep it in there. I grab my keys and hurry through the department. Past the ladies and past the medicine cabinet to a tiny room at the end of the corridor. It used to be the family room before they built the big extension, but now it just has two desks face to face, and two chairs.

We used to come here when something bad happened. When we lost a mum or a baby. When we'd helped a woman through a full-term stillbirth. When we had worked a double shift, and we could hardly stand. Or those days when we'd had a row at home, and we just wanted a good cry.

But always once a week to write our practice diaries. The rings from our coffee cups are still there, and a crumpled tissue on the table from when Mrs Thomas' twins didn't make it. Months and months ago, and no one has been in here because it's out of general use.

These desks are surplus now; not the clean, plastic flat tables we use in the offices. They are solid wood, and the drawers have dovetail joints and secret compartments. I slip my hand into the drawer, the slim compartment where sheets of paper were once kept, and pull out my diary. I haven't filled it in since Katie went. I feel further into the hardly noticeable alcove and pull out a notebook with butterflies on the cover.

I flick through it, and it is nearly full. I bring it back to the office. The date Katie was arrested is imprinted on my soul, but I need to check the days of the sample cases she is being tried for. I need to see if there is anything odd in the notes or in her diary. Anything I missed. The need to know all the details gnaws at me and makes me hungry for any snippet that will tell me why. Why she did it.

I go through Karen's report and check the notes again. Nothing. I cross-check with the dates in her practice diary, and mine. They match. There is nothing at all recorded that would point to the horrific incidents. But there is something. She has starred certain dates. Childish stick stars, boldly drawn on the corner of the date sections.

She has doodled hearts. I flick through and the whole diary is punctuated with delicately drawn flowers and illustrated hearts. It's joyful and not straight out of the pen of a serial killer. But what would I know? One of the sample dates is starred, but the others aren't. She's blocked a weekend off, but it isn't near any of the sample dates.

I flick to the back page, and she's written some musical notes. Katie lived for music. I can't bear to think about her trapped in a cell. No dancing. No singing. No laughing.

There's a circled phone number right at the bottom of the page that could belong to anyone. But the saddest thing is on the last page.

*Buy new practice diary.*

It's as if she hadn't planned to end her career. But she had. She was living a double life. I am tempted to wonder if she had deep mental health issues, but the scathing report paints her a calculating killer who was out to cover her steps. And I know that is how she will be described in court.

I push the diaries and the report into my bag and walk slowly back to the break room. Ian comes in and flicks the kettle on. I pretend to look busy, and he glances and decides not to disturb me. I feel the diaries in my bag. I know I should hand hers over, and possibly mine too, but I need something to remind me of her. To keep who I thought she was close. Because I miss her so much.

I need to get home. Tom was up again in the night and it's starting to be a habit. He won't talk about it, but the steady stream of journalists ringing the doorbell can't help. I check the rota and two staff midwives are here. Erica is meant to be taking them through the practice routine, but she isn't here.

I ring her. It goes to answerphone, but I don't leave a message. I can show them the basics, but I don't have time to go over everything. I check their HR notes and see they are both experienced. I check Erica's online log and it tells me she hasn't been here at all today. But I guess she doesn't have to now. Outreach means she doesn't have to be here at all if she has better things to do.

I text Karen.

*The staff midwives are here but Erica isn't. I have to go. Are you able to take them through welcome?*

I am, as usual, conflicted. I need to be with my family to weather the storm together. Present a united front and support each other. But I can't just leave. Especially now. It's like we say to the mums-to-be: *babies aren't on a schedule. They come when they want to.*

But I need to let go. I need to rest and think about something else other than this damned trial. I need to cook my family a nourishing meal and sit and eat it with them. Then watch a film with Tom while the boys sit in their rooms with earphones on. It's been so long, and I am pining for normality. My phone beeps.

*Of course. You go and I'll come down. You've done more than enough. But bell Erica to see if she's on her way, as I'm leaving soon.*

I ring Erica's phone again and it goes to voicemail. She must be out and about with one of her ladies. Or not. And now it is none of my business, as she reports directly to Karen. The two staff midwives come in and sit down at the next table. They get out their notes and begin to fill them in, chatting easily.

My phone beeps and Tom has messaged me a link to another article. This time it's a Facebook group. *Close Darkford Maternity Unit.* I scroll down and it's calling for the existing staff to be arrested on negligence charges. Two of the victims have commented and said no one noticed while they were being drugged. That no one believed them.

We checked. We fucking checked everything. Right down to the last microgram. I still don't know how Katie got hold of the medication. I can't work it out and, believe me, I have lain awake trying. I scroll down farther, and someone has posted a selfie of me and Katie from a night out at Christmas. The comment underneath says:

*Look at them enjoying themselves while women were dying.*

I message Tom back.

*Thanks, love. I'm coming home. I don't know how much more of this I can take.*

It sounds as if I am on the edge, but I am strangely calm. Numb. Like a cloud of bullshit has descended and all I can do is wait for it to pass and hope for the best. Except it hasn't even really started yet. There are four days left before the trial and it's just going to get worse. And if – when – she is found guilty, what then?

I set myself aside. My sentimentality has gone too far and now the label of 'killer' is being stretched over me. My heart suddenly cracks and breaks as I realise that's it. That. Is. It. The spell is broken, and I am no longer part of a team. No more crying over Katie. No more hoping this is all a mistake. This is serious now, and it's every woman for herself.

## Chapter Eleven

## Leila

I was awake at five thirty-seven this morning. It's hard to fall asleep at all these days, because I'm usually waiting for Ben to come to bed for hours. Then when he does, I'm worried he will roll onto me as he's so drunk. Then it's early morning and I want a wee.

So, I got up and tried to think positive. Monday morning. New week. Mum used to have affirmations on the fridge – *I am enough* and *everything will be OK* – and for a moment I regret taking them off. I removed them after she died, along with the frilled gingham curtains and the carved wooden tea, coffee and sugar pots. She liked cluttered, country-style kitchens. She said it made the place homely. I'm more of a pristine-white person.

I hear Ben stir upstairs, and my skin pricks with anxiety. I'm increasingly wondering each morning if today he'll be *nice Ben* or *horrible Ben*. The state of him yesterday tells me he will have a hangover and he won't be so nice.

I hear him run the tap in the bathroom and flush the toilet. Then my heart races at the sound of his footsteps on the stairs.

He appears in the doorway in just jogging pants, and, despite my angst, at the sight of his muscular bare torso I feel something warm stirring inside me. Love or lust, my hormone-addled brain can't decide as he kisses the top of my head on his way to the cupboard. I wonder if he meant what he said last night. That he will be here from now on.

He didn't like Erica. But then again, he hates all authority. I found that bad-boy very attractive, once. A rebel and goodlooking. Now he's more man-child. I watch him pouring his rice crispies and wonder how I could have mistaken him for a father figure. But here we are.

He smiles at me, slurping his breakfast.

'OK, bae?'

I cringe. *Bae* again. *Bae* from a world I'm not part of. That world is Instagram models and boys who pretend to have more money than they do. Late-night clubs, then after-parties. And I've seen what goes on there. Weed and whiskey and coke sniffed off women's backs. I know, really, that's what he's doing. Because he wants the best of both worlds. And the desperate thing is that I have no choice but to give it to him. It's that or be a bad mother, shouting and screaming and throwing bin bags full of his stuff out of the bedroom window.

I swallow hard. I'm trapped. I could ask him to leave but, one way or another, I have to see him again because very soon we will have a child together.

'Yeah. Good. Do you want coffee?'

He laughs. 'That would be great. Listen, about yesterday…'

I turn away so he won't see my worried expression. 'I only want to keep it all calm for when the baby comes,' I say. 'That's all.'

I turn back and he's staring at me.

'Course. Yeah. Course. I'll be around from now on. I mean, there are a few things I need to take care of today. Loose ends. But once that's sorted, I'm all yours.'

I want to scream at him. *All mine forever, or just until I'm busy with your baby?* But I'm distracted by a van pulling up outside. My phone starts to ring. It's Erica. I answer and move into the hallway.

'Leila?' she says. 'Good. You're up. The equipment's going to arrive soon.'

I open the front door. I can see curtains twitching as the neighbours marvel at traffic so early.

'They're here now. How much is there?'

She laughs. 'Not much. You'll be the first on their delivery schedule. I marked it as urgent.'

I freeze and go into worry mode. 'Why urgent? Is something wrong?'

She laughs again. She is very bright and breezy for so early in the morning. 'No, don't worry! But you are near your due date, so baby could put in an appearance at any time.' I can hear traffic in the background. 'I'm on my way round. I should be about twenty minutes. Then we can set things up and go over how we'll use it all.'

A man is walking up my pathway with a large box on a stack truck.

He smiles at me. 'Leila Summers? Well, I can see it's you who's in need of this. When's the happy day?'

I stare at the box. This is real now. My baby kicks as if to confirm and my hand goes to protect my stomach. 'A week or so yet. According to my due date. But who knows?'

He laughs. Everyone is in such a good mood today. 'Yeah. My wife was three weeks early with both my kids. You just never know. You could be holding it by teatime. Girl or boy? Do you know yet?'

I shake my head.

A second man, carrying another large box, stops behind him. 'You will soon, love,' says the second man. 'Where do you want it?'

I think fast. Not the bedroom – Ben will need somewhere to sleep, if I'm in labour all night. I panic. I should have had all this organised. There's the dining room. We eat at the kitchen table, and it's a private room at the back of the house. It's perfect.

When the boxes are all in place inside, the first man looks round and scratches his head. 'You'll need a bed in here. Shall we push this table back?'

I nod. A bed. I hadn't thought of that. I can feel my heart pounding and my face flush. 'Yes, please. We've ordered a bed. It'll be here soon.'

I'm lying to cover myself now. The truth is I'm not prepared at all. I don't even have many baby clothes. Or a bath. The second man wheels in what looks like a mini hospital crib. It's a plastic bubble incubator in a sturdy trolley. I sit down on a dining chair and catch my breath.

They hand me a consignment slip. 'Just sign here, love. And good luck.'

They make silly jokes to each other about *labour being the easy part* as I turn and sign the note on the table. When I turn back, Erica is standing behind them, tutting, and I hear heavy footsteps upstairs. Ben has decided not to join in with the jubilant arrival of my home birth kit. Once again, he's sloped off when someone – anyone who isn't one of his mates – knocks on the door, and no doubt he will hide until Erica leaves.

The steady deep bass of his American hip-hop starts and they all glance up. The two men raise their eyebrows and glance at each other. No words are needed. We all know what is going on. Erica picks up the consignment note and studies it.

'Thank you so much for prioritising this,' she says to them as they leave. 'We want Leila to be ready.'

'Right,' she says when we're alone, looking at the boxes. 'Shall we start?'

I sigh and sit down heavily. 'I'm not ready, Erica. I don't even have a bed ready. I can't give birth in our bed. I need somewhere—'

'Don't worry,' she interrupts. 'I will order a single bed. And afterwards I'll arrange for it to be removed along with all this. You're right. You need somewhere separate and private. Somewhere you can dismantle afterwards and put back to normal.'

'But I haven't even got baby grows. The baby's going to be in our room at first. So, the cot can go in there. But I still need all kinds of things.'

She shakes her head and smiles. 'Look. Shall I make some tea and we can write a list? Then you can order online. Even if Baby comes this afternoon, you can have things here by tomorrow. The miracle of Amazon.'

I suddenly feel lighter and I'm just starting to relax a little when I hear Ben's heavy footsteps on the stairs. He hurries into the room.

'What the fuck is all this?' He looks in disgust at the boxes, then jabs a thumb over his shoulder towards the kitchen. 'And why's *she* here?'

I back away from him to the wall.

'I told you. I'm having the baby here. That's what I want.'

I hear Erica stop stirring the tea. He moves closer and lowers his voice. 'Get this stuff out of here. You're having our kid in hospital like everyone else. You hear me?'

'Don't threaten me.' Anger flares in my chest and I step towards him. 'I will do what I want, when I want. What's happened to you?' I hold up my bruised wrist. 'How could you do this to me, eh? It's assault.'

He glances at the kitchen door, eyes wide. 'It was an accident.' He sounds rattled, but he doesn't back off.

I shake my head. I've heard it all before. 'An accident like when Deano hit Julia? That sort of accident? I told you if you ever laid a finger on me, it was over. Do you remember that?'

He looks at me and back at the door. I know in this moment I've crossed that line between childhood and becoming an adult: someone who could be a mother.

He is deflated. 'So, what are you saying?'

I step forward again until I am almost touching him. 'You are here full-time now, and not just until the baby is born. No friends round, no staying out. No middle-of-the-night phone calls about drug deals. Or you go.'

He erupts. 'You can't fucking tell me to go. I live here. I've got rights.' As he is screaming at me, Erica appears in the doorway, her expression serious. He turns his anger on her. 'Why did you have to interfere? Telling her to have the kid at home. I'm scared, OK? Scared something will go wrong—'

'Scared you won't be able to have Deano here, more like,' I cut in. 'I bet you thought you'd throw a party while I was in hospital, didn't you? Well, you're not. Because I'm having our baby here.'

He is silent for a moment. Then he drops his voice to a growl. 'I'll see a solicitor. You can't do this.'

'Well, shape up, then!' I yell. 'Be a man. It's your choice.'

He looks from me to Erica and back again. Then, finally, he steps away from me.

'You're only saying this cos she's here,' he says. 'It's not right. It's abuse, not letting me see my mates.' Then he turns to Erica and sneers. I've seen that look before. It's a calculated stare that is the beginning of something very cruel. 'You want to watch her,' he snarls. 'She's making out she's the Virgin Mary when she's the guiltiest in all this.'

His gaze is cold as it rests on me. 'She's a slag. I don't even know if that kid's mine.'

That's it. I lunge at him, hitting and screaming until Erica pulls me away.

His hands are in the air. 'See? I'm the victim here. Leave my fucking stuff outside, you crazy bitch. I'm fucking done here.'

He turns, and he is gone. Erica stares after him. I am shaking, but she is perfectly still. She speaks into the welcome silence. 'Are you OK?'

I check myself. I'm physically unharmed but inside I am destroyed. 'No. No, I'm not.'

She hugs me. 'Don't worry, I'll be here. I'll be here.'

## Chapter Twelve

### Sue

I'm sitting in the kitchen when I hear Tom's car pull onto the drive, fresh from the Monday morning school run. His key is in the door, then he pauses in the hallway. He will have seen my car parked two streets away, so he knows I am still here.

I shout to him. 'Want a cuppa, love? I'm just writing up some case notes.'

He comes into the kitchen and puts down a flyer he picked up from the mat.

'It's completely fucked up.' He still won't look at me. 'I don't think it's good for the kids, all this sneaking around. And it's only going to get worse.'

I grip my hands together in my lap. 'What do you want us to do?'

He is clouded by something I haven't seen in him before. He waits a long moment. Then the train I have been waiting for, the one that will hit my life full-on and blow it apart despite my desperate attempts to hold it together, arrives.

'I'm going to take the kids to my mum's for a bit. I've already talked to her. And… I don't think you should come with us.'

I am stunned. With no idea how to respond, I fast-forward over what I thought would happen in the next few weeks. Tom waiting for me at home to hold my hand after the long days in court. The kids happy that Mum is no longer working nights at the hospital. The five of us helping one another through this difficult time. How will we get through this if we're not all together?

'It's only until the trial's over, and all this resolves itself,' he says, gesturing out of the window. I can see two men sipping from takeout coffee cups in a car parked in front of the house. 'And you don't have to stay here. Surely you can stay at the hospital halls?'

I straighten. I could never do that. I'd be away from home. And alone.

'Why, Tom? I haven't done anything wrong. Why take the kids away from me?'

His face is set firm. Anger replaces contorted grief. 'It's not what I want, either. It's the last thing I want. But this is not about you! It's about the kids. And those people are not going to leave you alone, so… it seems the right thing to do. At the moment.'

I feel my face heat up. 'And what if it goes on for months? What then?'

I realise I am shouting. The air in the room seems suddenly thick. I stare at him, fuming. He says nothing, only blinks at me.

I lower my voice. 'What then, Tom?'

He collects himself, but his eyes are still blank. 'I should start work. I'll take the kids tonight, just for a few days at first, and let's review the situation each week. See where we are.'

But I can't leave it. I can't let him make this decision without me.

'Oh right,' I spit. 'Shall we have a review spreadsheet and save it in Dropbox? Is that the only contact I'll be having with you and the kids? Why are you fucking doing this, Tom?'

But deep down, I know he's right. He is protecting our children. I just didn't think it had got that bad. But then again, I haven't asked him much about how the school runs have gone. I'm always working at those times, and I've been so preoccupied with my own feelings about Katie and the mess she's made, maybe I didn't realise quite how tough this has become for my family.

He stands and looks at me for a second. I want to tell him he's right, I want to make up, but I can't bear to back down. Not until he acknowledges that this is a decision we have to make together.

He doesn't say anything. There's no angry come-back. No sign of him wanting to make peace, either. He simply stares at me, as if he's thinking. Then he leaves – not to his home office upstairs, but out the front door. I run upstairs and watch from the window as the people in the cars hold up their phones and take photos of him. I watch as he walks down the road, hands in pockets, and disappears around the corner.

I wipe away my tears with shaking hands. It's a done deal, then. He's taking the kids to his mum's house. I'll have to make an appointment every time I want to see them, because his mum will side with him. She's a lovely woman, but she doesn't agree with how much of the child-care in our family falls to Tom. She's never liked me working such long hours, and she doesn't understand that it's my vocation, not just a job.

All I can do is carry on. So I pull myself together, go back downstairs and open my laptop again. I log onto my dash-board and, as it opens, I do a double-take. I can usually only see my user area and the Ward Log. Now I can see everything. All the records. A window pops up, asking me to choose a new password, and I do. It relaunches and my new job title is now at the top of the screen.

Susan Springer – Deputy Team Leader, Maternity. Darkford General Hospital.

There it is. Proof that I'm at the pinnacle of my career. I search for the joy, but it isn't there.

The rest of my screen looks the same as before, except for a purple button at the side marked 'Budget', and invita-tions for me to complete seven new training modules. I click on the budget button and see a requisition I put through yesterday for extra PPI for the new staff midwives. I can also see all the orders made by other staff in the department. The total amount is displayed on the top line, and it's even more than I thought.

I scan the records to see how much Erica's home birth kit cost. I scroll up and down, but it isn't there. Clicking out of the budget, I navigate to her user area. Her meticulous note-keeping extends to this too – she has written up all the notes for Leila Summers, plus the order, and filed a consent form for the home birth. The weird thing is, Karen has approved it all and put a note on it. *Please put this through. See record 35698*. I know I'm new to the job, but I'm sure I should see anything that affects the department spend.

The order would make a dent in the budget – not a huge one – but, if lots of Katie's former patients want home births, it could become a serious problem.

I call Erica, but it goes to answerphone. I leave a message.

'Hiya, love. Give me a call when you can. I wanted to talk to you about the home birth costs. We need to look at the budgets before you book any more in. Anyway. Let's chat about it later. Bye.'

I look at the training modules I need to complete, but there's so much to learn and I'm not in any state of mind to absorb all that right now. My attention focuses on the other new files I have access to. All my colleagues' notes are there. With a jolt, I spot Katie's file, and I click on it before thinking. A window flashes up 'Confidential', and I immediately worry that someone can see what I've been doing. I close all my windows. I need to stop obsessing like this. It's not right. I need to calm down. I need to simply wait and see what the court decides. Most of all, I need to retain my integrity.

My phone beeps. Erica's name appears on the screen. I wonder why she didn't ring – I could use a friendly ear right now – but she's probably with one of her patients.

*Bit busy just now. None of the other ladies want home births. Just Leila. Don't worry. Speak later.*

That's me told, then. I'm alone. No Katie. No Erica. And now no Tom.

I go back upstairs, open the door to our eldest, Liam's, bedroom, and my heart aches. Our fifteen-year-old's computer screen is still glowing and his bed is unmade. I miss him already.

I could fight with Tom again, tell him he can't take the kids. *Or*, I think recklessly, *I could take them somewhere myself.* But where? My parents live in France. I can't go there and still do my job. Or see the trial out. And I would never do that to Tom. I can't bear not to be with him, either.

As I shut the door, I know I have to let them all go.

## Chapter Thirteen

## Leila

It's so hot. Mum loved July, when her garden was at its best. I look at my phone again. My heart aches for him, even though I know he's not thinking about me since I last saw him yesterday. I scroll through to his number. I look at his Facebook message account. *Last active 18 minutes ago.* A thousand scenarios run through my mind, most of them involving other girls, alcohol and drugs. Is that really what I want? Forever worrying about where he is?

He hasn't even asked if I was OK after he left. I go to ring him but change my mind and call Erica. She said I could. Anytime, she said. But she doesn't answer. I call again, but it goes to answerphone.

I'm shaken. I don't want to be, but I am. I can't stop crying. I've been checking my phone every second for his call. Erica stayed as long as she could after he left, but she had to get back to the hospital. Before she went, she set up the dining room and ordered a bed that she said would arrive today.

She is so organised, and it's like holding up a mirror to how useless I've become. It feels like my whole focus has been on keeping Ben here when it should have been on my baby. But I check myself. I've done the best for my child. I've kept appointments and made the effort. I'm not punishing myself. I can't, because I know it isn't my fault. I was here all the time, and where was he?

But deep inside, there's a hole. I don't know if it's because of my mum passing, or because of all this with Ben. All I know is I need someone here with me. I'm scared. There, I said it. Not just scared of the birth. I'm scared of everything to come.

I'd built it up in my mind. My baby would have everything I never had. A beautiful home – thank you, Mum – and a mum and dad who loved them. I would stay home and look after our child while Ben worked. I would get better at cooking and make sure I looked after everyone. I would plant flowers.

I look out over Mum's garden. Sobs wrack me. It still looks fine on the surface. She hasn't been gone long enough for it to become unmanageable. But the weeds are starting to come through. Stray raspberry brambles and self-seeded foxgloves are peeking through her carefully curated flowerbeds.

Not so long ago, I was planning a life with Ben and Mum. Daddy and Grandma. Mum is gone, but I know Ben will be back. This is the first time he's actually left. There have been rows, sure. But I could never have imagined it would come to this. He was so lovely at first, but I've ended up apologising more and more. Which means I've been apologising for his bad behaviour. It's a game I was willing to play to keep him.

The make-up sex was brilliant. The declarations of love and promises of a big wedding. The first few times I believed him, but doubt crept in slowly. I've started to cry whenever I see a wedding on TV or the bus goes past a happy scene at the village church. He's changed. He's not the man I was so happy with for so long.

I've had to play the game because now there's another person involved. Our baby. He's never before said outright he has doubts our baby is his. Anxiety floods my body as I wonder if he will start demanding DNA tests and I will have to arrange supervised visits. What if he wants to co-parent?

I feel dizzy at the thought of him taking our baby to Deano's flat. A tiny voice in my head mocks me. *What did you think would happen?* My father would talk to me that way. Belittling me and making fun. I can still hear him when I make a mistake. Was this a mistake? Was yesterday's argument a mistake?

I find the maternity unit number and press call. I need to find out when Erica will be here. A woman answers and I swallow hard. 'Hi. May I speak to Erica, please?'

'Who's calling, please?'

I almost end the call. Am I being super-needy? Is this what I am like with Ben? Is that why he's annoyed all the time? But I need to make sure I know how to get hold of Erica. 'It's Leila Summers. I'm one of her patients.'

The line clicks and I wait. And wait. Then she is back. 'I'm sorry, Erica is on outreach now. She doesn't work on the wards. But I can give you the outreach number.'

She reads out the same number Erica gave me. I put my phone on speaker and check. 'So, if you need her, that is the best number. But if you need the ward, give us another call.'

I know she is going to hang up, and I panic: 'Can I just ask… Erica has booked me in for a home birth. I wanted to know what would happen if I changed my mind. Or something went wrong.'

Erica's already told me, but I need to hear it again. I hear a keyboard tapping.

'Can I have your date of birth, please, Leila?'

I tell her and wait as she taps some more.

'Ah. Here we are. Yes, I can see you are marked for a home delivery.' She pauses. 'Ah. I see. Right.' I know she's seen that Katie was my former midwife. 'OK. Do not worry. I'm Pam. I'm a new staff midwife so I don't know about your record, but I can see here why you might be concerned. But let me assure you, we will be here if you want us. Erica is looking after you, and she has marked your file with everything we need to know.'

I feel my body relax. 'So, I can come into the hospital if I want to?'

'Of course you can. Talk to Erica about it and we will work to suit you. Please don't worry.'

I feel a smile form. I'm not alone after all. 'Thank you. I will talk to Erica. I'll ring her now.'

She ends the call and I try Erica again. There is no answer, and I think about leaving a voicemail, but in the end, I hang up. I need to stop all this worrying. Mum said she was proud of me for being so proactive, and that's what I need to be now.

I go into the back garden and sort through the tools. I find a long hoe and a trowel. I could plant some vegetables. For a second, I see the future. Something beyond all this mess. The greenhouse is empty now after a long winter and I could get some tomato plants and grow them. The thought of it lifts the sadness and I look over at next door's greenhouse. The couple who lives there – Mary and Don – are around the same age Mum was, and I know they got on.

I push the little gate between the houses. It's stiff with misuse – Ben didn't trust the neighbours and said they were watching him. It opens with a little bit of effort. Mum made a crazy-paving path to make it easier for them to knock on our back door. They would sit outside with cakes and cups of tea which, at the time, seemed boring, but I grew to like sitting with them.

Now, I can't imagine anything lovelier. Normality, whatever that is. Some calm to cancel out the constant worry and fear. I went round a couple of times after Mum died, and Mary did offer help. Now, I knock on the door.

The past year has been a lot, and I forgive myself a little. I see Mary through the glass.

She appears in her dressing gown. 'Oh, hello, love. I'm surprised to see you.'

I nod. 'Yeah. Sorry I haven't been round lately. I've been… well, Mum. And this.'

I haven't been round because I am embarrassed. Ben's late-night door slamming and whooping at computer games. The loud music, even during the day sometimes when he didn't get up for work. Arguing and me crying. She must have heard it.

She looks at my stomach, then back at me, and steps back a little. 'So, will you and your boyfriend be staying here? Or selling?'

She has heard it all, then. It hits me, as she looks past me to see if Ben is behind me, I have no friends. I've lost contact with the girls from school, even Rosie, my bestie. And I never fitted in with Ben's mates' girlfriends. They only tolerated me when Ben brought me out.

'Oh. I'm staying. With my baby. Do you know where I can get some tomato plants from? I'm going to look after the garden. It's what Mum would have wanted.'

Her features soften. 'Yes, she would. And I'm glad. I'm sure Don would help, if you wanted him to. If that's all right with your… boyfriend?'

I frown. I don't know if it would be, but that doesn't matter now. I think about telling her Ben has left, but what if he comes back? What if he realises he is wrong and this is just cold feet and fear of becoming a father?

When I first moved in, Mary would pop in for a cup of tea. She told me how much she missed Mum. But that stopped.

I say, 'Yes, that would be lovely. I'm sure Ben would be grateful too.'

She smiles. 'And you seem well looked after by the hospital now. That lovely young woman. Not the other one who was always on her phone in the garden, obviously.' She reddens. 'The dark-haired one who's always jolly.' She means Erica.

'It's OK. We know what's been going on. We've heard. And seen. But you need complete rest now and we don't want to bother you and the baby.' She moves closer. 'Otherwise, we would have come round when he was shouting yesterday morning. We didn't want to interfere. But, if you want us, you know where we are. Anyway, let us know about the garden. Probably best to wait until after the happy day.'

I feel much better now. Mary is next door and I have a string of appointments booked in with Erica. I finally feel like things are coming together.

## Chapter Fourteen

### Sue

They are gone and my heart is broken. We had our usual Monday tea, fried chicken, last night, then we sat the boys down and told them what had to happen.

'Will we have the football on at Grandma's?' said Daniel.

He and David are eleven and nine respectively, and they don't fully understand what has happened, mainly because we still haven't told them the full extent. I want my children to maintain their innocence as long as possible, and this would shoot holes right through it.

'Yes, son,' Tom told him, as I wiped away tears. 'But only if you've done your homework first.'

I thought I detected a hint of amusement in his voice that this was Dan's most pressing question, but I didn't find any of this funny. My heart was too busy splitting into two at the thought of spending days and nights apart from my children.

'Do I have to?' Liam said, glancing out of the window at the people sitting outside. 'I'm not bothered by that lot. I want to stay here with Mum, and all my stuff.'

Tom shook his head. 'It's not happening, mate. You can take anything you want from your room. You can sleep in the loft at Gran's. And it's not forever.'

His words had echoed around me. *It's not forever.* But it feels like it is. Early this morning, they got up and carted all their things out of the back door into Tom's people carrier. I helped and then kissed them all. They were sad but resigned. As I waved them away, right in front of the growing melee of reporters, I didn't break down. I didn't let them see my pain. I fixed a smile on my face, but as soon as my children turned the corner I ran inside. That's when the dam of emotion broke and left me in a sobbing, snotty heap.

Since they left, I've sat here and stared at the cars outside. There are nine now. I know they are only doing their jobs, but I bitterly resent them. The longer they stay, the longer I will be alone.

I didn't put up a fight at all. I let my family leave, and my home is completely deserted. I listen to the silence in the house. No distant beat of a radio. No shower running. No squeals of excitement from Dan and David playing together, or triumphant yells from Liam as he beats his friends at a video game. Just silence.

Why did Katie do this? I have a feeling Karen is protecting the hospital, and maybe herself. Wasn't she keen to get me and Erica out of the way? And she kept asking us to use the back door. It's either she's doing damage control for the hospital trust and we are collateral damage, or worse, like me, she wonders why I didn't notice. A niggle has grown over the months that she has questioned this officially and it will all be in that report, with all the stuff about Katie.

I can read what the papers say and listen to Karen's pieced-together reports, but I need to know for myself. To read the words, to see them in black and white.

I can't stay here. I need to find out what happened, so I can learn to accept that Katie did this. To stop the doubts for once and for all. I grab my keys, push my laptop into my tote bag, and pull on my work tunic. I've checked the staff rotas and Karen isn't in. Which means I'll be able to read the police report she said she had received. The one I haven't seen because I wasn't senior management. It will all be in there and I can finally understand how all this happened.

---

In twenty minutes, I am standing outside the department. I fiddle in my bag as Jenni Poulson, a duty health visitor, flashes her card and opens the door. I swing in behind her, pretending to press my card on the reader. I don't want it on record that I was in the department today.

I know this is wrong. I absolutely know I shouldn't do it, but the pull is too strong to resist. Once I know the facts,

I will be able to sleep and eat. And cope with the consequences.

Val the department admin on reception, grins at me. Then, 'Oh,' she says, checking the Tuesday shift sheet. 'You're not supposed to be here.'

'Yeah, I know,' I say, as breezily as I can. 'But I need to check who's doing what. I'm a bit worried that—'

She interrupts. 'Ah, yes. Of course. Worried about your ladies. Of course you are, love. Congratulations on your promotion, by the way!' She turns back to her computer. 'I'll just get the Ward Logs for you.'

'No. It's OK.' I step behind her desk and pull my laptop out of my bag. 'I'll look up what I need. Thanks, though.'

While she busies herself with her next task, I scan the sets of keys hanging on hooks beside her. The older offices in the hospital have locks, while the newer ones have pass cards. Karen's office is one of the older ones. She prefers her old oak desk and high windows to the square, white spaces favoured by some of the other senior managers. When I spot the keys I need, I place my tote bag strategically to block Val's view of them and wait until she is distracted.

Eventually, someone calls her into the ward to look at one of the new babies. She hurries away gleefully, and I grab the keys and drop them into my bag. No one is around, but I am aware of the CCTV camera Katie was caught on – thankfully, I know its reach doesn't extend this far down the corridor.

I walk back the way I came in, as if I am leaving the department, then duck into the side corridor. I hurry towards Karen's office and turn my key in the door. Once inside, I lock it. No one else has a key to this office except the security department – I'm counting on Val not realising the keys were taken from the desk and summoning them. I am shaking. This deception is new to me, and I don't like it. But I need clarity on what Karen knows, and what she's thinking.

I open the drawers of Karen's desk one by one and examine the contents. Her filing system is chaos. She is a clean desk campaigner, but I am relieved to see that she is flawed, like most people. It looks like she has just swept everything from her desk into the drawers.

I find the budget report easily and record 35698 is second from the top. It is blank. How can it be when I saw the figures on my laptop earlier? Flicking through the files, I see that Karen is seriously behind with her admin. I get a bad feeling in the pit of my stomach. Is she setting us up? Me and Erica? I can't believe Karen would do that, but then again I didn't think Katie would do what she did. And the stress on Karen is higher than ever right now – there has been talk amongst some of my colleagues that the victims' pressure group is bringing negligence charges against the hospital.

The police report has to be here somewhere. I know there was a hard copy, because she was reading from it when Erica and I were here the day she promoted us. I flick through more and more paperwork, until finally I see it wedged between a biscuit tin and the latest department spending report.

I pull it out. It's more than seventy pages long. The first part is Katie's statement. Her first interview. She answers most of the questions professionally and factually. But there are whole sections where she just says, 'I didn't do it'. The police interviewers ask her to say *no comment* instead, but she tells them that she doesn't want to imply she doesn't want to comment – because that isn't the case. She insists she will not admit to something she didn't do, and she won't lie by omission.

They show her the CCTV footage and ask her if that is her on the screen. She says it isn't. They tell her she wasn't home that night and ask her where she was, if that wasn't her. She answers simply, 'I can't say'. There is a note at the side of the page, handwritten, which says this is the only part of the interview where the accused showed any emotion.

The next part is statements from the victims. I skim-read them and they are all similar. Most of them remember nothing about the attacks. Some of them remember seeing a figure standing beside their hospital bed before they lost consciousness but can't identify who it was with any certainty. The next section is a printout of Katie's attendance, with the dates of the sample cases highlighted. She was on duty for all but one of the shifts – the one where she was caught on camera.

The next section starts with my statement. I can't stand to read it, so I flick through Karen's and Ian's. There are no damning statements about me in there. Next is Erica's statement. It is specific and straightforward but tinged with emotion – no doubt she was feeling guilty about whistleblowing. It details what she saw and when, how she put it all together and how she felt when she had to tell someone. She ends with how she couldn't believe lovely Katie could do this. That is a common theme.

Next is Adam's statement from the police's visit to their house. I can feel his desperation through the words. How he examined their life together for any clues she was capable of this.

Next is a list of items confiscated from Katie's home. A bag of work clothes and some hair for DNA testing. I do a double-take when I see the medication. Morphine. Scopolamine. She kept it at home. I can't believe it. Then I see the phone. I turn the page and there is a full report on it. I expect to see a list of patients' numbers, but there is just one. The police think it was a burner phone she was calling, and always in the park between her house and the hospital. No messages. Just calls. And the calls stopped when she was arrested.

I pull out Katie's practice diary from my tote bag and open it at the back page. I run my finger over the circled phone number, and it is the same. I punch the number into my phone, but then stop. No. The police will be watching. Of course they will. And this would implicate me. I read her statement again. *I can't say.* Why *can't*? Then it hits me. Because someone else *was* involved in Katie's crimes – someone she didn't want to incriminate. Or was afraid to.

I knew it. I knew she wasn't doing this alone. And, from what this looks like, with someone phoning her so often, at least twice a day, there was pressure on her.

Hiding drugs. Taking babies. This isn't something Katie could organise on her own. Someone was making her do it. She was scared.

This changes everything.

# Chapter Fifteen

## Leila

I'm in agony. I'm calling Erica and her phone is ringing out. She didn't turn up yesterday for our appointment and now I'm wondering if I should ask Mary if she will be my birthing partner.

My stomach tightens and I am sure the baby is coming. I google the symptoms and it must be the first stages of labour. But even thinking about having the baby right now, without Erica, makes it hard to breathe. I call her again. This time I leave a message.

'Erica. It's Leila. I thought you were coming round yesterday. Anyway, I think it's started. I'm going to dial 999 if it gets worse before you get here. And it's probably too late now, but I wondered if I should contact a doula?'

I end the call. I unlock the back door and nip through the little gate to Mary's house. I knock on the back door and wait. They are usually in during the day, and I can see her handbag on the table. I knock again.

The woman from the house next door to them comes out. 'Not seen her in days, love. Must have gone away.'

I look at her in her housecoat and slippers. 'Thanks. Did she say when she'd be back?'

She shrugs. 'Well, I didn't see them go. But they go to Scarborough sometimes. Anything I can help with?'

I don't know her. She moved in after I did, and I'm starting to not trust anyone. 'No. It's fine. I was just seeing if Mary wanted a brew.'

She goes inside and I go back to my garden. If Mary's not here, there's no one else nearby I can call on. Worry mounts and I have another pain. Ben hasn't phoned and I recognise from the deep longing in me that I am nearly at the point where I'd usually ring him. I'm starting to think I was too harsh on him. Yet I still can't stand the thought of him here with Deano while I'm feeding and bathing a baby. Another pain nags at me and I see my knuckles whiten, holding onto the kitchen chair.

My phone beeps and it's a message from Erica.

*On my way. I'm so sorry. My first Wednesday lady was late. Just stay put and don't ring anyone. It's all under control.*

It doesn't feel like it is. It feels like everything has come at once, crashing into me, and I am not ready for this. I pace up and down and try to focus on something else. But all I can think about is how I have let everyone down. Especially myself. I may not have got pregnant on purpose, but I wanted to start a family with Ben more than anything.

I thought it would change him. I believed him. But I am just as stupid as anyone else who believes someone who

112

won't commit. Because that's what it boils down to. I was just a convenience. At first it was the sex. Then I progressed to someone who would cook and do the washing, help with the bills, put him up in a bigger house. I should have seen it coming, but I wanted to please him. I wanted to be good to him.

Stress flares in my chest, and this is not the time. I google 'Doula' again while I pace, watching the window for Erica's car. Who knew there was a Doula Wiki? I take in the information I bookmarked:

> Doulas advocate for the individual's birth preferences and ensure their voice is heard. They can help facilitate communication between the birthing person, their partner, and the healthcare team. Their goal is to enhance the overall birth experience, promote a sense of empowerment, and help individuals and their families have a positive and memorable birth experience.

Empowerment sounds good. And I do want my voice heard. I am starting to think no one is listening to me. I am just starting to type 'how to find a doula in your area' into the search bar when a knock on the window makes me jump out of my skin. I turn quickly and see Erica beckoning me to the front door.

I hurry to let her in, but she is looking down the road. Tommy's van is approaching, and Ben is in the passenger seat.

She ushers me inside and shuts the door behind her. Another pain comes, and she sits me down on the bed in the dining room. She pulls up my leisure suit top and feels my stomach. Then she fetches a stethoscope from her bag and listens.

'All good in there. And I think these pains are Braxton Hicks. We'll keep an eye on them. But your body is practising for the main event.' She laughs at her own joke and goes into the kitchen.

But I am not laughing. I am thinking about Ben and what will happen next. I realise I am shaking. She returns with the tea and sits on the bed beside me.

'Look. I'm worried about your partner outside.' She stares at me. Her look is intense. 'Has he still got a key?'

As she says it, I hear him fumble to open the already unlocked door.

I freeze. I can feel the tension creep through my body and I want to hide. He stands in the doorway, hands on hips, sneering. He looks like he hasn't slept in days.

'I might have known Florence fucking Nightingale would be here. Anyways, I've come for some stuff. And I'll be needing that bank card for the savings account. Half of that's mine.'

Erica remains seated beside me. I am relieved that she isn't going anywhere.

He steps forward. 'Bank card. Now.'

Erica tenses. I breath harder now. I can hardly speak. But somehow I find the words. 'No. You're not having it. See my solicitor.'

I don't have a solicitor. But I tell myself I can find one.

He laughs. 'Fuck off.' He turns to Erica. 'You. Out. This is between me and her.'

Erica stares at him. 'I'm going nowhere. My concern is for Leila's welfare after the other day.'

She glances at my bruised wrist.

'Just give me the card then. And I'll be off.'

His arrogance is staggering. That money was mostly Mum's. Some of it was savings from my hairdressing job so I can get my own salon in time. But none of it is his.

'No.'

As quick as a flash, he makes a dive for my purse from my bag on the table. He knows I keep my card in there; he's gone through it for cash often enough. Despite my baby belly, I move at the same time as him and snatch my purse before he can. He grabs my arm and twists it behind my back. I grip my purse with my free hand.

He is screaming in my face. 'Give it to me. Now.'

I am an inch from his face and I can smell stale cigarettes and booze. I throw the purse to Erica and she catches it. He pushes me hard and I fall. Erica rushes towards me and he swings his arm back to punch her. But she straightens and stands firm. She is facing him off while I am trembling on the floor.

Still staring him out, she pulls her phone from her uniform pocket. She holds it up and punches in two nines. Her finger hovers above the nine key once more, and he lowers his arm and backs off. I manage to get up and sit on a chair.

He leans over me. 'I'll be back. I want that cash.'

He storms out.

We are silent for a long moment. Then Erica speaks. 'Right. Let's get all the spare keys together. And I'll sort out a locksmith. Better safe than sorry, eh?'

I hadn't even thought about that, but she's right. What if he tries that again after I've had the baby? Right on cue, another pain shoots through me.

'Yeah, yeah. Course. I don't want him just walking in. But after that, he might have learned his lesson.'

Erica scoffs. 'Well, you'd hope so. But you need to be sure. You want your baby to be safe, don't you? And you, of course.'

'Yes. I do. I was wondering, though. About a doula.'

As soon as I say it, I realise it's a trivial thing to bring up at a time like this. But she is ever-patient and nods thoughtfully.

'OK. Under some circumstances, and arranged earlier, it would work. But we don't have time, love. We need to get you organised.' She holds her hands out. 'If you give me the keys, I'll dispose of them. Windows, as well.'

I blink at her. 'It'll cost a lot to change all the locks. Do you know how much?'

She shrugs. 'I don't know, but it's not worth taking a chance. My first duty is to you, and when the time comes, the baby.'

I swallow hard, trying not to worry about how on earth I can afford this. This is going from bad to worse. 'Shouldn't we call the police? I mean, what if he comes back?'

'You could. But I don't know if they will do anything unless someone's witnessed him actually harming you.

They could question him but it's unlikely he'll admit it. You have bruises on your wrist, but the police need to see what happened. I should have called them earlier. I'm so sorry.'

I feel like hugging her. After all she has done, she is blaming herself. 'My god, Erica. It's not your fault. You did all you could.'

'Yeah, but I've not been as sharp as I should be these past few days. I've been a little bit nervous. About the trial. I know I told you I can't discuss it, and I can't, in any detail. But I do need to tell you something as it will mean me being away for a little while And I don't want you to worry. I have to give evidence.'

I gasp. 'She pleaded not guilty?'

Erica sighs. 'Yes. And it means I and lots of other people have to give evidence in court.'

A dozen scenarios run through my head. 'What if I start with the baby while you are giving evidence?'

She puts her hand on my arm. 'Don't worry. It will be a short appearance. I just have to state what I saw.'

I feel my skin heat up and my heart thumps in my chest. 'Oh, my God. You saw her do it?'

'I did. I'm the one who alerted everyone. I thought something was odd, so I kept a close eye on her. Then, when I had proof, I went to my team leader.'

She's a hero. I knew she was good, but she's saved those women's lives. And stopped babies being taken.

'I don't know what to say. You've… well. Saved my life, probably.'

She looks very serious then. 'I don't know about that, Leila, but I read her notes and saw the timesheets, and… no. I don't want to say it.'

But I know. I know what she is trying to say. That I would have been the next victim. I've known for some time that I had a lot in common with the others. I was just her type.

I hurry round the house and collect all the keys. Erica calls a locksmith, and they will be here first thing tomorrow morning. I know it's the right thing, but I worry what Ben's reaction will be when he comes back for his stuff.

I suddenly realise how scared I am. I knew I was scared of Katie. That is natural. But scared of Ben? That's not right. I knew he wasn't super-dad, or even super-boyfriend. But I never thought he would try to rule me by fear. There's no coming back from this. No way I could ever take him back now. The only way I'm going to feel safe is with him not here and with the house secure.

Erica is back. The pains have subsided a bit. She was right; they are probably Braxton Hicks.

'OK, I think we are all set,' she says. 'I'll leave you to get some rest now, if you'll be all right on your own?'

Panic grips me. I'm not all right on my own. Not at all. What if Ben walks back in? What if, this time, he brings his friends with him?

'Could you stay?' I blurt out. 'I'd feel safer if you did. Just until the locks are changed?'

She stares at me. 'It's not normal practice at all. But I can come round super-early tomorrow. But I'll have to pop out at lunchtime to meet a colleague about the trial. Oh, and I have appointments booked with some of my other ladies? But I can be here early. I'll book it in with my team leader.'

She opens her laptop and types. 'I've sent an email. ' She pauses. `I've also mentioned starting a safeguarding process to make sure we are both protected. If it carries on, I'm afraid I'll have to inform the police. That behaviour isn't acceptable.'

I feel tears well. This is the last thing I wanted, but she is right. The more people know, the better. She shuts her laptop.

'Don't worry. One way or another, it will all be fine. I promise.'

# Chapter Sixteen

## Sue

It's strange to wake up today to an empty house, because Sundays are usually a family day, starting with breakfast together. I've been so lonely the past few days with them gone and last night, when I called Tom, I could hear the boys in the background watching football with Tom's dad. The laughing and cheering stung as I sat in the empty lounge feeling more isolated than ever, especially with my new knowledge.

I try to remind myself that, even though it feels permanent, Tom and the kids staying somewhere else is just temporary. I'm being over-sentimental about something that's a practical solution. But, at the end of the call, I told Tom I loved him, and he didn't say it back. I can't remember the last time he neglected to say it back, so I feel unmoored.

I've decided to go into work today to keep me busy and my mind off this week. But I'm not going in until lunchtime, so I spend my morning preparing myself for what is to come. The trial starts tomorrow. I'm anxious and feel sick at the thought of what Katie did coming out in court but also relieved that soon this will all be over. Then I can issue a statement clarifying how I had nothing at all to do with this and hopefully things can start to go back to normal and I can have my family back.

I check my phone and open X. I search for my name and there are lots of posts about the trial that mention me and Erica. None of them actually says it in as many words, but the majority insinuate that we must have known. We must have suspected. And one line of argument is claiming that there has been a cover-up. That the women who initially complained were ignored.

I scroll down. One of them has sold her story to a national newspaper. There's a huge picture of her accompanying the article. I remember her. She was lovely. Just her mum there at the birth, because the dad wasn't in the picture anymore. I scan the article and then I realise I'm going to be late to meet Erica for our catch-up before I go to work.

Ten minutes later, I'm sitting in a Costa outside the hospital. I see Erica parking up outside and my heart lifts. I've missed her. I don't get to see her as much with her being on outreach.

She pushes open the door and grins at me. 'Hello, stranger!'

I stand up and hug her. 'Hello, you. It feels like I haven't seen you in ages. Are you OK?'

She nods into my shoulder and hugs me back. Then she sits down and leans on the table. 'It's going really well. I miss the ward. And you, of course. But the ladies I've been assigned to look after are nice, and I think I'm getting on top of it. It's all so new.' I suddenly feel tearful. She seems so calm and organised. She smiles kindly at me. 'Are you all right?'

The words escape before I can stop them. 'Tom took the boys to his mum's. There are reporters outside the house and after what Karen said…'

Her face clouds with concern. 'They didn't follow you, did they?'

'No. No, I've got a route out of the back of the house. They sit at the front.'

She shakes her head. 'Sorry, I just… I'm sorry Tom and the boys have had to leave. It's a terrible business.'

I take a deep breath to steady myself. 'And it's not going to get any better. I was reading about the trial today and apparently there's this lawyer called Lucy Norris who is shit-hot.'

She frowns. 'Oh. I'm not really used to… you know… courts. It's all a bit scary. So does that mean for the prosecution? Or defence? The lawyer?'

Of course. She has to give evidence. It isn't going to be easy for her. The article I read said Lucy Norris has defended dozens of misconduct cases and won. Her court skills are legendary.

'Defence. Look. I know some things. I don't think…'

She tucks her hair behind her ear. 'I'm already feeling nervous about having to stand up in court as a whistle-blower without having some clever lawyer trying to manipulate me to get Katie off.'

Her voice sounds faint and I realise I shouldn't have brought the lawyer up because it's going to be hard enough for Erica as it is. My God, how must she feel, having to stand up there? I already realise how hurtful it is to have your integrity in doubt. I pause for a moment to allow her to gather herself, before I broach what's been on my mind. 'You're right and I'm sure no one will doubt your word. It's really brave that you came forward as soon as you had your suspicions.'

She nods, grateful for my support. I hesitate, then voice my concern. 'I can't help think that someone was making her do it.'

She frowns at me. 'Seriously?'

'Otherwise, why would she have that second phone? Who was calling her?'

'I don't know. But one thing is for sure, if the police think she had an accomplice, it will be brought up in court. I guess we'll find out everything over the next few days.'

I know Erica is right and I hope that the truth does come out to help me understand and process everything that's happened. But until then, I can't shake this feeling that there's more to this than people are quick to believe. I want to show her the number I found and tell her Katie wouldn't do this unless she was forced to. But I can't, because then she'd know I've seen the police report. Which I sneaked into Karen's office to find. I wonder if I should share this weird feeling about Karen and how she always seems to be at the centre of things. Always around. I have suspicions about Karen that I can't quite put my finger on, and I suddenly feel very guilty. This has changed me. I would never have done anything like that before. I would never have sneaked into Karen's office. I pride myself on my honesty and integrity.

I pause before deciding it's best to simply agree with her. We got enough to deal with, and Erica and I need to stick together. We're a team, and right now that's comforting. 'I'm going to go tomorrow. I'll sit in the public gallery.'

She grabs my hand. 'Are you sure you want to put yourself through that? You know I can't come with you. I wish I could. But I'm not allowed in court until I've given my evidence on Tuesday. Will Tom come with you?'

I doubt Tom will, so I shake my head. I realise we barely do anything together these days, and that feeling of being unanchored rises to the surface again. Katie and Erica are my besties, and one will be in the dock and the other a key witness. Karen has already told me she won't be attending because she feels she is seen as a representative of the hospital, and she doesn't want to be seen to support Katie.

There is no one to support me. But I am compelled to go and see. I need to take in the facts rather than the speculation that's been making the headlines, and it feels like an important step to help me come to terms with what happened.

'Tom will be at his mum's with the kids. But I'll be fine. And I'll report back. Anyway, before I go into work, I've got a few things I need to run by you.'

She sips the coffee she ordered. 'Shoot.' She smiles.

I pull my laptop out of my tote bag. She does the same. This is my chance to talk to her about Karen and the missing records. I shiver. It's not just the records, though, it's her visiting Katie and keeping such a tight grip on all the information around the case. I can't help but think she has something to do with this. Or she's covering something up.

'So, part of my new job is to look at budgets. I can see you've put in your time sheets and submitted a fuel expense claim. But you know the other day when we spoke about the home birth? Well, I checked for the equipment requisition, and it's not here.'

She looks up from her screen. 'What do you mean? You saw me input it. And the equipment has arrived. It has to be logged there.'

I scan the log until I reach the correct page and turn my laptop around. 'Look, nothing is there. Other things from that day are there, but not that requisition.'

She looks confused. 'I don't understand. I input it myself. You saw me.'

'Yes, I did. Maybe it saved to the wrong place. But look at that note from Karen. She put it through without checking. I'm worried she's changed it or something. I'm worried she's… Have you got the reference? From the docket?'

She tenses and rubs her forehead. 'I put that information in. I don't know what happened to it. I don't have the docket with me. Now I'm on outreach, I can't carry everything around with me.' She seems overwhelmed.

This poor woman is giving evidence this week and I'm hassling her about a budget log.

'No, course you don't. Sorry, love. I wasn't getting at that. I think Karen's... well. I don't know. It just seems odd that she's trying to get us out of the way, and waving home births through. It's a difficult time for both of us. I'm sorry.' She's staring at her keyboard, but I duck down and catch her eye. 'Look. If it would feel better, come and sit outside the court tomorrow, and I'll come out and tell you what's happened. Neither of us needs to be on the ward.'

She shakes her head. She's fighting back tears. 'Not tomorrow. I have patient appointments I have to keep. But will you come with me on Tuesday? Seeing you before will make me feel better before I have to go into court.'

I touch her arm gently. 'Of course I will. It's a big thing.' She smiles at me through watery eyes. 'Whatever happens, we'll always be friends. None of this can come between us two. With everything else that's happening...'

My voice trails off. Exactly what else? I can't work out where Karen fits into all this. I know she saw that requisition. I saw the note. And now it's gone. Something is going on.

I have to admit it to myself. Maybe I'm only trying to avoid what increasingly seems like a solid fact that Katie did this alone. Not once, but several times. Yet my mind goes back and forth, a continuous argument with myself, because something else is not right. But Erica's correct about one thing: the police would have pursued every angle. The phone number could even be one of the ladies. Maybe her final victim.

I feel a tightness in my chest. Had Katie been ringing them out of work hours? Visiting them? Making them think she was their friend and gaining their trust? I read the notes from Erica's new lady. Leila and Katie had spent a long time together at Leila's home, and I realise Erica is right to be offering Leila a home birth if it will make her feel more comfortable: especially as it seems like she was being set up as Katie's next victim. I need to support Erica more. We are a team.

But I still can't imagine how Katie could do what she did. Tom has warned me not to judge people by my own standards, as I will only be disappointed. I've sometimes wondered if I was gullible, but I would rather be that than dishonest or just plain bad. I am not perfect. No one is. But I would do anything not to hurt another person's feelings, let alone hurt them physically.

Everything is falling apart. The next week is going to be a major challenge for all of us, especially Erica. I have a feeling that what we know now is only the tip of the iceberg.

## Chapter Seventeen

## Leila

I wake up just before nine. I haven't slept this well in ages. My phone alarm is flashing, and I don't need to check to know why. It's been on my mind all week. This is the day my baby is due, according to the hospital. What seems like years ago, I made a joyful entry.

*I will meet my baby today.*

This was before I found out the date is for guidance only. That, unless you can absolutely pinpoint the date your baby is conceived, the 'nine months' could be any time between eight-and-a-half and nine-and-a-half months. And even then, it could be earlier or later.

It was this uncertainty about when the baby might actually arrive that sent me into a spin in the first place. With neither me nor Ben driving, I freaked out about how I would get to the hospital in time. Back then, I thought we were different from the couples our friends have become. We wouldn't argue or storm out. We were different.

I lie in bed chastising myself for my teenage daydreams. I am not stupid, yet that's how I feel right now. I completely bought into the dream of happily-ever-after. Now it seems I am not that girl. But it will be OK.

I probably won't meet my baby today, as nothing seems to be working out as I thought it would. Ben isn't shaping up to be the partner I wanted during my pregnancy. But I feel a new sense of urgency to be ready and a belief that I can do this. I *can* do it. It's not excitement. It's more of a push to check everything is in place. At least the pains have gone. For now. And I feel so safe, because Erica is looking after me.

It's weird because I actually liked Katie. She made me feel safe, too. Looking back, she was brilliant after Mum died and I was lost in my grief. She told me Mum would always live on through me and my baby. We even talked about how she didn't have kids. She was always positive about the future, telling me the unexpected was around the next corner.

She didn't meet Ben, though. He was working then, and my appointments were always during the day. Looking back, I had company a lot of the time. Maybe that's why I feel so alone now. I'm going to follow the trial as much as I can because this is a lesson on how you can never tell what a person is really like and that I need to be better about who I trust once I've got the baby to look after. They've been reporting about the case on the local news bulletins, how more women have come forward. They've even started showing pictures of Katie. In a strange way, I miss her. Like I miss Ben.

But neither of them were good for me. I can see that now. Though Mum always said 'hold people at arm's length', she didn't believe in phasing them out. She said you should always give people a chance to change. I can feel my heart soften. Katie has gone. She's going to prison, and rightly so. But Ben is going to be part of my life forever, whether I like it or not.

I scroll through the photo gallery on my phone and look at adorable selfies of us. We had good times. Lots of them. I honestly thought he was The One. Have I been too harsh? Am I expecting too much? All this must have been a lot for Ben to handle, too. But I'd taken that into account and, to be honest, that's why I didn't end things earlier. People handle things in different ways, so I'd tried to give him time to get his head around everything.

I hear a light knock on my bedroom door. 'Come in.'

Erica pops her head round the door. She's here early like she said. I told her to take a key so she could get in, in case I went into labour. She looks fresh as a daisy. She's holding a tray with tea and toast on it. She sets it down beside me and folds her arms.

'There you are. Breakfast in bed. But don't get used to it.'

She laughs. I feel a little tearful. No one has done this for a while. 'Thank you.'

She smiles and sits on the end of the bed. 'The locksmith will be here soon. You stay here if you want. I'll sort it out.'

I nod and she disappears. I hear a vehicle and voices outside in the garden. I get up and peep through the curtains. Erica is dealing with the locksmiths. She's very efficient and I'm grateful for her helping me get organised. Pointing and instructing. That's how I will be soon. Making a home for my baby and going back to work. I feel like I'm finally finding a way to get out of this hole I am in. She's shaking her head – I guess she is telling them the reason why we need the locks changing. They are nodding.

It's all been such a shock. I'm still worried about what Ben will say about the locks. I put it out of my mind for the time being and go downstairs in my jumper and leggings co-ord that only just fits around me. I hear drilling at the back door, and Erica is sitting at the kitchen table with her laptop.

I smile at her, but when she looks up, she frowns. 'I thought I told you to stay upstairs. You need your rest.'

I sit down in front of her. 'I wanted to...' She tuts and shakes her head. I blurt it out. 'I wanted to talk to you about today. It's my due date, and it's made me feel... well, kind of worried. I'm wondering what will happen if, say, I start in labour tomorrow when you are in court.'

She nods seriously. 'I can see why you are worried, but we've gone over this. It'll be fine.'

Her eyes are wide and unblinking. I can just about see the screen on her laptop. A picture of Katie stares out, and the headline reads, 'Killer nurse due in court.' Of course, she is upset.

'Yes, sorry. And I know it's a bad day for you. I shouldn't have brought it up, I was just worried.'

She leans back on the Formica chair. 'Look. Baby will come when it's ready,' she says soothingly. 'And you've got me here to help, so we'll be ready.'

I nod and try to tell myself it will be OK.

Erica says, 'I know it's been hard. And you've had a lot to put up with. Your mum and that boyfriend of yours.'

'It's only a falling out, but he's my baby's dad and I know he'll support me.'

It's a gut reaction to defend him, one I have become so used to. I know this is not the case, really, but I'm not ready to admit it out loud yet. She raises her eyebrows as if to say *that's not what he said the other day*. We sit in silence until we're interrupted by the locksmith. He steps through the back door, dangling four keys on a string. 'Right, ladies. All done. And here they are.'

I get up to take them. He produces a card machine, and I push my card in and enter the pin.

The locksmith looks at Erica and takes in her uniform. He shakes his head. 'Terrible business. But we'll soon know how long she's got. Life, hopefully.'

He finishes the transaction and hands me the card and the receipt. She shows him out and then sits at the table opposite me.

'Right. Thank goodness that's all sorted out. You need to rest now. And hopefully that will be the end of your ex walking in and out.'

I blink at her. I suddenly feel defensive.

'I can make my own decisions. And I can decide if I want people in my life. He'll need to come and get his things, anyway.'

'Of course you can. But please, Leila, think of your baby. It's the most important thing now, not you or Ben. Not me or Katie. Like you say, it's your due date. Baby could be here any minute, and you need to be prepared. Your hormones will be raging right now, and that will affect how you feel.' She leans across and touches my hand. 'I'm worried about you and want to make sure you're in tip-top condition to have a smooth delivery. And I know it's not easy now the trial is starting. But let's pull together. Me and you. And when all this is over, you can make decisions about Ben then?'

Everything she says sounds reasonable. She is right about the hormones. One minute I'm fine, then the next I'm in tears. And I keep losing my temper. It's similar to what I felt every month before my period. A sense of impending doom. Then it would disappear, only to return a month later. That's when me and Ben had our worst rows.

I would hold in all the annoyance I felt at him and his friends all month and then I couldn't keep it in. It was as if I was suddenly brave and everything was clear and true, so that I absolutely had to say it. But he would call me names and shout 'time of the month' over and over again. It would make me angrier how he belittled me.

I even went to see my GP. She gave me progesterone, but it made me put weight on, which didn't escape Ben's notice. That's when the insults started. He'd poke my legs and call me a heifer. Then he'd make pig noises when I was eating. I stopped the progesterone, and the next month was hell. I lost weight, but I was angry all the time.

Ben continued to call me names. In front of people. It was as if I hadn't lost weight and he couldn't see me. A moment pops into my mind. It's something I have wiped away and replaced with thoughts of baby clothes and prams. We'd gone to see Phil and Julie. It was an attempt at a dinner party. I had a strong feeling Julie was having similar problems to me with Phil, who seemed to be a fixture in my lounge playing computer games.

Looking back, I can see that she simply wanted a happy relationship like everyone else on Instagram has. Their home was lovely, and she served up delicious food while we sat in silence. I'd worn a beautiful black dress I'd bought especially for the evening. She was wearing a scarlet Bardot-style dress. Ben and Phil had made the effort, too.

I'd started to scoop roasted baby potatoes onto my plate along with beef stroganoff. Ben snorted before the names started. 'Look at her. Oink, oink. Piggy, piggy, piggy.'

He pinched at my waist, and Julie looked horrified. I tried to laugh it off and ignore him. But he carried on. 'No one wants a fat girl. Put some of it back instead of piling it on your plate.'

Julie intervened. 'It's all right. Just leave what you don't want.'

Phil was laughing, and it all felt so wrong, although I could tell Julie was trying to make eye contact with me and check I was OK.

But Ben didn't stop there. 'That's her fucking problem. She wants it all. Can't stop eating. Fat as a pig.'

Phil wasn't laughing anymore. They were both staring at him and, for once, I knew he was out of order and everyone thought he'd crossed the line. In that moment I wanted to get up and walk out of the flat. I wanted to walk away from him and never see him again. Leave him behind. Go back to Mum's house, alone this time, and start again.

The thought excited me. It was like seeing a new beginning I hadn't glimpsed before. I promised myself I would do something about it as soon as possible. But I'd drunk too much, and we ended up having sex and that is the night I got pregnant. I know, because by then it was so rare he came home early enough to catch me awake, that it must have been.

When I found out I was pregnant, I tried to replace the memory of that night with a happier version, unable to bear the reality of how the baby had actually been conceived. He never stopped calling me names. I tried to think about all the times he was good to me, but they were getting less and less frequent.

Erica is right. I'm sitting here waiting for him to turn up and try to get round me, but he's had enough chances. If he's not going to be the partner I need and the father our baby deserves, then we'll be better off without him.

I go upstairs and sit on my bed. I'm going to ring him. Tell him how it is. Draw some boundaries. I should have done it before, but I didn't feel brave enough, worried he'd leave me.

I give my phone a scroll-through, summoning all my courage. But I stop. He hasn't contacted me. He hasn't rung or messaged to see how I am. Or our baby. All the things he said about being a good dad: they were lies. If I ring him now, I'm doing what I always do and crawling back. I'll end up apologising and he'll be horrible to me again. I need to break the cycle.

I can't believe he hasn't tried to get in touch. He never wanted me, and he doesn't want our baby. I feel a tightness in my stomach as I realise I really am alone now.

## Chapter Eighteen

### Sue

First thing on Monday morning, I'm sitting in the visitor gallery at Manchester Crown Court. I feel sick. The courtroom isn't what I thought it would be. I'd imagined an old-style, dark-wood-furnished room, but this is light wood and reinforced glass.

The row in front of me and to my right is occupied by a line of women who are holding hands. I recognise two of them and nod in acknowledgement, but they look away. Karen's words about not attending court hit me full force.

'If I attend, people will think I'm supporting her. And I'm not.'

That's what these new mums must think about me. I can't imagine what they have gone through. I want to tell them that I'm not on her side, that more than anything, I want the truth to help me understand and process everything that has happened and who is involved. I am hit now by a feeling that there are very few people I can trust. Erica. Tom. My children. Adam. I struggle to think of anyone else at all.

I look out over the courtroom populated by lawyers and clerks. I see a youngish, suited woman who I recognise from the internet as Lucy Norris, Katie's lawyer. She'll defend her case, although I can't see how she can with the evidence that's stacked against her.

My legs are shaking. Nerves do that to me, and I wonder if I shouldn't have come. Perhaps it will only make me feel worse. I promised Tom I wouldn't come. I spoke to the boys last night, and he grabbed the phone from Liam.

'You're not going to court, are you?'

I paused, not wanting to lie. 'I'm not giving evidence, so I might go and see—'

'I'd rather you didn't.'

I felt my hackles rise at him telling me what to do. 'I'll decide what I'm doing tomorrow. I'll go if I feel like it.'

He's called all the shots recently and I haven't done anything wrong. I could picture him nodding into his mum's old dial phone in her hallway.

'Of course. Sorry. I don't know what I'm saying. I'm worried.'

His conciliatory tone took me by surprise because I felt like there had been more distance between us lately, that he resented my involvement in all this.

'I know you are, love. But once this is over, we will be fine. It's only a blip that's neither of our fault,' I promised him.

He was silent. I heard the boys in the background and his mum talking about the TV to his dad.

Eventually he spoke. 'Sue…'

I interrupted. Whatever it was – another piece of advice or a veiled command – this wasn't the time for it. 'It's all right. Whatever it is will keep. I'll come over on Saturday and we can go out. A date. Like we used to. Somewhere secret. We've got a built-in babysitter now.'

I expected him to laugh and join in. But he didn't. He spoke quietly and his voice shook. 'Right, yeah. It's been hard on everyone. But I want you to remember that, whatever happens, I love you.'

The call cut off and I realised how difficult it must be for him having to look after three practically teenagers single-handed while his mum stuffs them with junk food and sugar and he's missing home. It's bound to take its toll. But it was his suggestion and that's why I wasn't going to let him put me off coming today, because this is something I have to do on my terms.

The gallery fills up and people filter into the courtroom. I am sitting directly opposite the dock, and I watch intently until the doors behind it open. Katie appears flanked by two police officers. One of them unlocks handcuffs and I feel my pulse quicken. I can't take my eyes off her. She is pale and thin. A shadow of herself. Her hair is longer, dark roots showing clearly through her trademark blonde. Her previous thick-rimmed, trendy glasses have been replaced with more staid frames, and she is wearing a grey tracksuit. She sits and lifts her head and my heart breaks at how ill she looks.

She catches my eyes and mouths to me, *I didn't do it*. But there is something else. She lowers her eyes and doesn't look up again. She was my best friend and I always thought I could read her but now it seems like she doesn't want to look at me, out of shame of what she's done. Even in that tiny box, she turns her body away from me. The lawyers are whispering to their clerks, and I watch her. Twitchy and outwardly calm, but the flush of her neck is a tell that she's nervous.

The jury of six women and six men are sworn in.

The expected 'All Rise' rings out, and the judge enters and motions for us to sit. I brace myself for what I'm about to hear.

Katie is sworn in. Her voice is small and not her usual confident tone. She simply states her name and refuses to swear on the Bible, so affirms to tell the truth instead. Her eyes are downcast until she stares directly at the judge as he speaks.

'Katie Withers. You have been charged with seven sample cases of attempted murder and attempted kidnapping. In a pre-trial plea hearing you pleaded not guilty to these charges. As a result, this court will consider the evidence of witnesses and the jury will come to a conclusion at the end of the trial.' He pauses and looks at the lawyers, both of whom nod to him. I half expected Lucy Norris to tell him Katie had decided to change her plea. But she doesn't. She smooths the robes over her suit and shuffles papers in front of her. He continues. 'Today's business will detail reports and two expert witnesses.

Tomorrow we will start to hear from other witnesses and other evidence will be brought. Each witness will be open to questions from both the defence and the prosecution. The first witness is Dr Luke Newton.'

It is underway and my mouth feels dry. I glance at the row of new mums. I'd assumed they were the sample cases, but surely they wouldn't be allowed to watch before they gave evidence? That's why Erica said she couldn't be here today. Dr Newton is ushered in and stands in the witness box. He is sworn in, and he explains to the court about the toxicology of the drugs given to the 'sample victim'.

My blood runs cold at these terms, and I see Katie shake her head slightly. I watch her as he speaks. She isn't looking at him. Instead, her eyes sweep the gallery. I wonder if she is looking for Adam or Erica. Or Karen. For a glimmer of support. But as I listen to Dr Newton, I see why no one is here to support her. I look around and spot her parents and my heart breaks for them as he speaks.

'The opiate medication was stolen from the maternity ward cabinet at regular intervals. On investigation by the staff, it was found to have been written down to waste, but an audit found it had not been signed out. This would have been inconclusive had a batch of medication matching the waste medication not been found in a bedroom at Katie Withers' home.'

I watch the jury. They have notepads and are writing down every detail. The gallery behind me has filled up now and there's a tense silence as we listen to proceedings. Some viewers have press passes and others have a visitor badge like me. Dr Newton finishes his statement and Lucy Norris stands up. She is small but imposing. When she speaks, her voice cuts through the courtroom like a knife, and everyone sits up straight.

'Dr Newton. Thank you for your very clear statement of fact. For the most part. My question is around the opiates found in my client's home.' She pauses. 'I have no doubt your expertise in toxicity is one hundred per cent correct and based on fact. I've seen the lab reports. But may I refer you to my client's statement on page thirty-five where she states she neither stole the medication nor took it to her home?'

He reads a report placed in front of him. She continues. 'And Mr Adam Withers' statement on page four listing the visitors to the house in the prior month?'

He reads the page and nods. She continues. 'So, my questions are these. Firstly, did anyone else have access to the medication cupboard in the maternity ward? And secondly, were any of those people visitors to Katie Withers' home preceding the incident in question?'

He is silent. I worried that something like this could happen and I would be implicated. He reddens, then speaks. 'Well, yes. Anyone authorised had access to the medication cupboard bu—'

Lucy interjects. 'So, did anyone see Katie Withers take the medication? Or could anyone else have taken it? You see, Dr Newton, I worry that this case hinges on the assumption Katie Withers did take the medication.'

He stares straight ahead. 'The statement says members of staff from the maternity ward were visitors to her home in the period before the incident.' He looks at the judge. 'I want to make clear that I didn't say Mrs Withers took the medication or put it in her home. My role here is only to state what the test results were.'

Lucy slaps the report on the desk in front of her. 'Exactly! That is exactly what I want to make clear, too. My client says she didn't take the medication. To your knowledge, did she take it? And did she hide it in her house?'

He purses his lips and shakes his head. 'No.'

'And could someone else have taken it? And put it in her house?'

The colour rises in his cheeks. 'Yes.'

She looks at the jury. 'Your Honour. I would like to request that the jury be directed to be wary of assumption and supposition and consider fact only.'

The judge nods in agreement and the prosecution lawyer stands. 'No further questions. Thank you.'

Dr Newton steps down but I feel shaken and my palms are clammy. I had access to Katie's home. We all did, so Lucy is right. At least six of us had been at Katie's in the previous month. And more before that.

I notice a man with a notepad looking at me, so I try to avoid his eye and keep staring straight ahead. Perhaps Tom was right and I shouldn't have come. The next witness is talking about mobile phone masts, and I lurch between wanting to run for the door and being transfixed by Katie in the dock, tucking her hair behind her ear meekly.

Lucy Norris is as good as everyone said she was. Only two witnesses in and she is systematically quashing any assumptions being used to implicate her client. I know it is her job to make Katie look innocent, but I don't like where this is going. If we all had access to that medicine cabinet, is there a case for hospital negligence? I can see now why Karen didn't want to be here if failings on her part are going to be brought to light.

I am transfixed by the to and fro of Lucy's questioning, one moment nodding at facts and the next shaking her head and shooting down supposition in flames. All the time Katie fidgets in her seat and I try to reconcile the woman in the dock with my best friend. Eventually, there is a break and I escape into the cool air of the corridor outside.

All I can think about are Lucy's words about assumptions and suppositions and how anyone could have taken the medication. And how we'd all been to Katie's the week before. My head spins with the endless possibilities. Putting two and two together and making five. How Jenni Lennon had been acting weird for months, then suddenly left. And Marion Stokes had stolen diazepam because she couldn't get a doctor's appointment.

Everyone had been so quick to assume this narrative of a childless nurse killing mothers to steal a baby.

# Chapter Nineteen

## Leila

I must have fallen asleep this afternoon. I check my body for any changes and feel a deep sense of relief that I am not in labour. But I am exhausted. I've checked all the pregnancy sites and they say constant tiredness is one of the main difficulties in the final trimester.

I will be so glad when I never need to hear pregnancy terms again. I've had a gutful of placenta previa and trimesters. But I'm loving reading about how to care for my baby once it arrives. I am only now finding out about how to bathe and how to change in the best way. I can imagine holding my little one, and I'm trying to be as prepared as possible. I've read every baby book I can get my hands on, and played the moment I can hold my child over and over in my mind. I cannot wait.

But I miss my mum. I know she would have loved all this and she would have been such a great helping hand to guide me in the early days after the baby arrives.

As I lie here on my bed, I try to feel her closer. I listen for her, but there is nothing. I don't know if there is a heaven, but I hope there is. I always imagine her sitting having a cup of tea with my gran. She loved her mum like I loved her. And it is only at this moment that I realise this baby kicking inside me will love me. Me. I might feel alone right now but I will be strong for my baby. I feel a surge of love and strength and I know it will all be fine.

I am ready. Sure, there will be problems. But I just need the birth to go smoothly and then it will all be OK once the baby is safely here. I listen for Erica downstairs. I feel like we argued before and I want to apologise. I don't expect she's bothered, because this is only a job for her. But she is going above and beyond, and I should thank her and listen to her advice because she's looking out for me.

I go downstairs, but she is gone. Her laptop and work things are still here, so she must have popped out. I look outside at the sunny garden. I could sit out there for a while. I push down on the new handle, but it's locked. I hadn't noticed, but the doors have the new kind of handles. I search around for the key, but I can't find it.

I rush to the front door. That's locked as well. I tell myself to calm down. I pace around. What if my baby comes now? What if I am all alone here, locked in, when…

My phone rings and it's Erica. I answer it.

'Leila. Listen. I'm so sorry, I've popped into town to get some food in for you but I've realised I've got both sets of keys in my bag.'

I breathe in, then out again, slowly. 'OK. So when will you be back?' I hear my voice, shaky and weak. This isn't the new, strong me.

I hear her breath, quick like she's been running. 'An hour. At the most. I was trying to do something nice to help you and I've gone and upset you, so I feel terrible about it.'

'No, it's a nice thought and I guess we've both got a lot on our minds.'

'I know, I think it's made me a bit scatty today, sorry, with thinking about the trial. I'll be back as soon as I can.'

She ends the call. I stare out of the window. She told me not to panic and I don't want to be ungrateful when she was trying to do something thoughtful. She's so organised and I want to show her that I can be like that so she knows the baby will be well-looked after.

I hear a ping and check my phone. Nothing. But another ping comes from Erica's computer. I look at her bag with the files inside. Curiosity gets the better of me: I want to know what she thinks of me. I bet she thinks I'm some kid who got pregnant by mistake and now I regret it. Nothing could be further from the truth.

I pull my file out of the bag. There are ways I can request my data so I really shouldn't be doing this. I've seen all the notices, but the book is in my hand now. There are pink flamingos on the front, and I've seen other midwives with these standard logs. Erica had it beside her when I had my appointment with her, and always brings it out when she checks me over.

My name is on the front. My due date today. I open the front cover. The first page is blank. I turn it over and the second page is blank, too. I quickly turn the rest of the pages. Erica has not written a single thing in this book. I pull the buff files out of her bag. They have the names of other women on the front of them and Erica's name in the corner. I open one. There are test results and reports.

I dig deeper into the bag and feel around for more baby logs. There are none. My mind races. She's spent so much time looking after me, sometimes I forget she has other patients because she makes me feel so well cared for. Her laptop pings again. I open it up and click on the messages. There are three or four from Karen Slater. I read the first one.

> Erica, can you ring me please? I need you to clarify something for me.

She's read it, but not answered. There's another message from Karen.

> Erica. Where are you? Give me a call. I need to run something by you.

I google Darkford General maternity department staff. I see Erica's name, and someone called Sue. Karen is their team leader. I close the browser and read the rest of the messages.

> Ring me as soon as possible. It's OK if you're
> at the trial. You're not in trouble. I need to
> clarify a detail.

And

> Erica. Message me please. I'm getting worried
> about you now.

I too feel worried for a moment, but check myself. Erica is a professional. She must have her reasons not to contact this Karen woman. Erica strikes me as someone who will do exactly what she wants to. I wish I was like that. It hits me that I might have been taking up too much of her time and she simply hasn't had a chance to respond. Ben accused me of being demanding. I resolve to be more independent and show Erica I can cope, because I know I can.

I look at the menu options on the laptop and my eyes rest on 'Client Records'. I click on it, hands shaking. I've always felt uneasy about these midwives judging me, worried what they would say about me.

I suspected they thought I was too young. I worried they would alert social services when they smelled weed in the house or saw any bruises on my arms. I'd seen it all before. Some of the girls who'd had kids with Ben's mates had ended up with them in care. It was usually due to neglect and/or drug misuse. I suspected some of them were relieved, because they had fulfilled the old adage of 'get pregnant to trap your man', consciously or subconsciously, and failed, then didn't want to be stuck with a baby.

I find my file and click on it. The first thing I see is Katie Withers' name on the top of it. It hasn't even been changed. Her notes, mostly exactly as she had read them back to me, are there. This will be why Erica hasn't made notes. These are long, detailed descriptions of our appointments. She describes me as 'a delightful young woman who will make a good mother'.

A huge sense of relief falls over me. But I scroll forward in the file for any mention of Ben. I read and read, but it is mostly details about my multiple scans and every visit she made here. She recorded the time she spent, and it looks accurate. She seemed so kind. It doesn't make sense that someone like her did those horrible things when she was only ever so nice to me.

I scroll ever forward until I grind to a halt. The date of the last entry is my hospital appointment. The entry is made by reception staff telling the system I was attending a special outreach appointment.

I scroll down but I see only dates. Erica has recorded nothing at all, which seems strange especially as I've seen her typing diligently whenever we have had a session. She made a show of typing after the argument with Ben and after we had words. She must have made them somewhere else. I click out of the file and look on the menu for other places she might have saved her notes.

I click onto the desktop and there is a folder named 'Leila'. I open it. There is a sub-folder named 'Equipment'. I open that and there is a requisition note for the things that were delivered. I feel silly for worrying, because she's always so organised. It makes sense that she has her own filing system.

Just because Ben has let me down, it doesn't mean that everyone else will. Erica has been brilliant and attentive with me since she took over as my midwife.

I hear a key turn in the door, and she appears in the doorway with shopping and a bunch of huge daisies. She hands them to me as she juggles shopping bags.

'Sorry, Leila, I feel like such an idiot for forgetting I had both sets of keys. But I'm back now. Did you want to go outside? I'll open the back door for you.'

# Chapter Twenty

## Sue

The corridor outside the courtroom, so quiet yesterday, is crowded this morning. I scan it for Erica and see the edge of her coat just visible poking out of an alcove. I hurry over, eager to meet her as planned to support her before she gives evidence. She is staring at her phone intently but puts it in her pocket as soon as she sees me. She smiles tightly and I hug her.

'Are you OK? You look nervous.'

'Do I? I'm ready to get this over with.'

'It will be better when we can all put this behind us.'

She fixes a smile. 'Exactly and I know what I saw. Hopefully it will be over quickly. They can't really quiz me on actual facts.'

It's true. She only has to say what she saw.

'Like yesterday. To be honest, it was a bit weird. That lawyer is…' I stop myself. The last thing I want to do is make her more anxious before she's called in. But she is staring at Lucy Norris as she walks along the corridor. Although she is small in stature, she has presence, and the crowds part to let her and her colleagues through. She doesn't look our way, but Erica's gaze follows her as she disappears through a side door.

Before I can make a comment about how it will all be all right, a woman calls out. 'Anyone giving evidence today come this way.'

She is rounding up people and I see Ian hurry towards her, rain mac over his arm. Erica looks at me. I go to take her hand, but she pulls away.

I smile at her. 'It'll be fine. I'll be in the gallery. Just look at me if it gets difficult. And I'll meet you here afterwards. You can do this,' I reassure her.

She nods. I see her phone is flashing, but she ignores it.

It's still only twenty past nine, and the session doesn't officially start until ten. I'm thinking about grabbing a coffee from the Costa across the road when I see Katie's mum and dad. Her mum, Rita, has lost a lot of weight and looks drawn. Her dad's usually cheerful expression is replaced with a tight grimace. They are walking towards me, and I have nowhere to go. I back into the alcove, but they see me.

'Oh, thank God. A familiar face. I thought I saw you yesterday and I'm glad you're here to support her, love. You know she didn't do it, don't you?'

I don't have the heart to tell her I am here for Erica. A scenario flashes through my mind where I find out one of my children killed someone. Or even thought about it.

Would I defend them? If I didn't, would I be a bad parent? Can you still love someone who has done something so terrible to another person?

I hug Rita. It's not her fault. Jim stands awkwardly beside her. 'The lawyer is very good.'

Rita adjusts the too-big suit she is wearing. 'She'd better be.'

An usher comes along and unlocks the door to the gallery and people stream in. My screen is still flashing as I push my phone into my bag.

I'm thankful Rita and Jim are sitting away from me. I couldn't bear Katie's pleading eyes on me and them together. I fidget around for some mints in my bag, hoping that sucking on one will make me less nervous.

It seems like an out-of-body experience to be sat here. One minute I'm drinking wine with Katie and running a busy maternity unit with my more-than-capable colleagues. And then it all comes tumbling down. I know life can be rebuilt, maybe in a different shape, but it will never be the same again, even if I can put what happened behind me.

I see Lucy Norris hurry into the courtroom, whispering to colleagues and pointing to a machine on a desk. She looks focused and I wonder if she thinks Katie has a chance of winning this case. Yesterday appeared to go well, but the more I think about it, the more she was trying to undermine assumptions instead of offering any evidence Katie was not guilty.

It seems increasingly desperate, and I am increasingly devastated. And then I see him and my heart lifts. My rock.

Tom is here to support me. He's sitting behind Rita and Jim. I'm slightly obscured behind a post and there are no other seats, so I can neither move nor get up and go to him. He looks pale, and he's staring down into the courtroom. I try to get his attention, but the jury is filing in, and Katie is back in the dock.

Tom is here to support me, and that is all that matters, giving me hope I can get through this.

# Chapter Twenty-One

## Sue

There is a pause while Lucy Norris organises her papers and someone brings her a box. Then Ian's name is called. Katie's gaze leaves the gallery and moves to the witness entrance. I can see she is blinking tears away, and she wipes her eyes.

Ian walks slowly to the witness box. He looks lost as he swears on the Bible. I can see his hand shaking as he holds it.

Lucy Norris stands. A screen on the opposite wall flashes to life as she wields a remote control. Then she begins her initial examination with Ian.

'Mr Bowers. You are a clerical manager at Darkford General Hospital, aren't you?'

He leans into the small microphone. His voice sounds weak and shaky. 'I am. For twenty-four years.'

'And you worked with Mrs Withers at the hospital?'

He pauses and looks at Katie. 'Yes. For six-and-a-half years. She worked in the maternity department where I'm a manager.'

Lucy Norris shuffles some notes. 'Mrs Withers is accused of drugging women in her care. And much of this case hinges on CCTV footage of a figure resembling Mrs Withers on the ward when she wasn't on duty, entering a cupboard where medication was discovered to be hidden, and going into a side ward where a woman was later drugged.' She sighs. 'And you supplied the CCTV footage of the evening, didn't you?'

Ian nods. 'Yes.'

'Were you there on the evening this happened?'

He reddens. 'No. There's a list of people who were on duty that night.'

She looks down at her notes. 'But you reviewed and recognised Mrs Withers on the CCTV footage, confidently making a positive identification?'

'Yes. It's definitely her in the footage,' he says confidently.

'With your permission, Your Honour, I would like to play the footage for the benefit of the court.'

The journalists are scribbling in their notebooks. I try again to get Tom's attention, knowing a smile from him will give me some reassurance, but he is staring straight ahead. The screen is filled with the corridor I have seen every day of my working life and an image of Katie walking away from the camera. I feel sick. We watch as she hurries down the corridor, then ducks into the cupboard.

Jim is whiter than white, while Rita fidgets nervously. There are murmurs in the gallery and an usher asks for quiet.

Lucy Norris winds the footage back and freezes a frame with Katie's shape large on the screen. The jury is transfixed, and every muscle in my body is taut, with a shiver running down my spine at this incriminating freeze-frame.

'So, you are one hundred per cent sure that is Katie Withers?' Lucy turns her attention back to Ian, pointing at Katie in the dock. 'This woman here?'

He looks at Katie carefully. 'Yes. Absolutely sure. It couldn't be anyone else, and her key fob was used that night. It's all in my statement.'

'Yes, it is. And everyone who was shown that footage recognised Katie. Yet...'

I see the prosecution barrister straighten. He turns to his colleague and whispers something.

But Lucy continues regardless. 'My client has never admitted this crime and has pleaded not guilty, constantly maintaining her innocence. In her statement, she repeatedly said she couldn't disclose her whereabouts that evening. Her husband, in his statement, confirmed she wasn't at home, and he thought she was at work.' She turns to the judge. 'Your Honour. I have a new piece of evidence to submit. About Mrs Withers' whereabouts on the night this crime was committed. May I submit it to the court?'

She hands a file to the prosecution and the barrister hungrily reads it. The judge considers it for a moment, and

I realise I'm shaking as the silence is filled with tension. He looks through the file Lucy has presented him with and calls the prosecution to the bench. He covers the microphone with his hand, and they exchange words.

All the while, the image of Katie is large on the screen. Her long blonde hair and figure magnified for all to see. She is mid-step and I only realise now how much I have missed the ward over the past few weeks. Her presence was always such a comfort to me.

I look at Tom again, but the prosecution barrister is back in his seat and Lucy is straightening her robe. At a gesture from the judge to continue, she presses play and a different scene flashes on the screen.

The date and time in the corner are time-stamped 27/05/2023 19:16. Katie is walking down Market Street in Manchester. She's wearing her zebra print jacket and ankle boots with jeans and a black top I haven't seen before. She's carrying a huge tote bag. Her hair is straightened. Her face is clearly visible, and she is half smiling. She disappears around a corner and Lucy pauses the footage.

Lucy turns to Ian. 'Do you recognise that woman?'

He nods. 'Yes, it's Katie. But that was much earlier on—'

She interrupts. 'But that's her? Just yes or no will do,' she says firmly.

'Yes,' he replies.

She motions to someone at a desk at the back of a courtroom and another image flashes on the screen. This time she is entering a restaurant. The overhead CCTV catches her face in close-up, and I see she is wearing the bee earrings she kept for best. She is laughing with the reception staff and nodding. She pulls her phone out and speaks into it. But it isn't her phone. It's a larger, black iPhone. She always used to have a Samsung phone, the same model as mine.

She turns away momentarily. Then she ends the call, and the server directs her to the bar. He brings her a pink gin and tonic. We watch as she looks at the phone and then at the door. She sips her drink and then her face lights up. She must have been meeting someone. Adam has always said he was at home that night, so I'm confused as to who it would have been.

A million thoughts race through my mind. I'm shocked that she would even think about having an affair and I feel betrayed that she didn't tell me – I always thought we were best friends, so why did she feel like she couldn't confide in me? But most of all, I'm confused as to why she hasn't said this earlier when it could have cleared her name.

She is waiting and looking out of the window. Suddenly a man walks in behind a young couple. He looks familiar. The shape of him. The black jacket that I've brushed down and hung in the wardrobe. I can almost smell him. She stands up and envelopes him in her arms, kissing him and laughing. My world collapses around me at the sight of Katie kissing my husband.

I tear my eyes away from the screen and look at her in the dock. Her hands are over her face, to shield her from view. I turn and look at Tom. I cannot think straight. My head is spinning. He doesn't look at me and still hasn't noticed I'm here. Because I realise that he isn't here for me.

His expression is a contortion of pain as he stares at Katie and, in that moment, I know it's Katie that he loves.

It's her.

Ian is staring at me. He is shocked and pale, but Lucy seizes her moment to clear her client's name. 'So, Mr Bowers, do you recognise the woman in the footage?'

'Yes. It's Katie Withers,' he confirms before glancing back at me.

'Thank you. This footage was retrieved from The Lotus Flower and shows Mrs Withers entering at 19:39 and leaving at 10:32.' She points at the desk in the corner. 'Next, please.'

I watch as she and Tom stumble into a hotel lobby and then he kisses her at the reception desk. A concierge comes over and shakes his hand. They laugh and chat. He knows him. This is not the first time. They look like they are regulars as the room key is handed to Katie and she joins in the fun. My blood runs cold at what's unfolding before my eyes. Her arm snakes around my husband's waist. This can't be happening. I am weak and shaky, like I'm not really here. I was at home that night with the boys. The police had asked me my whereabouts in a statement I'd given.

I thought we were a unit. A family. I trusted him. I thought we were forever, just as we'd vowed all those years ago. I even blamed myself for him not being able to sleep lately, feeling guilty for what I was putting the family through being caught up in this case.

They are getting into the lift and then the footage switches to a long hotel corridor. He carries her tote bag, and she opens the door. And in they go. Another stab in the heart at the ending of my marriage. I panic at the thought of telling our children. As if it hasn't been bad enough, Mum and Dad are over. I reel as I start to understand why he took them to his mum's. He always intended to save her. And he wanted to spare them the scene with me that he never got round to.

The footage continues, where they emerge from the hotel lift the following morning. Fresh-faced and showered. The time stamp says 07:30.

Lucy Norris stops the footage. 'Mr Bowers. Do you recognise the woman in the footage?'

'Yes. It's Katie Withers.'

She turns to the jury. The prosecution barrister is pale and angry. 'Katie Withers could not have been at the hospital that night. I have multiple witnesses from the restaurant and hotel who will say they saw her that night. The hotel submitted footage for the whole night, and she did not leave at any point until the morning. I'm sure you will question why these witnesses didn't come forward previously. The answer to that question is that the… gentleman in the footage booked everything under a false name for… secrecy, and this certainly worked. They simply did not realise his paramour was Katie Withers until they were asked for the footage by the police who had been informed by,' she pauses to check her paperwork, 'Mr Springer.'

She turns to the judge. 'So, I ask you, Your Honour, to consider acquitting this defendant as the bulk of evidence rests on Mrs Withers' identification on the 27th of May in the maternity department at Darkford General and we now know my client has a confirmed alibi for her whereabouts that night. It, of course, begs the question of who *did* commit this crime, but that is for another hearing and not this one.'

The judge motions for both barristers to come forward and they confer. Then the judge stands.

'This court is suspended. I am recording a mistrial. Mrs Withers, you are free to leave.'

The shock is palpable and the gallery breaks out into animated chatter and gasps. The journalists dash out of the door to go file their stories about this dramatic turn of events.

The court rises as the barristers and clerks follow the judge into chambers.

I watch as Katie is led out, and she looks up at Tom. Her parents are hugging each other and, as the gallery clears, I see him. Tom. He's sat there with tears running down his face. I wait for him to turn and say he is sorry, but he doesn't. Because I really don't think he is and now I understand why there's been this distance between us.

I can't stand to sit here any longer, so, unsteadily, I get to my feet and hurry out into the corridor. My phone is flashing, and I foolishly hope it's him telling me it's all been a mistake, because I really am that stupid.

But it's Karen.

# Chapter Twenty-Two

## Erica

This tea is awful as I sit here in the court witness room, desperate to escape after the mistrial was declared. Who would have thought little Miss Perfect wasn't, after all? Not me, that's for sure. But no matter. I have to get out of here. The other witnesses are milling about aimlessly having been dismissed, but I have a plan. I always have a plan. I'm always one step ahead.

While the clerks are busy answering pointless, speculative questions about the trial from the other witnesses, I see my opportunity to slip away. As I go through into the adjoining room and open that door, I see everyone streaming out of the public gallery. Sensing my chance, I place myself in the middle of the melee and allow it to fade me into obscurity. I keep my head down as we pass the CCTV camera I noticed earlier. Always in the background. Always staying calm. We hurry along the corridor and out onto the street, until I can finally walk to my car and to safety. I'd parked on a street in the city. No camera-ridden multi-storey car parks where they record your reg number for me.

I know I am more intelligent than average and I use that to my advantage. This whole exercise has been planned with precision, including this possibility that Katie might not be found guilty at trial. I admit it was one I thought had only the faintest possibility of happening. I'd studied all of the midwives on the ward, but especially Sue and Katie. Sue is one of those nauseating people who always does the right thing, so I knew she'd be no good.

I rely on people not being so black-and-white to do what I need to do. A bit of wriggle room for the occasional misde-meanour or lie. But Sue always seems straight up. The only slight issue was a hint of a temper, but she held it down well. God knows I tested her. All the stepping back and making her do the work. Pleading ignorance and deferring to her. Oh, I had my reasons. But I wanted to see how far she could go.

Quite far, it turned out. Verging on the stupid, really. But lovely old Sue was always so patient and trusting. I would have loved to have seen her face when she found out about her best friend Katie and her husband. That wasn't even on my radar, because Katie also appeared to be a boring goody-two-shoes. Her, and that Adam, played the perfect couple even though anyone could see they desperately wanted a child. Katie would have done anything for a baby, and that's what I capitalised on because I knew the media would latch onto that narrative.

And that made it all the easier to hang this on her. Those women started to complain, and it was only a matter of time before they started looking into everyone, so I needed a scapegoat. I just speeded it up and made sure nobody would suspect me. I produced some evidence that pointed in a different direction. It's my modus operandi. I've done it before and got away with it. Only this time, it hasn't been entirely successful.

But what I *have* done is cover my tracks. People might think it was me – and by people, I mean that fuck-up Karen. She'll put two and two together and see that it could only have been someone with a key to the medication cabinet, and that Saint Sue had an alibi. But they will never be able to prove it. And, even if they do, it won't matter because it will be too late by then. I'm going to make sure nothing will spoil my plan. Everything will go ahead just as I have it set out.

I reach my car and get into the passenger seat. I check my phone and see three calls from Leila and a couple of calls from Karen. And a message. I open it and see a copy of a Royal College of Midwives membership card with the name Erica Davies on it. And a picture of a woman who isn't me. She stares out at me. I have seen her eyes stare at me before. But I shake the image from my mind, not wanting to dwell on that now.

I scan the message. Karen is going on about having sent the award to the RCM and them sending this back.

*Probably just an error,* she's typed. I snort. That's the problem with people – or rather, a clear advantage and why I can exploit people. Everyone is too polite. They want to be politically correct or avoid upsetting someone. But the real reason they very rarely say what they think is that they are afraid they might be wrong, so they are too scared to call anyone out.

All those times on the ward when I didn't have a clue what was going on, I simply busied myself in the background so that nobody would say anything, knowing they wouldn't want to be seen to question my competency. I made myself useful in the things they hated. The mundane tasks. The unexciting dirty jobs that took the glamour out of the moment.

Sue and Katie were so grateful for good old Erica. Emptying bedpans and writing the logs. Fetching medication and inserting cannulas, which I have to say I was very good at, bearing in mind I was working purely off that time I had my appendix removed. I'd watched the nurse intently as the needle went in, and stored it for later. Because I always knew deep down that knowledge would come in useful someday.

All of them were hungry to be the centre of attention, the star of the show. Happy to receive flowers and chocolates from grateful mums or proudly plastering cards telling them how wonderful they are on the wall in the maternity unit. They did me a favour. I was watching and waiting. Trying out my procedure and waiting for the perfect opportunity.

And I found that opportunity in the kind of women who came in and demanded a private room and then spent half the day straightening their hair. Asking for the baby to be taken to the nursery 'because they need their sleep'. They were clearly not going to be mothers making the sacrifices a baby needs. I was almost there. I'd even got the dose almost right. I never intended to kill anyone, I just wanted them to know how I felt to want a baby so much. I wanted them to realise what it was like. Because I think that is sometimes worse than being dead.

Anyway, Karen is hardly going to message me with *Hi Erica – if that's your real name. Because it looks like you have faked ID and lied about being a midwife.* If she said that and it all turned out to be a terrible mistake, I could sue her, so she's running scared. Instead, she is dancing around the issue and giving me an opportunity to sort out this unfortunate misunderstanding. As if I ever would. Because what good would it do?

I have a couple of breaking news alerts on my phone:

**Midwife accused of murder goes free**

and

**Killer midwife case ruled a mistrial**

It won't be long until people's attention turns to the killer who must still be out there. At this very moment, the hospital board and police will be anxiously scoping the department for who could be responsible. I watch a video showing journalists streaming out of the court to write up their stories, followed by all the ordinary people who were rammed in there. I look for myself, but I'm hidden amongst the crowd. Another thing I rely on.

Then I see her. Sue Springer. Saint Sue. Pale as anything, looking shaken up as you would be to find out your husband and best friend had been having an affair. She didn't see that one coming and she has no idea what's going to happen next.

I know I'll have to deflect the attention away from me. All the hours spent logging shifts and medications and writing up notes so meticulously when, in reality, I've sown my little seeds everywhere. This particular one about Katie grew at an unprecedented rate once it got going. But it wasn't the only one, because I've learned to always have a Plan B.

I have a feeling that second seed is about to sprout. The one with Saint Sue's name on it. I have to smile, because this is just too perfect. Without any pre-empt from me, she has lost her husband and her family. No support for when I go in for the professional kill. And, by then, she will be too weak to fight. And everyone is going to buy this story – the scorned wife trying to frame her husband's mistress.

I climb over to the driver's seat. It's time for me to leave and continue with my plan. I call Leila who answers after just a few rings.

'Leila. It's Erica. I've got some very bad news. The trial has been stopped on a technicality. Katie has been released.'

I hear her gasp. 'But don't worry. It's all over the news so don't switch the TV on until I get back. Don't answer your phone unless it's me. I don't want you getting stressed. I'm coming over.'

I end the call. I can still do this. This is a small blip. Nothing is going to stop me. I just need to make a few adjustments and speed things up so everything still goes to plan.

## Chapter Twenty-Three

### Sue

I hurry against the crowd that's filtering out of the public gallery, looking for Erica. But when I find the witness waiting room, everyone has left.

I stand still for a moment, trying to take in what just happened to my marriage. It is only too clear. What I don't know is what happens next. I always wanted things to go back to the way they were, but now I realise that, even though Katie has been released, I'll never get my best friend back.

I stumble my way out of the court and onto the road outside. Erica isn't here, either. I know she was worried about today so, after what's happened, perhaps she's gone home. I walk down a back-street, trying to remember where I parked my car. I feel dazed by this morning's revelations, still barely believing what I saw.

I'm disgusted by Tom and Katie. I can't believe I thought that Katie was my best friend and that we were there for each other. I cringe as I remember venting to her about trivial things in my home life; how she had handed me a gin and listened or offered a shoulder to cry on, because that's how close we were. I shake my head – what a fool I was to think she was like the sister I never had. I'd always tried to be there for her when she and Adam were having trouble conceiving, reassuring her it would happen and what great parents they'd make. And, whatever was happening in our personal lives, it always felt like we were in it together on the ward.

I stop in the middle of the street. Katie had wanted more than anything to be a mum, and I realise now that she will be step-mum to my kids. She will put my boys to bed and help Liam with his homework. She will go for burgers, a replacement me in the family snaps. I can't deal with the idea of the person I confided in and trusted swooping in to take my place.

My phone rings, and it's Karen again. I feel bad for ignoring her other calls so decide I'd better answer it.

'Sue. Where are you?' she asks, sounding worried.

I can see my car and I walk towards it. 'I'm still in town.'

'Can you wait at the courts? I'm coming over there.'

'Is everything OK, Karen? Only I've had a bit of a shock and—'

She interrupts. 'Just meet me at the court entrance. I won't be long.' She hangs up.

I get in my car, needing a minute to think. My own world feels like it's come off its axis so that I can't understand the bigger picture. My head throbs. My whole body feels weak. I realise I am exhausted and likely suffering from shock.

If Katie has been cleared, then it means that it must have been someone else on shift. It was only really Katie, Erica and myself that had access to the meds cupboard. We could have signed the meds key out to someone, but it would have been obvious if that had happened on a regular basis at the relevant times. I look at my reflection in the rear-view mirror. I am pale and I have dark circles under my eyes. If it isn't Katie, and it isn't me, that only leaves one person.

No, I must have got it wrong. Maybe someone took a copy of the key. It can't have been Erica. She was always so busy in the background, helping us and being so calm with the patients. I know this, but everyone else does not. If they suspected Katie, does that mean that they're going to come after me next? I jump out of the car and hurry up the lane back to the court to meet Karen.

I spot her yellow coat in the entrance. She's talking to a police officer. I am tempted to walk over there and explain that, if it wasn't Katie or me, there's only one other person it could have been. But if Erica set Katie up, who's to say she won't do the same to me? I need to find her. Perhaps I can get her onside and find out what she's planning, but I'll sort out whatever is going on with Karen first.

She doesn't smile as I walk towards her, just nods in acknowledgement. 'I need to speak to you about the awards. We always write to the RCM to let them know who wins each year. They publish it in their magazines and send a congrats letter and all that. So, I looked up Erica's RCM number on the system and sent it along to them with that photo from the night and the article.'

She pauses for breath, and I'm confused by what she's trying to tell me, why she's bringing this up.

'Yeah. Go on.'

'So, they sent an email back with Erica Davies' registration card and photo.'

She grabs her phone and shows it to me. I look at the message and the photo. That woman isn't Erica. The name and background are hers, but the photo is a different lady. People can lose weight or change their hair colour, but there's no way this can be the same person.

'Maybe they got the photo mixed up? It happens,' I try to tell her. It's the first thing I think of.

But Karen shakes her head. 'Wouldn't she have had to show her pass at the exams? And to the agency when they approved her for bank?' she points out.

I think back and, yes, from memory that is exactly what happens. I can't think of a way a different photograph could have made its way onto Erica's records. Perhaps I should tell Karen what my worry is – that only the three of us had access to the meds cupboard so that points to one person now. But, after the way Karen has been acting, I'm still not sure I can trust her. It's like she's been trying to push me to one side or blame me, and maybe she's changed the budgets to try and make me look like the incompetent one.

I stare at her, my words shaking. 'I thought you did the background checks.'

She nods and stares back. 'And I thought you had. Looks like we were both wrong. And that we'd better be sure next time.' She pauses. 'All we can do now is tell the truth and hope that Erica has a good explanation for this mix-up.'

I hurry back to my car, eager to find Erica to get to the bottom of this. I want to know why she has someone else's ID and who is behind the druggings. Not for me, or Karen. Or Katie. Not for fucking Tom. But for those women and their babies.

---

When I arrive at the hospital, I park on the road outside, grabbing my tote bag from the back seat, and walk through the grounds. I scan myself in and run up to the department. I'm hoping to see Erica, but if not, I have a good idea where she might be. It all makes sense now. The missing requisition. Her never being where she says she is.

I go to the break room and get my laptop out. I log into the system and desperately try to remember the lady's name. Linda? Laura? I scroll through the records and there is nothing familiar allocated to Erica. I pull Katie's practice diary out of my bag. I flick through it, carefully avoiding the back page with the doodled hearts and phone number which are painful reminders of her betrayal. *Come on, come on.* I can't find it. I try to think when it would have been.

Months and months ago, and it will be in here because Katie was always so good at keeping her records. Then I see it. Leila. Leila Summers.

I look up her name in the system. There is a Christine Summers and a Helen Sumner. But no Leila. I try again but, again, nothing comes up. No record at all. She must have been registered with the hospital before this. I move to the register for Darkford General Hospital and type in her name again. It appears, along with her date of birth. She is just twenty.

I scroll down to her address which is listed as '7th Floor Catford House, Newton Heath'. That can't be right. Both Katie and Erica mentioned she lived in a rural, out-of-town location and that it would be a problem for her to get into hospital, which is why Erica claimed she'd decided on a home birth. I do a general search. I try different spellings of her name, but she is not registered with the maternity department.

I remember her being here last week. She was one of the first patients Erica was assigned at her outreach clinic. I bring up the records. It would have been that morning, right after Karen told us about the promotions. She would have been Erica's first lady to speak to. She was placenta previa. It's all coming back. Erica went for a scan with her. The appointment archive comes up and there are three ladies listed that morning. But no Leila. I check the scan records but, again, I find nothing. My heart beats faster and I feel a knot in my stomach as I realise it's like Leila has never been here.

I know that records don't just disappear, so Erica must have deleted them. I run through to the locker rooms, but Erica's is locked, as I thought it would be. I open my own, reaching in and finding a boot amongst the cluttered chaos.

I hammer at Erica's locker. It dents but does not open until I hit the lock hard. Then it bursts, and I am disappointed to see a very neat space. Folded tunics and a hairbrush are neatly placed on top of a towel. I pull everything on to the floor to go through it. Then I realise to my horror, if it was her, she had dressed up as Katie. She must have that hair – a wig – and identical trainers to Katie's somewhere. I grasp at a sports bag pushed down the back of the locker and tear it open. But the only things I find are a water bottle and a notepad. A pair of pink trainers are tucked down the side, but no sturdy black Nikes like Katie wore. I sit on the floor beside Erica's things. All I can do now is go to the police and tell them what I think. But what proof do I have?

## Chapter Twenty-Four

## Leila

*Come on, Erica. Where are you?* My brain is in overdrive as I pace around my living room. I peeked at the news on my phone, even though Erica told me not to, and see that the trial's been stopped. Thrown out of court and Katie released. It didn't say why, but I can't bear to look at it. That Katie's face is everywhere again and now she's going to be out there. I've made what seems like hundreds of cups of tea and stationed myself by the window, watching for Erica's car.

She called to say she was on her way ages ago. I don't know where she is. And to make matters worse, I feel weird and I don't think it's only the stress or shock of what happened with the trial. My tummy is tense and there is pressure when I stand up. I feel really uncomfortable.

At first, I thought I'd overdone it cleaning the kitchen. I want to be completely ready when this little one makes an appearance. I love this house and want it to be in order. It's my one comfort at the moment and my only connection left to Mum.

As I wait for Erica to come back, I check my phone again. I'm a bit surprised I've not heard from Ben. I know things aren't good between us right now but surely, when he sees about Katie, he'll want to check I'm OK? I scroll through my contacts and find his number. That's when I see 'unblock number' at the bottom of the screen. That's strange, because I definitely did not block his number.

I unblock it and, after a few minutes, a message comes through.

> It's me, babe. I understand why u don't want to take my calls and I'm not coming round with Nurse Pratchett there. I saw what happened with that midwife on the news and I just wanted to say I hope u r OK? I'm down in London with Jakey but if u want to talk drop me a message, yeah?

My heart sinks. How could he have gone to London with his mate when I'm at my due date for his baby? I've been such an idiot to think he'd be there for us. Maybe Erica is right and I'll be better off without him.

I look at the text again. It's pathetic of him to claim that Erica is all that is keeping him away. If it only took that one thing, he must not have cared that much to start with.

It doesn't sound like he'll be wanting to play much of a role in our baby's life. I was worried about him wanting shared custody, but that would cramp his style and get in the way of his fun. He is unreliable and immature. I don't want that in my life. I need people who will support me and help me.

Erica's car pulls up. I feel relief and a little bit of joy. Instead of parking on the road like she normally does, she turns into the driveway and her car disappears towards the garage. I hear the creaky automatic door begin to lift and wonder why she's putting her car in the garage.

I sit and wait until I hear the spare keys in the back door. When she appears, I want to hug her, but I don't because she is holding a huge box.

I smile at her instead. 'Thank God you're here. I was terrified.' I let out a huge sigh of relief.

She puts the box down on the kitchen worktop. 'What a day. I was about to give evidence, and then it was all stopped. Apparently, the police made a mistake with some of the evidence and it's all been thrown out. Are you OK?'

I touch my stomach and her eyes follow my hand.

'I don't know. No pain, but my tummy is tight as a drum. And I want to wee when I stand up. Is that all...'

I hesitate and she immediately begins fussing around me. 'Come and sit down. It's all normal. You need your rest now. It sounds like that little one is getting ready to make an appearance.'

She smiles brightly, but I feel overwhelmed. I'm not ready for the baby to come yet. She holds my hand as I lean back in Mum's chair.

'It's OK. I'll be here. I've brought some more things from my flat, so I don't have to keep going backwards and forwards.' She gestures at the box. 'And I think there are some ginger nuts in there, if you want a cuppa to calm you down.'

I watch her busy in the kitchen, looking after me. She reminds me a bit of my mum. Cheery, but with a sadness behind her eyes I can't ask her about. Mum used to say I was wistful, and it's that. As if she is thinking about something else some of the time, which is understandable with what's happened today.

'So, what will happen now? With Katie? Will you have to give evidence again?'

Erica comes through with two cups of tea and a plate of biscuits. She sits down opposite me.

'I don't want you to worry about all that right now. I've delivered hundreds of babies, and I can see that your time is very close, so you need to focus only on that.'

I'm shaking. I don't want to appear soft or silly, but I need to tell someone about the doubts I'm having. I speak quietly and slowly. 'I'm scared. I'm wondering if I should go to hospital after all.'

I see a twitch at the side of her mouth. I've seen it before, when Ben was here. I think it's when she's annoyed.

'That is your choice, of course. Although, as you can imagine, with all the staff changes, it's a bit chaotic. But I can book you in, if you like? I'll phone up and they will allocate you to someone else.'

I freeze. 'But… I thought you would be my midwife? You said…' I hesitate, scared that Katie might be my midwife again.

'I am on outreach. If you choose a hospital birth, you will be allocated to one of the midwives on the ward. I don't know which one, because they are all new after… Well. After all this.'

It seems hopeless. Whatever I do, I will be afraid. Another problem hits home. 'How would I get to the hospital if you aren't here?'

She shrugs. 'I expect you would call an ambulance and hope they get to you in time.'

She stares at me, unblinking. I'm back to the same problem I started with, where I can't get to the hospital easily. I look around at the carefully set up area in my dining room with all the equipment she's sorted out for me. She has gone to a lot of effort. And what option do I have, really? I flex the tension out of my neck.

'Are you sure it will be OK?' I ask hopefully.

She smiles. 'I absolutely wouldn't have suggested it if I didn't. And I have a backup plan.'

I think back to the blank pages in my pregnancy planner and Erica's notebook.

'Can I see it? Just to put my mind at rest?'

She nods enthusiastically. 'Yes, of course. It involves other staff, so it's back on the ward, but I'll get it printed out as soon as possible.' She takes my hand and strokes it, which calms me down. 'Everything will be fine. But you need to relax now and stop worrying. I've created the perfect space here for you to have a home birth. And, if there is a complication, because I'll be here, I have my car to get up quickly to hospital if needed.'

She takes a sip of her tea and dunks a ginger nut. Erica is right. She's a professional and she'll be here if anything goes wrong. I need to focus on the baby and doing what Erica tells me so it arrives safely, although I feel the huge weight of what a responsibility that is.

'To be fair to you, there's been a lot going on and you've not had an easy time of it.'

I open my mouth to ask her if she blocked Ben's number. She's the only person who could have. She's the only person who was here, but it makes no sense why she would have done that.

Before I can ask, she says, 'And losing your mum. I feel so sorry for you, Leila. Sorry she's not here. From what you've told me, she'd have been a brilliant grandma. But we can do this. And I've got a plan. From now on, this place is like a health spa. Pure relaxation.'

She hurries to the box in the kitchen and comes back with a pile of DVDs.

'I've brought a selection of movies we can watch, because you need to put your feet up.' She places them in front of Mum's ancient DVD player and paces up and down. 'We need to avoid the news on the TV. It will only upset us, and stress isn't good for the baby. Just happiness and nice things until this little one comes out.' She stops, hands on hips. 'Do you know there are studies that have shown that women who relax and have a rest before child-birth have a better experience?'

I nod because what she's saying makes a lot of sense. The top of the pile of DVDs is *Mary Poppins*. I almost giggle. Erica looks a bit like the picture on the front. Grey mack and hair curled tightly. Come to think of it, she is a bit like Mary Poppins. Someone magical who has arrived in my life to make things better.

'So. Tea and biscuits,' she says, handing me my mug. 'Then we'll settle down and put our feet up.'

I take the cup and sip. She's right. The warm, sweet tea is comforting. Erica is smiling and, by the time I have finished the cup, I am feeling much, much better. Everything feels like it's in soft focus, and I forget to ask her about Ben's number being blocked.

# Chapter Twenty-Five

## Nicola

M y old flat is probably the last place I should be right now. But once this is done, I will be home and dry. It's highly unlikely the police will find this place straight away, because it's registered to Nicola Green. My hospital mail goes to Erica Davies, and I have the little key she kept in the top pocket of her uniform. The one that opens her PO box and allows me to collect all her mail. So, they'll go there first.

I never killed anyone. I had no control over what happened when I left her. Although she deserved everything she got. I never meant to get pregnant. I was on the pill. In those halcyon days when I still believed things might be fine, I was willing to wait to bring a baby into the world at the perfect time.

My boyfriend Mark and I had talked about it. A small wedding with family first before we started trying. I hadn't told him at that point about my family and how they had abandoned me. I pretended they were busy in big-time jobs and my sisters and brother lived in faraway cities. It was entirely possible. He told me that we would be the only family each other needed.

The morning I found out I was pregnant, I'd been to nursing college and then come home on the bus. I'd checked the chart for my period, and it was three weeks late. I remember being angry because this wasn't part of the plan – we were supposed to get married first and do things the traditional way. Yet I still felt a spark of excitement. Something that was rare and precious. I held onto it as I stared at the 'yes' on the pregnancy test.

I remember the night I told Mark and how I'd tried to do everything right. How I'd pictured this moment. Even making his favourite dinner of steak and chips.

'I know you're shocked, babe. But here we are. We're going to be parents.' I grinned, knowing as soon as I'd seen the test result that it was right next step for us.

'This isn't the right time, Nic. Not at all.'

I stopped pouring a beer I'd picked up for him. I gripped the glass so tightly I thought it was going to break. *When is the right time, then?*

'I know we'd talked about getting married first but we always wanted a family, so we can make it work.'

He looked me right in the eye. 'There's something I need to tell you. I've been… seeing someone.'

'A therapist? It's OK. I know you have those nightmares.'

His face turned a deep shade of red. 'Nic. Come on. You know what I mean. I've been… I'm sorry. I really am, but

I'm leaving you. Especially...' He paused. I dropped my arms to my sides. Rhythmic sobs deep in my chest surfaced for the first time. He continued, 'I can go with you for a termination.'

I sank into the chair and watched him get his things together. He did it quickly, like he'd been rehearsing it for a while. Then he was gone.

Mark might had gone but I told myself I was going to keep the baby. I'd dropped out of nursing college to get ready to become a mother. I wanted more than anything to be a mother. Until that was taken away from me too. A month later, I woke up and found blood all over the sheets. I was scared and didn't know what to do or where to go I rang my GP, and he told me to go to the maternity unit at Darkford General. I had an ultrasound, and the consultant confirmed I had miscarried. I would need a procedure called a D&C: dilation and curettage. To remove tissue from the womb. My baby. In the days between the scan and the D&C operation, I realised this was her fault. If this other woman had never come into Mark's life, we would still be happy. I wouldn't have been stressed and then I wouldn't have miscarried. He wouldn't have sent me a leaflet for an abortion clinic, and he wouldn't have blocked my number.

Her Instagram was public so I could still see them on there. That's when I made a plan and decided she had to suffer in the same way I had. An eye for an eye. She'd pushed me too far. They both had.

I followed her. I listened to her talking on her phone. I watched her sitting in cafés googling jobs. I went through her bins and found a letter from the RCM. People really should be more careful with their rubbish. She was looking for work. Phoning agencies and applying. But her being a midwife made it all worse – she was supposed to deliver babies into this world, but instead she'd taken away mine.

It wasn't long before I was pressing the buzzer to her flat with a clipboard in my hand. She'd answered quickly.

'Erica Davies?' I asked.

'Yes. Who is it?'

I checked to see if there were any cameras, but there was nothing. Just the old-style buzzer.

'I'm from Wright's Properties. I've come to do an inspection.'

She buzzed me in, but she was standing in her doorway. I watched her face for any sign of recognition, but there was none.

She leaned forward. 'Have you got some ID, please?'

Of course I had. I'd done my homework and thought of everything. I flashed her a plastic badge on a lanyard, identical to the one the Wright's Properties representative had presented to me as he showed me a vacant flat in the same block. She motioned for me to follow her in.

'We've had some reports of mice and… well. Rodents. So, I wondered if I could have a look around.'

I scanned the place. It was a mess. I thought of Mark's almost OCD cleanliness and had a moment of premature triumph over how he was slumming it after me, before I remembered why I was here.

'But, before I begin, you might want to take my number.'

I gave her a fake card and, as she smiled, I realised how pretty she was. I could see why Mark liked her.

'Thank you. Where do you want to start?'

I laughed. 'I'd like to have a look in that cupboard behind the kitchen. We think they're coming up through the stairs. If we find any trace, I can get the pest control to come and lay some bait. Do you have any pets?'

She shook her head. 'No. Not allowed.'

I smiled. A rule keeper. How quaint. 'OK. So, I'll need you to come with me so you can see I'm not damaging your property.'

She unlocked and opened the cupboard, then placed her keys on the table behind her. I was close to her. Close enough to smell her citrusy perfume. *It's your fault*, my brain screamed as I pulled out the syringe and stuck it through her sweater into her arm.

I pushed her into the cupboard. She was drowsy as I took her phone. I closed the door and locked it.

She wasn't dead. I didn't kill her. And if she had deserved to get out, she would have done.

I sat at her kitchen table and played back the footage from the tiny camera on my lapel that had recorded her opening her phone. I needed the passcode. I unlocked the phone and sent Mark a message.

I'm sorry but I don't want to see you again.
Please do not contact me. This has been a

> mistake and I can't be in this relationship
> anymore. I need some time so won't be
> answering your messages or calls.

I turned and saw myself in the mirror on her kitchen wall. Flame-haired and heavily made up. If anyone had seen me, they would not describe me as dark-haired, natural Nicola Green. I took a tea towel and pushed the heavy table against the pantry door. She deserved it. She'd stopped me from having what I wanted most in the world.

I went back weekly and checked her mailbox in the corridor of the block. I was already checking her emails on her phone and, when she got the job at Darkford General, I saw an opportunity and took it. It was fate, really. Mark did try to contact her a few times, but he gave up surprisingly easily, which saved me having to deal with him, too.

I grab the hospital records I have been keeping here and push them into an Aldi bag-for-life. I open the wardrobe in the corner, pulling out the trainers and blonde wig that I'd kept here so nobody would find them. I was so sure this would work, and I'd set it all up so perfectly. But what I hadn't factored in was Katie being a lying slut.

It's strange being back here, but I know it will be the last time. This place has served me well, but it's time now to leave it behind. I must leave no trace. That's what the past has taught me.

I've collected baby clothes for a long time now and take out the small suitcase from under the bed. Little shell-edged layettes and frilly dresses. Romper suits and tiny, tiny hats.

No patients have noticed they have gone from the ward as they are showered with baby gifts for their little ones. I only took the best which would be good enough for my own baby.

I'll drop those hospital records in a bin somewhere remote so nobody will find them. I know exactly the right place. Where I went to hide away when things got bad at home. And where I'll be again soon. And the wig and trainers? I'll pop them in Sue's locker. Prim and proper Saint Sue in the frame. She's walked right into it and won't see it coming. Finding out her husband is having an affair with her best friend gives her the perfect motive. This evidence will seal the deal.

The police won't come here for ages. They'll go to Erica's when Karen tells them about the stolen identity after I've gone missing. And when I anonymously tip the police off, they'll go to Sue's locker and find all the evidence they need to keep them busy with her instead of looking for me.

By the time they come here, I will be long gone.

## Chapter Twenty-Six

### Sue

I've woken up this morning having barely been able to sleep with a sense of dread about what happens next. I miss the kids, but I don't want to face them and keep what I've found out from them. And now Katie has an alibi for that night, it's obvious someone was trying to set her up. I know Erica has something to do with it. The only evidence I have is a missing docket for equipment and a photo on a membership card, which doesn't feel like enough proof.

I can't face going out because the journalists are still on the street. There's even more interest in the case now everyone on social media is talking about how the midwife who's been deemed 'innocent' was having an affair.

I want to hate Tom. For all the deceit. For pretending everything was fine. But all I can think about are the first days of the pandemic. We'd heard about it already. Me, Katie and Erica, who was fairly new then. It was the day of the annual staff conference that we realised something serious was going on. It strengthened us as a team. But all that time she had been with my husband.

The meeting was at an office block near Piccadilly Station. I met Katie at the tram stop and we rode in together. Halfway in, Karen rang. She was already at the venue. Her voice sounded deep and stressed. 'Sue. Hi. Look, can you go to Boots and pick up some hand sanitiser and face-masks? I know it's ridiculous because we work at a hospital but...'

I wasn't laughing at Katie's handbag peanuts anymore. This was serious. 'But what?'

She paused. I could hear her breathing. 'Someone who is already here has just said there is a Coronavirus outbreak at the school their daughter goes to. It's closed. We can't be too careful.'

We went to Boots to buy facemasks and hand sanitiser. The assistant looked at us as if we were mad and it was all a conspiracy theory. But none of us shook hands that day. It wasn't long afterwards we were told ladies would have to give birth without birthing partners and restrictions on ward visiting would happen.

Then one of our anaesthetists got COVID. She was admitted to the COVID ward and the maternity unit was closed. The three of us sat in the break room and we did not need words. We knew something bad was coming. Everyone else we knew was working from home. But we were key workers. We had to be here. We *wanted* to be here.

Erica had carried on regardless. I thought she was brave. Now, although I can hardly comprehend it, like I could not with Katie, I realise she had a motive to be there. Something beyond the duty of care and the compulsion to help others. At the time, I admired her. Not like me and Katie, pale and worried.

One day, when Erica was at a mentor meeting, Katie sat beside me. Closer than we were really allowed, but not touching. She spoke gently. 'I'm scared. I know I shouldn't say it. But I am absolutely terrified.'

I was, too. By then, we were in the middle of the first lockdown and people were dying every day. Three of our ladies had the virus, and one of them had died. She was due to deliver. It was unthinkable. We taped up our visors and cuffs and carried on.

I had slept in the spare room instead of moving into hospital halls. Is that when Tom's head turned? When he was at home all the time and I was sleeping apart from him?

She couldn't have been seeing him then. It must have been after the pandemic that I'd comforted her through when she'd told me that she was terrified about what was going to happen. When Tom told me work had picked up and he was on the road again so away some of the time.

I can't believe it. I can't believe she would do this. I expect myself to be upset that Tom has broken our vows and left me. People do that. But Katie and I had more in some ways. We had an unspoken language. When things got too much on the ward, when the ladies were screaming for their partners or we had to test newborns for COVID, I would seek out her eyes. They were the only things visible in the PPE that was sometimes black bin bags, but they were there, as mine were for her.

One day, we opened a side ward and the young mother who occupied it was dead. She'd complained of a severe headache the day before and we'd taken her baby to the nursery. Katie and I stood at the door with her baby girl in a plastic crib. Katie let out a loud sob. It was almost unbearable. Almost. But childbirth is something that can never stop under any circumstances. We had to close the ward for deep clean for the fifteenth time since the outbreak.

Katie volunteered to come in and bottle-feed the newborn baby. She was so kind and selfless. Which is why I am shocked to the core that she has done this to me.

Tom only moved with the boys temporarily to his mum's, so I never imagined him not coming back. But now it seems like there's no other option. I have two missed calls from Tom and a message, which I open.

> I'm concerned you will tell the boys what's
> happened. I want us to tell them together.

I should probably take my time and try to be amicable about this for the sake of the boys, but I'm just so angry at him.

> Who do you mean by 'us'?

There is no way he's bringing Katie into this. It's going to be confusing enough for the boys to understand that we're splitting up without telling them that it's for someone who was like an auntie to them.

His reply is immediate. You and me. Us. I'm not a monster, Sue.

I almost laugh. He isn't going to dictate what I say to my children. There will be no carefully prepared statement or agreed words. I will tell them what I feel like telling them. And I don't want to be anywhere near him after what he's done.

There is no us.

I hear a car outside. Doors slamming and people talking. Surely it can't be Tom because he wouldn't have been texting and driving. There's already journalists lingering outside, so the thought of more arriving makes me feel sick. I peer out of the window and see two uniformed police and two plain-clothes emerging from a car. All the energy drains from my body and my knees buckle.

I run downstairs to answer the door, eager to not give the journalists anything else to write about. One of the plain-clothes officers steps forward. He shows me his warrant card.

'I'm DC Ben Marple.' I recognise him from the initial news reports. 'Susan Springer. I am arresting you on suspicion of attempted murder and kidnapping. You do not have to say anything. But it may harm your defence if you do not mention when questioned something which you later rely on in court. Anything you do say may be given in evidence.'

I step back and I feel lightheaded. 'You've made a mistake. It's Erica. You have got her, haven't you?' My voice is high-pitched and the words tumble out.

His face shows no emotion. They are all staring at me, and, from their expressions, I can tell that they think I did it. As they handcuff me, I feel almost outside of my body. This can't be happening, but when I look down it's *my* hands that are bound. The journalists who have had little to see for months are suddenly out of their cars and filming on their phones. This is exactly the kind of fodder they're going to love writing about.

Liam had his laptop with him and, even though we try to limit screentime, there's no way they won't see this. I feel sickened at the thought of them believing their mum could have done something like this. And what are the other kids going to say to them at school? The police now think I have a motive. If Erica set Katie up, she's done it again somehow to implicate me. But this time there's a motive that makes it look like I was out for revenge. Katie stole my husband, so I set her up, framing her for the attempted murders they think I have committed.

I am bundled into the back of the police car, and I can't breathe.

# Chapter Twenty-Seven

## Leila

Oh, my God. I feel like I've been asleep for ages but what's weird is that I can't even remember going to bed. Erica must have made me go lie down and then thrown a cover over me. As I come round, I feel groggy, like I used to when everyone was smoking weed in the same room. I can hear Erica in the next room talking on her phone, so I go to put the kettle on.

The garden looks lovely in this early morning sunlight. It's that kind of golden light that makes you feel all good and warm inside. I switch on the kettle and then go to open the back door. It's locked. I look around for the keys, but I can't see them. Erica must have put them somewhere safe because she knew I was worried about Katie being released. I go to check my phone messages to see if there have been any more developments.

But my phone's not in my pocket. I always keep it in my dressing gown pocket. It's my lifeline. I start to panic.

What if I dropped it somewhere? I can't remember the last time I went out. Erica has been so helpful doing all my errands for me so I can put my feet up. Erica is still talking on her phone.

Then I feel the pressure in my tummy. This is different to the pain I had yesterday. The shape of my bump has changed, and it feels lower. I scoop it with my hands and go through to the lounge where Erica is talking still. I stand in the doorway and listen.

'... and it needs two bedrooms, please.' There is a pause, then she laughs. 'Yes, that will be perfect. Send me some pictures.'

When she sees me standing there, she ends the call.

'Awake now, are we? You were asleep for ages. Sleepyhead. I've just been booking an Airbnb for a little break. Me and my friend.'

I'm not really listening to her holiday plans because my heart's thudding now and there's something I need to talk to her about. 'Can I have the keys, please? I want to go outside. And have you seen my phone? I can't find it anywhere.'

She fusses towards me. 'I'm not sure wandering about is good at the moment. You know what pregnancy hormones are like, you've probably put your phone some-where you can't remember. But please take it easy. You're past your due date and...'

I stare at her. My mouth is dry, and my head fuzzy.

'Give me the keys, Erica,' I say, trying to be firm, but my voice falters.

I think about saying *or else* but realise how helpless I am. I have no mobile. And Mum had the house phone removed years ago. What exactly am I going to do?

'I might as well tell you.' Erica sighs, sitting down on a dining chair and clasping her hands in her lap. 'If you're going to be difficult. I didn't want to bother you with it, but your neighbours have been burgled. Someone smashed their porch window and broke in. Apparently, they called the police, and *they* said to be careful because they might be back. So I'm not sure it's a good idea going outside right now or leaving the door unlocked.'

I struggle for air. The room feels like it's closing in on me. I was trying to build a safe home for me and the baby, but I haven't been doing a good enough job, if we're living next door to a house that's just been burgled.

'You know, love, I'm only thinking about you and your safety. But I'm sure the garden is safe in broad daylight. Let me help you look for the keys, because a little fresh air might be good for Baby too.'

I feel a little calmer. I sink back into Mum's chair. I can feel my baby kicking. So strong and alive. I cannot wait to meet this little person. I went to lots of classes early on in my pregnancy. All suggested by Katie. That's why I couldn't believe she was so horrible.

I had trusted her, really. But when she kept disappearing off and giggling on her phone, it made me feel like I wasn't important. I told her I was uncertain about all this. That I thought I might be too young, but she told me not to worry. She told me younger women have turned out to be excellent mothers. But then she would drift off and whisper in corners. And why shouldn't I have believed her? She was a professional.

I'd trusted Ben too, even though I was always suspicious of where he was going and when he was coming back. He had no set routine, and it made me nervous. I'd constantly wonder who he was with, especially when his phone was off. But I never really thought he would leave me.

And now I am suspecting Erica. She's doing everything she possibly can to make sure I am safe, and I'm accusing her in my mind. It just doesn't feel right. I know there are good people, and Erica is one of them. My mum was one of them too, and I wonder for a moment if Erica has been sent as my guardian angel because she's been so good to me.

Erica returns with a cup of tea she's made for me. 'Right. I need to go out and get some supplies.' She is pulling on her coat, and I stand up unsteadily. 'Rest up and have a nice cup of tea.'

I blink at her. 'I don't think I feel like tea right now.'

'I put sugar in it to perk you up a bit. It will help,' she promises and motions for me to take a sip. I do. 'I'm only going to the supermarket and the hospital. I'll be back in a couple of hours.'

'But what if the baby comes? We haven't found my phone yet so how can I call you?' I ask anxiously.

'I would be very surprised if anything happens before then. I'm sure your phone is somewhere close. I'll ring it,' she offers, and I'm reminded again how calm she is, always having a plan for everything.

She scrolls to her contacts and presses my number. I hear it ring out on her phone. She turns the volume down and we listen. It's very quiet.

I sigh. 'It's probably on silent. I'll check upstairs in a bit, because it can't have gone far,' I admit.

She smiles. 'OK. But don't go wearing yourself out. Is there anything in particular you fancy? I can pick it up for you.'

I shake my head. 'No. But you get back as soon as you can.'

As she leaves, I remember I should have asked her to fetch me some orange juice. If I can find my phone, I could text her.

It's bound to be upstairs somewhere. I take it one step at a time. I feel a little woozy so the sugar in the tea must not have worked yet. I grip the handrail and it takes me a full minute to get up there because my bump is so big and heavy at this point. Once in my room, I feel behind all the pillows on the bed and look under the covers. It's not there.

My bedroom feels like it's changed. Erica's moved things around. There are some holdalls pushed against the wall and I peek inside. She's laid out the baby clothes I've bought and the nappies so everything is ready. The beautiful white romper suit with yellow satin edging which is the special first outfit I want it to wear because yellow was my mum's favourite colour. So tiny. I button it up. My baby will soon be wearing this.

I reach farther back into the drawer and find a white shawl. It's beautiful. Shell edging and seed pearls. I don't remember ordering this but I'm getting more forgetful lately. Deeper and farther in there are tiny cardigans in lemon and an expensive-looking coat and hat. It's the softest wool I have ever felt, but again, I wouldn't have bought anything this expensive.

I look at the label on the coat. It's Ralph Lauren. I take it through to the spare room where my laptop is set up and type 'Ralph Lauren baby coat' into the search engine. It must have cost a fortune. The Windows icon whirs and then it tells me there is no internet.

Mum was always moaning about it cutting out, which I guess is what happens when you live somewhere remote. Ben bought a dongle, so I open the desk drawer and search through the wires and plugs to find it. I plug it into the USB socket, and it flashes up the password. The internet signal lights up and I am in business. The notification tells me there is £1.69 left on the dongle. That will be enough. The search engine appears and finds a whole screen of Ralph Lauren baby coats. I scroll through and find the exact one. It costs £190. It's lovely if Erica wanted to surprise me with a gift, but surely she wouldn't have bought something so expensive for us?

While I have signal, I check my Facebook messages. I suppose I am hoping for Ben to have sent me something. But he hasn't. I check his profile. It's just posts about cars and games and weed. It's a bit juvenile. Like a teenage boy. Not like someone who's just about to become a father.

My baby kicks in agreement and I murmur to them. 'We'll be OK. Just you and me. We'll be fine.'

I am starting to feel drowsy like before. I need to find my phone and ask Erica to get me some juice. I click on my Samsung account and on the 'locate my device' icon. A map flashes up and I recognise the red marker as where I am now. The one-road-in-one-road-out village. The app draws a line to where my phone is. A thick red line that connects at the end with the location of my phone. I zoom in to see that my phone is in the carpark at Morrisons supermarket.

Erica must have taken my phone. I go through every excuse I can find for it. Perhaps it fell in her bag or she picked it up by mistake. But that doesn't seem right, because she knew I couldn't find it so she should have told me. I feel a wave of panic. I google 'Katie Withers midwife'. I know I am opening a can of worms, but I have a gut feeling that something isn't right. My mum told me to always rely on my instincts. There are hundreds of results, even some new posts today. I click on the top article.

**Midwife exonerated in courtroom drama**

> The case against the Darkford General
> midwife accused of doping women to steal
> their babies was sensationally thrown out
> yesterday. The second day of the trial
> presented new evidence after a witness came

> forward to show Ms Withers had an alibi for
> the date one of the key crimes was committed.
> Police confirmed they are investigating.

If it wasn't Katie, then it must have been someone else and Erica didn't mention any new investigation to me. I am suddenly cold and shivering. What if she is…

It's all starting to feel too wrong. I have to get out of here.

I click on my Facebook conversation with Ben. You have to help me. Can you get over here as soon as possible?

There is a green circle beside his name. He is online. I wait for the blue tick to appear to tell me the message is sent and the icon to move down to show he has read my message. I will him to see it and read it. But then I remember it's Thursday. He'll be gearing up for his usual Thursday night early weekend exploits by having a lie in and then getting high. It could be hours until he sees my message, and even then, he'll probably ignore it. The hard fact hits home that I am on my own. Even Mary next door has gone on holiday so there's nobody to help. There must be someone I can contact, but the internet is disconnected again. I click repeatedly on the dongle icon and there is no balance. Zero.

I go downstairs as fast as I can. If Mary is away, I'll try some other neighbour or perhaps the police will be here looking into the burglary. I have to get away from here. Away from her. But as I scan the coffee table for my keys, I realise they are gone again.

I scream, but I know no one will hear me through Mum's triple-glazing. If the keys are missing, Erica will have locked all the windows too. I feel weak and woozy like yesterday, and then suddenly everything starts to feel hazy. I see the white china teacup with a red rose and a gold rim. A saucer and a silver teaspoon. The tea made and brought to me by Erica, with a biscuit.

I am so stupid. It's her. It was her all along. And I was too stupid to see it.

## Chapter Twenty-Eight

## Nicola

I know next to nothing about childbirth, but I've been around it enough to know it won't be long until Leila goes into labour. I've watched and learned and, of course, I went to nursing college, so I know the basics. But, as usual, no one understood my priorities, so I had to drop out.

In this world, you're on your own. I left home when I was sixteen but that didn't matter to me because I knew I was going to meet someone and have a child and love it so much. I would be the opposite of what my own mother was to me and that was going to make amends.

As I'm shopping at Morrisons, I check my phone to see if there are any updates since the charges against Katie were dropped. I fully expect to see something on the news about a woman who had been drugged and pushed into a cupboard being discovered. Part of me wonders if Erica managed to escape and has simply never looked back, getting as far away from here as she can.

The thing is, as the months went on, I started to think about what could have happened to her. I had her phone, just like I've got Leila's now. Her mother sent her brief messages, and I replied saying I was busy and would try to visit soon. I made up a secondment in the US which I posted about on her Instagram. Most of her followers were acquaintances rather than close friends.

It turned out that Erica only had one real friend. Which was one more than I had and more than Leila has now. A girl from school called Susanna. She lived in France with her husband and baby and would message often. I studied the previous messages and soon picked up the tone of the conversation. Always one step ahead.

For the right person, it can be so easy to make them disappear. No one missed Erica. It turned out her mum and dad were separated and her dad had a new family to keep him busy. I saw them on her Facebook account, playing happy families and ignoring her. Her mum tried a few more times. I wondered if she would visit. Maybe she did and thought Erica wasn't in or was ignoring her. And that's why I know that nobody is going to come looking for Leila – the boyfriend made a good job of isolating her from what friends she did have, and it was easy enough to get rid of him.

I expected to find something awful, but there was nothing when I went back a few months later. No smell. No flies. Just a table pushed in front of the pantry door where I left her. I remembered when I had viewed a similar flat in the building. How I looked for small spaces and hidey holes. Back then, it was so I could hide in her flat and surprise her, but the pantry was cool and made a popping noise like it was sealed when the lady who showed me round opened it. I felt very pleased my plan had worked out so well since then.

I went through her admin. It felt like a gamble going to Darkford General because Erica had just got a job through an agency, but everything worked out. By that time, I'd started work at the hospital and was having my salary paid into her account, so the rent and bills went out automatically. It was a stretch keeping up Erica's life and Nicola's life, but that is what I am good at. Keeping pretences up. Keeping my cool when everyone else is panicking.

That's why I'm so good: because I stay calm. And I can be like putty; sticky and shaped by those around me. I never fitted in. Never. But I learned to mould myself into the shapes of others, so I wasn't conspicuous. And soon I was a beloved member of the team. I was in the right place.

Because my future child was right there. I watched the mothers, some of them enchanted by their babies and some of them ambivalent. It was clear from the outset that there were some who were completely disinterested and wouldn't make good parents. Too young. Too worried about their appearance. Too easily distracted. Just like my own mother so I knew all the warning signs and could spot them a mile off.

I was able to get the morphine easily enough by faking waste reports, but I had to buy the scopolamine. Incredibly, it was freely available online, and I bought it from different sites on Erica's credit card so nothing could be traced back to me.

I'd read about Twilight Sleep, and it was perfect because I didn't want to kill anyone. All that with Erica was an accident. I only wanted to knock them out while they were in labour, so they would remember nothing.

But I had to perfect the dose. It was risky; I knew that. Although I had my back-up plan. I am always one step ahead. And in this case, there was a Plan A, and B, and C. So, I found myself where I am now, in a side ward at the hospital with the key to the medication cupboard. It was easy this time. I know this place so well that I know how careless and distracted people are. Not those two, Katie and Saint Sue. They were on the ball. But the others, well, let's say they would just run in the direction of the latest fire.

And that's why I know my plan today is going to work so well. My keycard is still working so Karen hasn't suspended me yet over the ID mix-up she's discovered. I walk into the empty break room and push bread into the toaster, jamming down the lever. I've made sure the toaster is positioned right under the smoke alarm, so it will be quick to go off. As soon as the alarm goes, everyone evacuates the building.

I hurry to the medication cabinet and open it, scooping what I need into my tote bag. Leila should be asleep for a while because I put a good dose in that tea. I don't want to give her too much or I won't be able to assess her threshold. But I think it will be OK. She is very close now to giving birth, although she won't suffer.

She is not ready to be a mother. And that baby doesn't deserve such a waste of space for a dad. Leila is a nice enough girl, but stupid and gullible. She swallowed the story about Katie hook, line and sinker. And just like Erica, she was isolated and easy for me to pick off.

In some ways, it was easier being Erica than me. I tried her clothes and make-up on, and I had my hair cut like hers. I sometimes stayed at her place, and I would see other residents in the morning as I left for work. None of them questioned me as I opened her mailbox and unlocked the front door. Just a lot of good mornings as they scurried to the next distraction. But I had focus. Oh yes. Complete focus. I knew by then that, if you keep your head down, you are anonymous.

The only slight blip was three months later when there was a buzz on the door intercom. It made me jump because, in all the time I had spent there, no one had ever pressed that buzzer. Then I heard a familiar voice. Mark was telling Erica how he thought she had gone away, but someone had seen her leaving the building in her yellow coat and they were sure it was her. I moved closer to the speaker and listened.

*'Look, I know you don't want anything to do with me. I don't know why, but I will respect you. I only want you to know how much I love you. I think about you every day. I know you were worried about Nicola and what she would do. And that's understandable. I should have suggested we move away so she couldn't watch us.'*

I was shocked. They knew I'd been watching them. Unfamiliar panic tore through me. Mark had seen me.

Really seen me. He knew who I was. And how long would it be until he put two and two together? He was stupid, yes, but not completely unintelligent. He went on.

*'If you would just give me a chance, I'd marry you and move away with you. I don't even know if you're in. I know you told me not to contact you, but I will send you one more message, then, if you don't respond, I'll leave you alone. I love you, Erica. And I'll never forget you.'*

Erica's phone pinged and there was almost an essay from Mark in Facebook messages. It made me very angry. But it confirmed that I was doing the right thing. I was almost glad I hadn't had a baby with him. What kind of father would he make? A voice inside me reminded me that he was disposable and wouldn't have been around long enough to make an impression on our child, if he didn't match up.

I carefully composed a message. It took a few days to make sure it didn't disclose any information that gave me away. But eventually, after studying all their messages to each other, I came up with the perfect fuck-off.

Mark. Thank you for your heart-felt message. I wasn't really expecting it as I asked you not to contact me. I had good reason. I did meet with Nicola, and she told me she was pregnant. She also told me you offered to give her money for an abortion. You didn't mention any of this to me, even though we were close. So, I can only conclude you wanted to hide this side of you

> from me, and if I am going to be with
> someone, I need honesty.

I took a chance on him not telling her about me and our baby. There was nothing in their long message history about it, just Mark calling me a psychopath which is completely wrong as I barely score on the Hare scale. But there was a lot about truth and love and trust. I adore watching people and finding out what their deal-breakers are. You can always find an opportunity to use it against them. Hers was lying. And now I'd lied, too.

I saw the message icon turn to 'read' and waited to see if he would respond. I pictured him in our flat, head in hands, wondering how he could have fucked it all up so badly. Then I simply continued as Erica.

And now I'm almost at mission completion. Thanks to this little fire alarm diversion, I've got all the medication I need to make sure Leila remembers nothing about this birth. I've packed prostaglandin and oxytocin. I know the dosage for the Twilight Sleep because I had time to test it— that didn't go exactly to plan, but it doesn't matter. And I have used the labour-inducing preparations dozens of time.

I am almost there. I've covered my tracks and I'm ready to be a mother at last. All I need to do now is go and get my baby.

## Chapter Twenty-Nine

### Sue

I'm sat in the interview room now waiting for my solicitor to turn up. I'd been in touch with them before about representing me at a potential malpractice case brought by a woman whose baby didn't make it, but it got dropped. I know this is going to be more of a fight.

All the police officers are looking at me in the same way. They've confiscated my phone and have a search warrant for the house, so I can tell that they think I did it somehow. They spoke to me in measured tones that hardly covered a sour taste in their mouths. I asked when I would be interviewed, and they explained the length of time they had and that I would be spending the night in the cells.

As they walked me down, the police officer asked me if I had a dog. Or a cat.

'No. But I have three children.'

He didn't miss a beat. 'And are they at home now?'

I stopped in my tracks. 'I wouldn't leave my children alone.'

He stared straight ahead and blinked into the brightly lit corridor. 'We'll be searching your house this evening and we need to make sure our officers are safe.'

He took off the handcuffs and shut the cell door. I stood there for a while, wondering how it could have spiralled to this. But I know how. Because of her. Erica. The more I think about it, the more I see how she did this.

She made me and Katie believe she was learning from us. That she was our willing pupil. But the truth was, she didn't know what she was doing. Who is she? Karen's revelation about her RCM pass tells me she is not Erica Davies. But who is that woman?

I woke around 3am with a deep sense of foreboding. She was grooming Leila. I can't remember her exact due date, but she's close. That's what all the equipment was for. She's going to deliver her baby at home and then…

I banged on the cell door loudly. Other prisoners shouted for me to be quiet. But I kept banging until someone came. As the door opened, I rushed at it and the two officers grabbed my arms.

'But you don't understand. I know who did this. I need to speak to someone.'

They remained steely calm. The kind of calm that could simmer over any moment into violence. They let go of me and I sat down hard.

'She could be doing it again right now. Please.'

The tallest officer nodded. 'You'll have an opportunity to speak to someone in the morning. For now, please be quiet. There are other people in here. Have a bit of consideration.'

They slammed the door shut, and I felt cheap and dirty. As if I had spoiled everyone's day. As if it really was me who had done whatever Erica had. I don't even know the full extent. But I have an idea of what she is planning.

This morning an officer came and ushered me to an interview room up the corridor.

I feel so stupid as I'm sitting here. They've got the wrong person. I shouldn't be in here. Erica should. She's set me up, and I didn't even see it. I played right into her hands. After Katie's case was thrown out of court, I had my suspicions, and maybe I should have gone straight to Karen or the police then, even though I worried it wasn't enough to go on. Instead, I've sat back and made it easy for her to strike first. Now she's framing me somehow, just as she framed Katie. I am still feeling shaken when two men arrive with my solicitor. They sit down opposite me, the solicitor James Potter takes a seat next to me.

'I'm DC Mearns and this is DC Stafford. We've reopened our investigation, and we want to ask you a few questions.'

I stare at them, arms folded.

My solicitor whispers to me, 'Don't worry, Sue. Let's get through this interview. You don't have to answer any questions you don't want to.'

I think about Katie and her 'I didn't do it' statements. I'd always thought it was odd she maintained she wasn't guilty, but now I realise I'm going to be in the same situation, trying to plead my innocence and people not believing me.

'For the purposes of the recording, DC Stafford and DC Mearns are interviewing Susan Springer with her legal representative, James Potter, present. Recording started at ten past ten.'

DC Mearns takes a deep breath in. 'So, Susan, as you know, your colleague charged with sample crimes of administering drugs to women at your hospital has now got an alibi for a key date. Which means it must have been someone else working at the hospital.' I nod. 'We would like to make this easy for you. Did you do it? We know you have the medical knowledge to administer these drugs and you also had access to the medicine cabinet where they were kept.'

James motions for me to answer.

'I didn't do it. You can ask my hus… ex-husband. And people who were on duty. Ask them. But I know who did. It was Erica. Erica Davies. And I think she's planning to do it again right now with a patient who's having a home birth.'

I try hard to keep my voice calm but I sound shaken. DC Mearns reaches into a holdall on the floor and pulls out a blonde wig and some trainers. Katie's trainers.

'Do you recognise these items?'

'Yes. They are the same kind of trainers Katie wears. Whoever impersonated Katie wore them in the CCTV footage I saw in court. It was Erica who pretended to be Katie.'

He passes an A4 piece of paper to my solicitor and another to me. I read it. It states the date and time a search team broke into my locker at the hospital and found the wig and the trainers underneath a bag containing morphine boxes. He slides some photographs of the morphine boxes across the table.

'We've sent them off for forensics. But these are the boxes we found.'

I know how this looks. Erica has done a good job of making me look incredibly guilty with all the evidence now pointing in my direction. But I'm not going down without a fight. 'Weren't these the same boxes you found at Katie's? So, did she have them, or did I have them? Or more likely, it seems the real person responsible for this has been planting evidence around,' I say defiantly.

'So you have no idea how these or the wig and trainers came to be in your locker, then?'

'The only time I've seen that wig or those trainers before is in the footage. We all know the combinations to each other's lockers. We're standing next to each other when we get changed. She knows my code. You've got the wrong person.'

A flicker of irritation sweeps over both their faces. I hear my voice, calm and professional now. 'Besides the things that have been planted in my locker, which lots of people have seen me open so could have taken the code, have you found anything else?'

'We've sent some items from your house for forensics—'

James interrupts. 'What items?'

DC Mearns slides another list over to us. They've taken my uniform and some black trainers. Some tramadol Tom was prescribed for his bad back about three years ago.

DC Mearns resumes his questioning. 'Can you explain why you had Katie's diary in your bag?'

'Because I didn't believe she did it. I found it in the space we used as our office to fill out our practice logs. I wanted to check something about a patient,' I say calmly.

'And you didn't think you should come forward to the police with this as a piece of potential evidence?' he challenges me.

'I thought the police must have already examined it and returned it,' I say evenly.

DI Mearns changes track. 'When did you find out that Katie was having an affair with your husband?'

I flush red, still embarrassed at how I found out in such a painful way. 'I had no idea, so I learned of it during the trial when the new CCTV evidence was presented,' I say faintly.

'You didn't find out earlier and then set her up out of revenge? It seems like a very strong motive to me.'

I try to suppress the anger that's rising inside me. I'm hurt by the affair, but I still don't understand what motive they think I have for administering the doses to mothers in the first place.

'Like I said, I found out about the affair during the trial. And I'm not sure what motive you think I had to administer the drugs. I've worked at the hospital for years. I've even won an award for distinguished service, so why would I suddenly start drugging patients I'm pledged to protect?'

They are silent. Still reading the report. I wait a moment, then I speak up again. 'Erica must have put those things in my locker. They weren't there the day before when I went to the hospital.'

They sit up. 'Why were you at the hospital?'

I have to tell the truth because that's the best chance I have of getting out of here and helping them to catch the real culprit behind this.

'I broke into Erica's locker. I knew it was her. I was angry about what happened at the trial. I realised she must have set Katie up and she'd probably be coming for me next, so I had to do something. You have to believe me. She has an outreach lady, and she spends all her time there. She ordered equipment for a home birth, then, when I looked for the requisition docket, it was gone. She said she'd forgotten to file it. But when I looked on the system for that lady's address, all *her* records were deleted too. There's no trace of her.'

DC Stafford raises his voice. 'But you didn't think to tell anyone?'

I shake my head, ashamed. 'You don't understand. This all happened over time. And she had an excuse for everything. It all seemed unconnected, and mistakes do happen. But now… now Katie has been proved not to have done this, it's starting to look like Erica has been grooming this lady. There's another thing too. My boss, Karen, told me the RCM confirmed that Erica Davies is not the same woman who's been working at Darkford General. Please talk to Karen and she can confirm that. And, if Erica's planted those things in my locker, will you be able to check the CCTV at the hospital or the keycards? Erica would have had no reason to be at the hospital so, if she has been there, it's because she's been there to plant evidence.'

The door opens and a uniformed officer beckons the two detectives. They switch the recorder off and leave.

'Do you know where Erica, or whoever she really is, lives? Or the patient she's been spending a lot of time with?'

I shake my head. 'No. I had no reason to look. There were just a few things that seemed a bit odd about the home birth and how it got signed off. But it wasn't my patient. Erica was assigned to her, and she'd always seemed above board before then. The hospital has just promoted her, so she's fooled everyone.'

The day she was offered the outreach post comes into focus. How she insisted on home births for those ladies who had engaged with Katie because they would be nervous about coming into the hospital. How she sounded full of authority as she ordered the home birth kit. How her explanation of the missing requisition sounded so convincing.

James has his mobile in his hand. 'Look, Sue. I'm afraid this is all over the internet. Snaps and videos of you being led from your home. I have to warn you that, if they release you, the press will be…'

'My children.' I fight back the tears that are threatening to form. It's going to be devastating and confusing for them. No matter how big a cheat Tom has turned out to be, I hope he'll protect them and maintain my innocence.

James looks at me. 'I know this is an extremely difficult situation. But when this is all cleared up, you'll have a strong case for wrongful arrest. They should have simply asked you to come in for questioning. This has seriously damaged your reputation.'

I've been so focused on fighting to defend myself, I hadn't even thought of that erosion of trust and how this is going to be perceived. Pregnant women put their trust in their midwives to deliver their babies safely. But nobody will want me to deliver their child now. I will lose my job. And I will be all alone to face a future where I have been accused of harming newborns – the thought of which makes me sick to my stomach after all those years of service.

But I don't have time to process all this, because they return to the room and sit opposite me.

DC Stafford speaks very softly. 'You are free to leave, Mrs Springer. I am formally ending this interview at this point. If we need to ask you anything else, we'll give you a call. You can collect your belongings at the desk. The next steps are that we will be back in touch to take a formal statement depending on further evidence.'

'What's happened? Have you found Erica?'

They look pale and serious, and I sense something has shifted.

'We've had some new evidence that corroborates your story and we're pursuing a new line of enquiry,' DC Stafford tells me.

But will it be too late?

# Chapter Thirty

## Nicola

I've gone back to Erica's flat and wiped over every single surface, so there is no trace of me. But I'm worried I'm on borrowed time now that Karen will be snooping into the RCM records.

I know it's only a matter of time until the police come and search this flat. It's almost perfect as it is, but I need to add some finishing touches to keep them off my trail.

It's amazing what you can get away with. As long as you're not leaving the country and don't look wildly different to the photo ID you have, there is rarely a problem. I've used Erica's passport and ID a few times, and people might give it a cursory glance, but they don't look that closely. Of course, I had full access to her utility bills. So, I was able to open multiple credit card accounts and treat myself, too. I kept an eye on them, of course, making sure I stayed within limits. No need to raise any fuss.

I sit down at the table with my blue surgical gloves on and write out an itinerary. I google train times on Erica's phone and write them on a stark white sheet, along with the address of an Airbnb. I even supply them with a carpark, leaving the breadcrumbs I want them to follow. I press deep with the ballpoint pen, so it makes a clear impression on the sheet underneath.

Then I leave some documents I printed out in a drawer where they will be easily found. They are mainly receipts and bookings. I look around. I will be sorry to leave this place but it's time for me and my baby to have a fresh start far from here.

Erica's clothes will be collected up and sent for testing. They will scour every inch of this place for any trace of me. I tingle a little with the excitement of how clever I've been. They could be outside now. And there's only one door. I like living on the edge and I've found something I'm good at, even though my mother used to make me feel like I wasn't special.

I am done here. I rip the white note from the pad and take a last look at this particular scene I'm leaving behind for the police to find.

I shut the door and lock it. I pull my hood over my hair and check the mailbox for the last time. Old habits die hard, but there are always new habits to be made, and I'm so close to everything coming together like I planned.

I drive away and find myself going to my old childhood home as it's the last time I'm going to be in the area. A couple and their young children live there now. I've seen them going in and out, the ghost of my childhood self watching their happy family. I left this place as soon as I could at sixteen, but I've never forgotten it. I know every inch of it. Every inch of the garden and the drive. And the house. I went back just before my twenty-first birthday. I'd written to Mum asking her why she did those things to me. I suggested, if it had been him influencing her, we could talk. She never replied.

I even called, but she put the phone down as soon as she knew it was me. I want to think it was him, but it wasn't. She locked me away so she could have her new life. She could have had me adopted or sent me to live with my grandmother in Ireland. But she didn't.

I stand in front of the house, and it all floods back. The locked room. Then being locked outside, because they knew by then I was too scared to tell anyone. As I got older, I knew they had a point. I *did* think bad things, and I *did* do them. But only when people deserved it. She'd shaken me and screamed that I couldn't be judge and jury any more than she could. But she already had, and that was the point.

School appointed a psychologist. I was the first pupil to see her. My mother came with me and squeezed my hand tightly as I went in so I would know not to say anything about how she treated me. *Be a good girl* turned into a confusion of lies as I smiled and told them everything was fine. Then it would still be the same. Locked in my room. Or worse. Locked outside on a freezing night.

I walk up the path and past the back door. Still no gate. Gross stupidity, because it gives people like me access. But people are stupid. She was. My mother. I retrace my steps up the side of the garden to a turfed area. I dig deep with my heel and find the metal. There is no sign that this was once a coal hole. The grass is seamless now. But I'd slipped inside on the nights it was too cold. It was dark and wet and deep. It smelled of mould. And I came out dirtier than I went in, my knees scuffed and bleeding. I'd go inside the house when I was allowed and scrape off the grime before I got into my school uniform. It was while I was in there I would plan. I knew what I needed to do. And somehow, the planning made it worth it. Instead of my mother dragging me to my bedroom, I would go up there voluntarily and scheme. I would open the back door and step onto the icy grass before they pushed me outside. I don't think they missed me.

I stood here that day long ago. Then I knocked on the back door and she let me in. She took her time making a pot of tea. Perfectly silent. I felt the excitement build, and I watched her stir and pour it into china teacups and saucers from her best tea set. The one with the red roses and the gold rim.

'I like your new hair colour, Nicola. It suits you.' She paused. She couldn't look at me. 'I'd like to put it behind us, Nicola, if we can?'

I'd nodded. 'Yes. I'd like that. I'd like us to be back in each other's life. The garden is looking great. Do you want to show me what you've done?'

I saw something flash across her face, then she agreed. We left the full teacups on the table, and she led me up the path.

I pointed at the cherry tree. 'How beautiful!'

She took a step towards it and then she stumbled and dropped through the grass I had replaced after opening the coal hole door. I heard her heels clatter down the steps and then silence.

I whispered into the darkness, 'You know how it feels now, don't you?'

I shut the door and replaced the grass. My heart beat fast and I felt elated. There had been no need for a struggle, and my plan had worked perfectly. I hurried back into the house, poured away the tea and washed the cups, replacing them exactly where they had been. I took her bag and keys and packed an overnight case with essentials. Finally, I placed a letter on the kitchen table. It explained how she was leaving because she had never agreed with how he had treated her or Nicola. That she wouldn't be back.

I stand over the coal hole now. Just like with Erica, I waited for news of a woman being found or someone coming to arrest me when she escaped. I figured it would have been worth it, because she deserved to suffer.

But it never happened. I almost wanted it to, so that I could tell everyone what she did to me. But, as time went on, I realised she got what she deserved.

I look down at the grass. *I won't be back, Mum. I'll be caring for my baby and doing a much better job than you ever did with me.*

## Chapter Thirty-One

### Leila

I am awake. I listen, eyes closed, to see if she is in the house. I tense, listening for a creak of a floorboard or sounds of her moving around. She could be sitting right here, beside me. I feel my pulse quicken at the thought, and then my baby kicks.

I open my eyes, but she isn't there. I don't know how long I passed out for or how much time I have. I feel weak and light-headed, although my baby is moving so I take that as a good sign it's OK. I feel relief that whatever she's been drugging me with doesn't seem to be having an effect on my little one.

I can't let her do it again, though. I get up as quickly as I can manage and pad upstairs. Mum had an alarm clock on her bedside table, so I can check the day and time on that. But as I go into her room, I see it's gone. I look out of the window and a car passes. I bang as hard as I can. I even wonder if I could smash a downstairs window.

But I have no chance of climbing through the high cottage windows. My back is hurting and, because I'm full-term, my range of movement is restricted. I have to try, I tell myself. I go back downstairs and look around for something heavy. Mum was fond of delicate ornaments, and I kept her Capo di Monte ladies lined up in a display cabinet.

I feel groggy and I have terrible backache. I don't think I have the strength to hit the heavily glazed windows with anything.

I know before I go to look that Mum has no tools in this house. We don't have anything that could help me because she didn't believe in DIY. She had a man to come in and do odd jobs so maybe he brought his own.

I wish Mum were here now. I wish I had listened to her and then none of this would be happening. Another car passes and I bang on the window again. I hurry around to the kitchen and look for the neighbours in their gardens, but no one is around. This place is so isolated. It's beautiful, but so far from anything. I pull out a knife from the drawer and try to prise the back door open. But it is solid, and I make no progress.

I pick up a wooden stool and try to fling it at the kitchen window. But it bounces off a worktop and hits my arm. I jump away to avoid it and my back hurts even more. I pick up the knife again and try to lever open one of the top windows. At least someone might hear me shouting. But it doesn't budge. I'm starting to feel like I'm really trapped in here and frightened about what's going to happen if nobody finds me.

I have another idea that could be my last chance. I bang on the wall with a rolling pin. I haven't seen Mary or Jack for ages. Erica said they'd gone away, although she could have been lying. I decide it's worth a try. I scream as loud as I can and continue banging, making as much noise as I can in the hope they'll hear and come rushing over.

'Help me. Please. Mary. I need help,' I cry desperately.

It's no use and I catch my breath. I have to face it. She's going to come back at some point and… What am I going to do then? I realise how much I'm shaking, terrified at what she might do to me. Is she going to kill me? Is that what she was going to do to those other women? But she didn't kill the others, so maybe there's still a way I can get out of this alive. Even though Erica told me not to, I'd read every article about what had happened at the hospital. I'd read every online post and watched every TV news report. I recognised all the corridors and the rooms they showed. We'd had a tour of the maternity ward, and it seemed like a safe place, which is why all this was even more shocking.

She drugged the women, but they woke up. Just like I have. I remember the expensive baby clothes I found in the drawer that she's bought, and I have goosebumps working out why she is doing this. She wants my baby. My arms cover my stomach to protect this precious new life. I am scared enough about giving birth, but this is unthinkable that she would take a piece of me. If she lets me live, I will tell the police. So why would she risk that?

I feel a twinge of pain deep in my tummy. Please don't let it be starting now. I don't want to give birth here, alone. I should never have agreed to do this at home. I could have changed my mind and said I wanted to go to hospital. Then she couldn't have trapped me, so that's why she was so clever at talking me out of it. Although, after she drugged those other women, maybe the hospital wouldn't have been any safer.

I realise, even though I have no chance of getting out of here, I still have the knife in my hand. I know what I have to do. I feel sick at the thought because I am not a violent person. I have never hurt anyone intentionally in my life. But if it's a choice of me and my baby, or them, I'll do anything to protect us. I just can't figure out how. There is nowhere to hide in this house which would help me gain the advantage of surprise.

I never used to be able to get away from Ben when he brought his mates over here, because there was nowhere to go. And now an even bigger monster has come along I need to hide from. She pretended she was protecting me when, really, she was manipulating me all along. I realise how easy I made it for her and feel another pain in my stomach. This time it feels like it's pressing in on me. My hips ache with the weight and I sit on the bed. I need to think quickly. Where would I be able to surprise her? Fear makes my skin tingle as I try to come up with a plan to save myself.

The bathroom could work. I can't hide behind a door because I'd have to move quickly which I can't. The bathroom has some towel hooks beside the door. I could duck behind there and wait for her to come into the room, then…

I try it out. She will see my feet. I pull a footstool over and cover them with it. I feel sick and my head is spinning. I don't know if I can do this. I desperately want to believe that I can because it's my only chance, but all the strength has gone from my body, and I am in a cold sweat. My back is aching worse than before, and I am wondering how long I will have to stand here – maybe for hours – when I hear the key in the front door.

She's here. I try to take deep breaths to calm my beating heart. The front door opens and closes quietly. I hear her footsteps on the hallway tiles, her black brogues padding along in the familiar space she's made herself at home in. She throws the keys down on the coffee table. I wonder if I can lure her upstairs and then run and grab them. But it's a pipe dream because I can't run anywhere. The ache between my legs is heavy and I feel like I am going to pass out from the pain which comes and goes in waves.

She is in the kitchen. I hear her flick the kettle on and rattle cups.

Then she shouts, 'You awake? I'm making a cup of tea. You stay up there, and I'll bring it up.'

I think about every scary horror film I have watched where someone is being pursued. All the scenes when I hid behind a cushion or made Ben hold me to feel safe. Nothing was as terrifying as living it out for real now. Yet I steel myself, because I have the advantage. She thinks I am still drugged up in bed. She has underestimated me. She doesn't know what I am capable of.

*Come on, Erica, come on.*

I will her to come upstairs. I hear her making the tea. Then all is silent. Did I leave the drawer open when I took the knife or did I shut it? I don't hear anything for a moment, which is strange because I thought she would have been coming upstairs. Then I see a shadow passing the door. My heart feels like it's beating outside of my chest. She must have taken her shoes off, knowing that the creaky floorboard on the second to top step and then outside Mum's bedroom would give her away.

I hear her rustling in a cupboard. She is moving things around and noisily pushing things into Mum's pine dresser. The floorboard creaks again, and the shadow passes the door towards my old room. I can see the back of her from here. I could step forward and… no. I have to wait until she is super-close. I can't mess this up. I only have one chance.

My throat is tight, and my mouth is dry. She peeps around the door and then she laughs.

'Oh! So, you're playing that little game, are you? Where are you, Leila? Where are you hiding?' she calls in a soft sing-song voice which makes me shudder.

She goes into my bedroom and switches the light on. My knees buckle, but I make myself completely still. I watch because, when she emerges, she will be facing the bathroom door which is ajar, and I don't know if I am invisible.

I hear her opening the wardrobes and dramatically drawing the curtains open.

'Not here? Where then?' She laughs again.

I see her through a gap in the towels. She is smiling. I hadn't noticed it before, but she has very white teeth. She doesn't see me. She looks into the room, but then turns and hurries downstairs.

She quickly realises, like I did, that there is nowhere to hide down there. She checks the back door, rattling the handle, but all the doors are locked.

'Where are you? I know you're here somewhere?'

Then she is climbing the stairs again, but this time she doesn't take care to be quiet. She races up to the landing, back to Mum's room. Now is my chance. One step after another, she is nearer and nearer. I grip the knife so tightly I think I will burst a blood vessel. Then she is standing on the landing right in front of me.

I force my foot forwards. Then the other foot. But then I feel a warm sensation on my thighs, a waterfall running down my legs. I look down and it is spreading across the tiles, pink and thick. I look up and my eyes meet hers.

She is grinning. 'So, there you are.'

# Chapter Thirty-Two

## Sue

I am watching it live on TV. I've been home for a while now, and rejecting calls from Tom. I'm shaken and shocked, but I cannot take my eyes from the TV screen. The police are erecting an incident tent around an address not far from Darkford General. It seems like there are new developments in the case and I only hope they're getting closer to the truth and finding Erica.

My phone rings. It's my solicitor and I answer, eager to know why he's calling.

'Sue. It's James. I wanted to let you know I've looked into the position with your employers. They can't dismiss you for this. You've done nothing wrong.'

I watch the TV screen as the news anchor gesticulates and speculates. It doesn't feel like I've done nothing wrong after the way I was led out of my house in handcuffs and bundled into the back of a police car. That image is going to haunt me forever.

'I'd advise suing for wrongful arrest as you have a very strong case. I'd also consider making a public statement to avoid further reputational damage.'

I nod into the phone until he has finished speaking, then thank him.

I message Karen saying, Thanks for the support. I'd expected more, to be honest. Understandably, I'll be taking a couple of weeks off. If you have any issues with that, talk to my solicitor.

She doesn't respond. I still feel exhausted and broken by what's happened – that I could even be considered guilty for a second. If I thought that the past months have been a nightmare, the past few days have been much, much worse than I thought was even possible. I know I'm still suffering from shock. I need to give myself time and try to hold it together. I don't even know if I will go back, but it will be my decision. Everything will from now on.

All I want is to be at home with my children, and for the police to catch Erica before she harms anyone else.

I scroll through my messages and see the most recent one from Liam.

> I've seen what they are saying about you on socials
>
> Some kid at school showed me on their phone, and I told Gran I wanted my phone back to message you. I don't know why we still can't come home, because I miss you. Let me come home Mum. I'll make you a cup of tea

> and tidy my bedroom. I don't know where Dad
> is. I want to be there with you.
>     I love you, Mum. Whatever's happening we
> can sort it out.

As I re-read it, I feel my eyes mist over. I'm the one that's supposed to protect the kids, not the other way around. I feel so guilty for what I've put them through.

Now I've had chance to start to pull myself together, I message Liam back.

> Thank you love. I am home now. What you
> wrote means the world. I'll explain it all later,
> but, yes, you can come home after school
> tomorrow. I'll ask Gran to drop you all off here.
> Then we can get on with our lives. I love you.
> Mum x

He messages back a string of emojis, which makes me smile for the first time in a while. Maybe we can somehow get through this. I text Tom too.

> Meet me at the house in an hour. We need to
> talk. Just the two of us.

He sends a thumbs-up back. The sun is in that place in the lounge where it shines on my chair. I sit here, warm and still, and for a minute I start to feel better. But then the TV reporter announces gravely that a body has been found in the flat of Erica Davies. My stomach tenses in knots at what she's saying, and I start to cry as the wave of shock hits me again.

The camera pans to a block of flats with a communal entrance. The reporter holds his finger to his ear.

*Reports are coming in that the body in the flat has been there a while. The woman who has been allegedly posing as the occupant of this flat has fled, according to media speculation. We're going over to the newsroom as a police press conference has just started.*

The screen flashes to a large room stuffed with reporters, and DCs Stafford and Mearns sitting at a table. DC Stafford speaks.

*Following fast-moving enquiries, we have established that a thirty-year-old woman, Nicola Marie Green, has been posing as qualified midwife Erica Davies. Sadly, Erica Davies has been discovered deceased today at a property on Solent Road. We have reason to believe that Nicola Green has fled to London.*

A photograph of Erica flashes on the screen. But this isn't the woman I've come to know as Erica.

It finally hits me. The woman on the RCM's photo ID: she's dead. And the woman I have worked with and thought I knew and could trust, is a stranger to me. I was only just starting to realise what she was capable of with drugging our mothers on the ward, but *killing* someone?

I take my laptop and log into the system, frantic about the mother who requested the home birth. If the police are closing in on whoever this woman posing as Erica really is, I'm worried what she'll do as she becomes more desperate. I check all the records again for Erica's appointments and client list. I check for the ladies who have been flagged up as previous patients looked after by Katie. I tell myself I might have missed the woman I'm looking for when I was in a panic. But she isn't there. And neither is the equipment requisition. I told them. I need to tell the police again until they look into it because, if this woman has killed once, then...

I'm so scared and anxious that I start to feel sick. Then I see Tom's car pull up outside. This is the last thing I need to be dealing with right now, even though it was my idea to talk so that the kids could come home.

I watch him walk up the path and get his key out. He looks nervous, the way he would look when we went to parties with people we didn't know. I always enjoyed meeting new people, but he was unsure and twitchy. I still can't believe that the only man I've ever loved and thought I'd be with forever has done this to me.

And then he is here. It's weird how someone I thought I knew so well now seems distant and like a stranger. He has his hands in his pockets and hesitates over whether to sit down or not. I cannot speak. I am suddenly overcome with sadness. It's not even about his infidelity. It's about the record collection we share and the places we have visited together over and over. Our default bars and cafés. Our favourite meal and takeaway Thursday. The memories we have and I thought we would keep creating together. And, at the forefront, our children.

I turn off the TV so we can have this out properly.

'You could have told me,' I begin.

He drops onto our worn sofa. 'I couldn't. I...'

I shake my head. 'She told you not to, didn't she?' He nods. I feel the prick of anger. 'Willing to go to prison to save... what?'

'It wasn't like that,' Tom says, but his voice is faint and weak, just like he's become. 'She was protecting me, not you. I'm sorry, love. We didn't know what to do. And they had so much evidence, all she could do was keep denying it. They built a case. But she kept believing that, in the end, they would find out it wasn't her. When it went to trial, I went to see her because I couldn't sit back and let her go to prison for something she didn't do.'

I look at him. 'So you played the hero and tore our life apart to save her?'

He lowers his eyes. 'I knew she didn't do it and you couldn't believe it either. We were just going to... then... I don't know. It all went mad and I couldn't tell you. You were already upset. And the kids...' He wipes his hands over his face.

I snap at him. 'So, if she had gone to jail, none of this would have come out? You would have carried on living with me and seeing her? And I would never have found out?'

He shakes his head. 'Yeah. I mean. No. She begged me not to tell them. She's ashamed. And embarrassed. We both are, because we never planned for this to happen.'

'But when you realised you were going to have to come forward to save her, you didn't think you should tell me first? Instead, you let me find out by watching footage of you in court with everyone else, being absolutely humiliated as I realised my marriage was a lie.'

'I came forward and then the police requested CCTV from where I'd said we'd been. I didn't know you'd be at the trial. I hoped you'd stay away like I told you. You have to see that it's all completely fucked up. The thing is, if she got life, then…'

I am speechless. I nod. Yes. If she was found guilty and sentenced, then we would have carried on as before. Unbelievable. They'd both been in on it. As if it was a game and me and the children were the consolation prize. None of it makes sense. But none of this mess does. They've both betrayed me, having an affair behind my back and I'll never be able to forgive them. Especially Tom who's been too spineless to tell me the truth.

'You know there's no way back from this. And you're going to have to tell the kids what you've done, why we're splitting up and why you won't be living here anymore.'

'Right. What do you want to happen then?'

I snap bitterly, 'Oh, now you care about me and what I want, do you? I thought you'd have it all planned. Your new life with Katie.'

He opens his mouth to speak and I stand here impatiently to see what he's going to say.

'I need to tell you the truth. I owe you that, at least.' He stops to gauge my reaction, but I am unmoved and don't feel like I can believe what he's saying. 'I love her. I'm sorry. I can't help it. I fell in love with her. I didn't want to hurt you and God only knows I especially didn't want to hurt the kids.

But that's it. Adam's already living at his sister's, so I can stay with Katie at her house for now until we all work something out.'

'I want the kids to come home today,' I tell him.

'OK, I really didn't want to take them away from you, I was only trying to protect them from the trial and all the journalists.'

'Well, I think, after recent events, I need to be with the boys and they need to be back home so it doesn't feel like everything has changed,' I say firmly.

'Will I be able to see them?' he asks, his voice breaking at the thought of being separated from them.

I think back to Liam's message. *I love you both.* I want to scream at him that, no, you cheated, and you don't deserve them. That he's the one who's walking out on us and leaving the family. But, as much as he's hurt us all and will have to explain that to them, he's still their dad.

I nod, realising that, even though I'm heartbroken, we'll have to find a way to parent them together. 'Yes. Of course. We'll set something up.'

He stands up and I realise this is how it ends. No big argument. No cruel recriminations. He pauses and, for a moment, I think he is going to say he is sorry and that it's all been a mistake he wishes he could take back. But he doesn't; he turns and walks out. I hear the door close behind him, and that is how our marriage ends.

# Chapter Thirty-Three

## Leila

She has tied me to the bed set up in the dining room. Both my hands are bound with rope to the headboard, and I can hardly move. My back is aching badly and every so often I feel an overwhelming, crushing cramp in my pelvis. I've never felt pain like it. This can't be normal, not from any of the books I've read. It can't be.

Erica is in the kitchen. She's brought a trolley and rolled it to the side of the bed. I crane my neck to see what she has and what she might be planning. I've been terrified at what she's going to do next since my waters broke last night and she managed to take the knife from me.

I've lost my chance to stop her and get help now I've gone into labour.

She makes me a cup of tea in the china cup, but I don't drink it. I force my mouth closed as she raises the cup to my lips.

She tuts. 'Have it your way.'

I pull my arms to release myself, but another pain comes. I scream and Erica hovers.

'We'll need less noise, please, or I'll have to give you something. You must stay calm so you can safely deliver the baby.'

I wait until the pain decreases, then I plead with her. 'Please. I won't say anything. Please let me go. I'll give you my baby, if that's what you want. Please, I will never breathe a word to anyone. Please stop this, Erica.' I try to sound confident. But my voice falters.

She laughs. 'What do you think is going to happen? I'm not going to kill you.' She says it mockingly. Like I'm ridiculous to think it. 'I've never killed anyone, and I wouldn't. But you have to admit, this was all a mistake. Getting pregnant with that… man.'

She stares at me, waiting for me to say something. She is judging me like I worried they all would at the hospital because I was going to be a young mother. All the time she has been pretending to help me, she's been planning this.

She sips her own tea. 'I'm only trying to help you. I could see the mess you got yourself in so I wanted to help you. I know you're not ready to be a mother.'

I have to fight back. 'I'm going to love my baby so much and give it the best life. The pregnancy might have been a surprise, but I am ready. I can do this. I'm going to be a good mum, like my mum was to me.'

'You can't cope. You couldn't even manage to get to hospital, whining about it. The helpless little girl act. Except it wasn't an act, was it? You really are helpless. Stuck here in the middle of nowhere. Did it ever occur to you that you could have moved nearer?'

I feel my temper rise. 'This is my mum's house. I want to stay here so I can bring her grandchild up here. It's supposed to be a safe place for me and my family, but you've spoiled it. You're not fit to be a midwife.'

She laughs callously. I tense. No contraction, just anger at this bitch who's tricked me. She checks her phone. It's a different one to what she's had before. I strain to hear the low volume as a video plays, but I can make out the words 'Darkford' and 'Nicola Green'. I hear a man's voice saying they think she's fled to London. I feel more desperate than ever as I start to piece it together, that she isn't who she told me she is.

She watches the footage. 'I'm not a midwife. I'm a trained nurse, well, partly, but I'm not a midwife.'

My blood runs cold. I'm trapped here with her and she isn't even a midwife. How can she help me give birth, then? What about my baby? I panic as fear consumes me, but I will myself to stay calm for my baby's sake. I think about the first time I met Erica in the maternity ward. How she was super-kind and put me at ease, confident I was in safe hands. She must have had this planned all along.

'Why me?' I whisper.

She puts her phone down and stares at me. 'Because you remind me of how I was once. Before I wised up and realised you need to take what you want for yourself. My God. You let that guy walk all over you. He didn't even turn up for your scan and you were still making excuses for him. I was with someone like him once. But you live and learn. He went off with someone else and I made sure she regretted that.'

I snap back at her. 'You said you wouldn't harm anyone. You said that.'

She shifts in her chair. 'The thing is, people have a choice to be nice or not. And when they're not, they try to blame it on someone else. They try to say someone made them do it. But I'm not buying that.'

There is a change in her mood. She was laughing, but now it's like a switch has been flicked and she's all fired up. I need to keep her talking, find out anything that could keep me safe until help comes.

'What happened to you, Erica?'

She wipes a tear. 'That's what the do-gooders say, *it wasn't your fault, you're a victim*. They have an answer for everything. But in this world, you have to help yourself. Defend yourself. No one is going to rescue you. You have to make your own happiness.'

I need to say the right thing. Get her to untie me, convince her I won't be so stupid as to try anything. Keep her busy until they get here, make her trust me.

'I'm sorry someone hurt you, Erica. But I'm not going to do that. I've welcomed you into my home. And now you're not being very nice to me. You have a choice. Please untie me so I can be more comfortable to keep the baby safe and calm.'

She stands and towers over me, but her expression is vacant and glazed over. Her jaw is set, and she pulls up the cover over my bump and smooths it. 'You don't know anything about me. And you don't want to. Like I said. I have never killed anyone. And I won't kill you. You'll have the same chance as all the others. If it's meant to be, you will be fine. And if not...'

I try to sit up. 'What others? What do you mean I'll have the same chance? You can't get away with this. You can't.'

'But I can.' She smiles. 'And I have. The thing is you have to plan things. And you didn't, did you? If you hadn't been so pathetic about not being able to get to the hospital, none of this would have happened and it would have been someone else.'

'I'm twenty years old. This is the first time I've had to do anything like this and I'm going to manage.'

She is shouting now. '*Had* to? No one forced you to sleep with that waste of space. That's the problem. You make it sound like someone forced you. And now it's someone else's fault. People like you have babies and aren't in the least bit prepared. It will be the child that suffers while people like me who want to be a mother...'

She turns away and stares out of the window. What has happened to her to make her this crazy?

Another contraction comes, bigger this time. She moves over to the trolley and comes back with another strap. I think she is going to tie my legs, but she pushes it between me and the bed and around my stomach. Then she presses a button and looks at her phone. She is monitoring the contractions, so at least she knows to do that. She seems to be stepping into action. I have felt them stronger and closer, but I have no idea how near to giving birth I am.

She goes back to the trolley. She snaps on a pair of surgical gloves, and I pull my legs tightly together. No. I can't bear it. I can't let her touch me. I think about kicking her squarely in the face, which might knock her out, but then I'd be all alone. And I can't give birth with my hands tied. My baby, helpless and alone. As terrified as I am, I need her here.

Another contraction comes unexpectedly quickly. She spins around and checks the monitor on her phone. Her face is concentrated and, despite her admission that she is not a midwife, it seems like she knows what to do. However she got the job, she *has* been working at the hospital. She unrolls a green strip and I hear the clatter of metal. She places a metal dish on the trolley, then disappears. I hear her going upstairs and then the creaking floorboard outside my mum's bedroom. She reappears a long minute later with some white boxes and begins to unwrap them.

I can see the lounge window through the adjoining doors from here. I see the top of a bus drive by. I wonder how long it will be before someone arrives. But will it be too late when they do? Will it be days after she has gone with my baby and left me here tied to this bed?

The strain of trying to release my arms and holding myself rigid has taken its toll, and the last bit of energy I had drains from my body. I tell myself that, if there is a God, he will realise this can't happen and stop her somehow. As she measures out liquids, I try to think what I have done wrong in my life to deserve this. I've made mistakes but I never hurt anyone.

As she flicks a syringe to release the air, I silently pray that, whatever happens to me, my baby will live and be safe.

She turns to face me. 'It's time. This Twilight Sleep is a method that has been used for over a century to help ladies give birth without any pain.' She comes towards me, and I twist my body away from her, but another contraction claws at me, stronger than before and I go limp. She wipes a damp swab across my thigh. 'Nearly done, Leila. Don't worry. This is for your own good.'

# Chapter Thirty-Four

## Sue

'Have a good time.' I smile as I wave the boys off into Patricia's car. It was nice to have them home last night and eat a takeaway for tea all together, but I want to keep things as normal as possible for them until Tom and I decide what to tell them. I'm grateful to Patricia for taking them to the football tournament today, which has been planned for a few weeks.

I'm struck by how empty the house feels without them as I close the front door. I suppose this is how it might be from now on – them having a weekend day at Tom's and me pottering around by myself.

I should probably clean and do a load of washing, but I can't just sit around here. Something is badly wrong. I can't get the young blonde girl out of my head. Erica, or whoever she is, had us all fooled.

My phone rings. It's Katie, but I can't speak to her. I can't. Simply the thought of it makes my stomach flip. It's not the first time she's tried to call me since she's been released. I've been ignoring her calls.

I might go for a walk and I'm about to go upstairs to grab my bag when the doorbell rings. I'm surprised to see DC Mearns on my doorstep.

'Sue, I didn't get a chance to apologise about the arrest. You have to understand we needed to look at everything. But I'm hoping I can come in and ask you a few questions following up on what you told us in your interview.'

I wonder if I should call James to get his advice but decide to show him in.

'We've confirmed that the woman who's been posing as Erica Davies is in fact a Nicola Green,' he explains.

'So she's not really a midwife?' I gasp and he shakes his head. When Katie was in the frame, I never quite believed she could have done it, but at least she knew what she was doing. Someone who doesn't could easily give the wrong dose and women could have died. I shudder at the thought.

'You mentioned when we interviewed you that you were concerned about one patient in particular. Can you tell me more about her?'

'Erica was promoted and assigned to outreach. She told me she had this lady, Leila, on her list. She ordered home birth equipment.'

He pulls out a folder and passes me an A4 page. I immediately recognise it as the outreach list.

'One of our experts has interrogated the hospital system with the cooperation of the administrators. We've visited each of these ladies, and our liaison officers have spoken to them. As you can see, everyone who was in contact with Nicola Green has been contacted pending interview.'

I read the list. I run my finger down it, searching for Leila. But she isn't there. Of course she isn't, because Erica, or Nicola as she's really called, wiped her from the system.

'But she deleted the records. Leila wasn't on the system. But I saw them together for a first appointment at the hospital. And she talked about her.'

He nods. 'This has been a very stressful time for you, so thanks for telling us what you know. We're going to look into this, but we're also pursuing another line of enquiry for a thorough investigation.'

'I understand that, but I really think this woman could be in danger.'

'We'll look into this, but we are very confident that Nicola Green is no longer in this area due to evidence found at her property. And, rest assured, we will find her.'

I look at the list again. 'But you are going to look again for the missing record and check this other patient is OK? I haven't imagined her.'

He stands. 'I'll add it to the notes. Thanks for your time, Sue.'

I show him out, wondering if I have got it wrong. Perhaps Erica has really left knowing it was only a matter of time until the police were onto her. But I can't help thinking back to the day Erica argued strongly for home births. I thought she cared, but now I can see she was setting this up.

I want to let it go. I do. But all that information *has* gone. Why would she go to the effort of planning this, only to leave before the woman gave birth? Because she was originally one of Katie's patients, I don't know any details about her case, and Katie's diary only had logs of their appointments, not when she was due.

And then I know what I have to do. Katie is the only person who will believe me. And she's the only person who knows where Leila lives. It's the only way.

I pull out my phone and see her name in my call log. All the reasons I should not do this roll through my mind. Tom. How she betrayed me. What she did to Adam who was a friend of mine too. I don't know if she'll even answer because I've ignored so many of her calls. All I know is, if I don't do this and Erica takes that child, I won't be able to live with myself.

I call her and it rings until her voice is on the end of the line.

'Hello? Sue? Look—'

I interrupt her. 'I don't want to go into everything now, I'm not ready to. It's actually about Erica.' I wonder if Tom is there with her and if they're cosily playing house, but I try to focus on the important matter at hand. 'She's… well, you know what's happened. I think she's with one of the ladies. Leila something. But I'm not sure the police are going to look into it. They think she's already left the area.'

'Leila Summers? How…' Katie trails off

'After you were arrested, Karen put Erica on outreach. She ordered a home birth kit.'

'I know where she lives,' Katie says. 'I can't remember the exact address, but I can take you there. If you—'

'I'll pick you up in five.'

---

Katie gets into my car, but looks awkward and doesn't meet my eye.

'I never meant to hurt you,' she says at last, breaking the silence we've been driving in for a while.

Though it stings, she sounds sincere. I noticed, when she got in the car, she has lost weight and has dark circles under her eyes. No matter what she's done with Tom, she doesn't deserve the hell she's been put through in the last few months.

'No, I don't expect you did,' I concede.

She says quietly, 'I could give you that you-can't-help-who-you-fall-in-love-with shit. But I won't. It was already over with Adam.'

I want to scream at her, *so you thought you'd take my husband?* I'm so angry and upset but I'm grateful she's finally being honest and not trying to patronise me. I've been wondering why the staff at the hotel never came forward earlier, but it's dawned on me their affair must have been going on for a while. They would have been just another couple sneaking off to a hotel. Probably using false names. The staff would have greeted thousands of people. We are more anonymous than we think. She and Tom capitalised on that.

'I don't want to talk about this right now, I'm not ready. I only called because I want to make sure that woman's OK.'

She doesn't speak again until we reach a sign at a crossroads. 'Take a right here. It's up this road.'

She points at the house. It's a pretty cottage with a lovely garden.

As I pull up outside, I say, 'I don't know what we're going to find here. But thanks for doing this. It must be hard coming back here.'

She nods. 'I really wish it hadn't all turned out like this, but I know I have to live with that.'

We sit there for a moment. This might be the very last time I am alone with her. There's so much I think I should tell her, like how I felt when she was arrested and how I worried about her being in jail. I want to tell her how much I've missed her.

But all that is trumped by her betrayal with Tom.

'Shall we?' I mutter.

She leads the way and knocks on the front door. When nobody comes, she tries again, banging louder. Then she tries to open the door, but it's locked.

'She lives here with her partner. Maybe they've gone out,' Katie reasons.

I call through the letterbox, 'Leila? Are you there?'

'Come on, let's try the back door in case they've got the TV on and can't hear us,' Katie suggests.

I suddenly worry that we're going to sneak around someone's home to find them having a cup of tea in the kitchen. I'll look crazy if we're wrong, but I have this gut feeling that something is off. We walk around the stone path to the back door. Katie tries that as well. Then she shouts.

I peer in through the back window. And stop dead. I can see a bed with a surgical trolley at the side of it. Some implements we are familiar with, and a syringe. And, tied to the steel headboard, are two thick ropes.

Katie is shaking next to me. 'Oh, my God. My God. We're too late.'

# Chapter Thirty-Five

## Nicola

I am finally starting the new life I've been dreaming of. Our new life. She is beautiful. I'm driving a new car with her safely tucked in her car seat to our mini-break before we travel to our forever home. Finally, she is here beside me. She has the most perfect button nose and tiny fists that she stuffs in her mouth. She is everything I ever dreamed she could be.

I couldn't have timed it better because it's all over the news, of course. Poor Erica. Poor man-stealing Erica. It's been interesting to hear the reports about her. I never knew who she was, really. I might have had her passport and her documents, and her home, but all I knew was she was the reason I lost my boyfriend and my baby. Turns out nobody cared enough about her to check she was OK.

I have to admit I did enjoy watching as Mark was frog-marched out of his flat and taken in for questioning. It went very well with my afternoon cup of tea and biscuit. All I can hope is that some journalist gets hold of the story and it all comes out. How he dumped me when I was pregnant and threw me away like an old rag. Then how I miscarried. I sincerely hope it all comes tumbling out. In fact, I might call a journalist myself to start the ball rolling.

When I settle in, of course. I've selected a beautiful Airbnb nearby. I thought it was better to stay in the area while the police followed my wild goose chase to London. As if I'd be so careless as to leave the real address on the notepad.

There are a couple of things niggling at me, though. I have a plan worked out for the future and I know me and this little darling happily sleeping away next to me are going to be happy. But it would have been better to slip away more quietly. I've had to leave more loose ends that I wanted. The incident with that nosey old witch, Mary, trying to interfere, coming to see Leila, left me with no choice but to make sure she and her husband wouldn't bother us again. I didn't kill them. Because I'm not a killer. She would have poured the milk into the tea. I had no control over how much she put in, or what happened next.

I allow myself a moment to remember how far I have come. And how it all started.

My mother didn't merely send me upstairs. She locked me away. She had to take me to school, but I spent the rest of the time in my room. I could hear my brother and sisters downstairs, laughing and playing, but I rarely saw them. They would be in the kitchen as she led me down the stairs and out of the front door.

I sometimes caught a glimpse of my sister's red hair and my brother's boots as they disappeared through the kitchen swing door. I wanted to see them. I guess I loved them. That feeling of wanting to look after someone. Wanting them to be OK. Wanting to do things for them. Missing them.

But now I have my own special girl to look after. And I'm not going to make the same mistakes that my mum did, being besotted with my stepfather who was a piece of work.

I'll have my own family now. Just me and her. I have thought of everything. It would be better to go abroad. Maybe France or Austria. But not yet. Once the fuss has died down, I will slip through the net. I have chosen my new identity correctly this time. No confusion.

It all started with the list of women dopey Karen gave me. I checked all their records and picked three who had not changed their addresses. I checked on the electoral register online – you have to pay, but it was worth it – and bingo! Leila Summers still lived in a grotty dive of a tower block, as far as everyone else was concerned. But, according to her record, which diligent Katie wrote up oh so diligently, she lived in a cottage at the end of the A34, right out of the way.

Naturally, I followed the other two possibilities up to assess my options. One lived on a sink estate and had no real interest in looking after a child – as far as I could see she lived with her mum who would inevitably become the baby's stand-in mum when she couldn't be arsed to look after it. But that was a no-go because the mum was going to be in my way.

The other one had a rottweiler of a partner who would have been difficult to get rid of completely. He dipped in and out of her life, leaving her crying and screaming. No concern for her unborn child. Teenage tantrum after teenage tantrum.

That's why Leila stood out and was the best of the bunch. Weak and pliable, and that pathetic excuse of a bloke I knew wouldn't stick around. I look in my mirror at her now, tied up like a chicken on the back seat. Out for the count. As soon as I saw her picking at her nails in the hospital waiting room, I knew I could help her. I am doing her a favour. If I hadn't staged an intervention, she'd still be doing all Ben's washing now and cooking his friends fry-ups for their hangovers. And what would have happened to this little one? I know I can give her a much better life, and that's why I had to act.

I approach the turning for the forest. It's strange being back here, only a mile away from the area I grew up in. This patch of wild land with a river running through it cuts it off from the edge of the city. I'd come here after school on my own. It was the only place I felt free. Although I knew it might be dangerous to go there alone, I felt safe knowing nobody could find me.

The phone rings and my little one twitches at the noise, so I hurriedly answer.

'Hello. Is this Leila Summers?' the voice booms out on speakerphone.

I check the back seat. 'Yes. Leila here.' I smile, not lying. 'Who is this, please?'

'This is Kathy from the Airbnb. I just wanted to check what time you'll be arriving? If it's later on, I can leave a key for you.'

'Oh, not sure. I'm afraid it might not be for another hour or so. Is that a problem?'

'Not at all.' And I smile at how well this will work out, not having to see her. 'I'll text you instructions for the key pick-up. Sorry I can't be there in person—'

There is an almighty scream. 'She's not Leila! Call the police. She's got my baby—'

I snatch the phone from the dashboard cradle. 'Sorry. I'm listening to an audiobook. I've turned it down now. Thanks for leaving the key. I'm looking forward to my stay.'

I quickly end the call. My skin prickles. I turn off onto the woodland path and stare at Leila in my rear-view mirror. I had to bring her. I couldn't leave her at the house to be found eventually and blab. And I'm not a killer. But I do have a plan for her.

'You'll pay for that,' I snarl, knowing I should have gagged her.

'You'll pay for this. You're going to hell,' she shouts.

I laugh. 'Oh, really? I think it's you who will go to hell. You're the one who couldn't think of anything except your lazy boyfriend. You're the one who couldn't even be bothered to prepare for the birth of your beautiful child.'

She screams again and my baby stirs.

Leila is wriggling and writhing but she'll not be able to free herself from these bindings. I was sure I had given her enough sedative to knock her out for the journey. Everything was going so well. The Twilight Sleep worked perfectly, and she was adequately supple throughout the delivery.

I pull up, seeing the steel shed left by the people who built the estate. It looks like a half container, something they forgot to tow away. Over the years, it has become consumed by brambles, and even a tree has stretched a branch over it. But its blue walls, so out of place in this green and brown, are unmistakable.

I would bring my dolls here and pretend we were a proper family. I would even bring food and stockpile it, thinking that, when I ran away, I could live here. But Mum always spoiled it by locking me in my room, and, by the time I returned, the food would be rotten or eaten by animals.

I always knew that I would bring my own child here to show it and say goodbye. My way of making peace with what happened and putting it behind me so it didn't ruin my new life. And that is what I am going to do today. My little one is still asleep. I gently lift her up and cuddle her.

'She'll never be yours. You're not her mother. You never will be,' Leila whimpers. 'Don't hurt her. Please.'

I've had enough. It's time to get rid of her

'I would never hurt a child. Never. How dare you? I did all this for her,' I say as I fuss over the baby.

I need to get away. I need to end this now and start my new life before it's all tainted. This should be perfect. I bring the baby seat round to the boot and open it. I place my treasure inside and cover her up with a pink blanket I rescued from the maternity ward. She clenches her fist. She is adorable. Just one more step and we will be off into our new life.

Leila is quiet now on the back seat. No doubt she has a plan. She will be thinking about how she can overcome me. Because it worked so well last time when she hid in the bathroom. But I am always one step ahead. I walk around to the side door nearest to her feet and let her think she can kick out at me. I open the door and, sure enough, she kicks with both legs.

Anticipating it, I duck to one side so she is kicking at thin air. How futile. I take a syringe out of my pocket and take off the end protector. I stab her thigh with it. Hard and fast, and then I slowly push the plunger down. The kicking fades and, as she grows still, I feel more powerful.

I check her pulse, which is still strong. This won't kill her. But, with the combination of no food or water and the length of time she will be sleeping, it will weaken her. I doubt she will survive. I pull her legs and drag her out of the car to the ground.

I lug her through the leaves and unlock the door to the steel cabin. It's rusty and creaks open. I drag her inside. I slip a spare key under a plant pot on the make-shift table where I used to sit my Barbie. It's emotional, really. All the time I spent here, and now I can never come back.

I put the syringe into her hand. I debate whether to give her a second shot to make sure, but that would spoil the game. Like the others, if she is worthy, she will survive – although nobody has to date.

I lock the door behind me and don't look back. This part of my life is over now. I go to get my daughter.

# Chapter Thirty-Six

## Sue

'This is my fault,' Katie wails.

'You dial 999. I'll try to break in and see if Leila's in there.' I peer again through the window but it looks to be a deserted house.

Katie pulls her phone out and I grab a piece of stone from the rockery. I take off my jacket and wrap it around my hand, then hit the window hard with the stone. It takes three strikes to smash it. I drop the rock and clear the glass. I can hear Katie talking on the phone.

'No. There's no one here. Just a lot of equipment. No, there's no threat of violence.' She starts to shout. 'Yes. A crime has been committed. Look, just get someone here. Quick.'

I climb in through the broken window and Katie follows.

'Don't touch anything,' I say. but she picks up a sheet of paper headed 'Twilight Sleep'.

We check each room and shout Leila's name, but it is futile. We run upstairs and find the bedroom in disarray. There are clothes strewn everywhere, including some baby clothes. But Leila is not here, and neither is Erica. Nor a newborn baby.

We go back downstairs and survey the scene in the dining room, with all the equipment from the missing requisition. What's happened to Leila?

I turn to Katie. 'How long did they say they would be?'

'Five minutes.' After a moment she speaks up again. 'Sue, please can we talk?'

'I really don't think there's anything to say,' I tell her, trying not to get upset.

'I didn't mean any of this to happen. Honestly, you have to believe me.'

I shrug. 'So he made the first move, did he?'

She lowers her gaze and I know from her silence he did. I roll my eyes at the thought of dependable old Tom in his slightly flared cords. Tom, who I considered my partner for life, making a move on another woman. It stings. I stand awkwardly in the heavy silence that fills the room, waiting for either the sirens to arrive or for Katie to gather the courage to answer me.

'Remember that time I burned my arm?' she starts. 'On a baking tray? And I had a day off? I came back in and I was on light duties for a day. I asked Erica to see how far my lady was dilated and she disappeared for a bit. Said she was going getting some gloves. But the gloves were on the ward.' I do remember, but we were busy, and it passed me by. 'I reckon Erica was googling it. I don't think she had a clue.' She nods in the direction of the bed and the equipment. 'Which makes all this all the more worrying.'

My stomach churns. 'I asked her. I asked if she wanted me here. When she booked the home birth in. Karen was trying to get us off the department so the press wouldn't surround the hospital. So she put Erica on outreach.'

Katie looks at me, horrified. 'Oh my God. She was fucking clever, whoever she really is. All that watching and waiting. Even when I was in there, in that cell, I didn't suspect her. Or you. I couldn't work it out at the time. I wondered if it had been bank staff or someone who'd since managed to move on. But I'm starting to see how she did it now. She was trying it out. The dosage.' She walks over to look at the vials, open on the table. 'She was waiting for the right person. Someone she could isolate and control. And then... this.'

I feel shaken as it all starts to make more sense. 'For the record, I didn't believe you did it.'

'Where are they? You'd think they'd be here by now, wouldn't you?' she mutters.

Something else catches my attention. A small china teacup with red roses and a gold rim. Just like the ones in the staff room at the hospital. My knees buckle. 'Katie. Come and look at this.'

She sees it straight away. Her expression clouds over. 'Oh my God. She was doing it right in front of us. Bringing them toast and tea in nice china cups. We thought she was old-fashioned and fussing over them, trying to make them feel well looked after. And all the time…'

Blue lights are flashing behind us. They try to open the front door and we shout so they come around the back. I open the back door to let them in.

Trembling, Katie quickly tells the police everything I'd already tried to. 'The property belongs to Leila Summers. The maternity equipment is from Darkford General. It looks like the woman you were looking for, Nicola Green, has delivered Leila's baby and taken them both.'

'We'll need to take a statement. But leave this to us now and step outside, please.'

'We'll wait in the car.' I point to it.

My legs are shaking as I walk away towards my car.

'I can't believe it. That she did that. That poor woman. And her baby. Leila is lovely. A bit naïve but really lovely. You don't think she's…' Katie stops herself.

The horror of this is only now sinking in. There was plenty about that room that tells me things did not go to plan for Erica. Blood and swabs. Syringes. It looked like she'd given her adrenaline. God only knows what has happened to Leila.

The police believed Erica had gone to London but I hope they can quickly change track and find her. The realisation of what she is capable of races through my mind. Those teacups. She'd brought them into work 'to make it nicer for the ladies'. I'd thought it was very sweet, and thanked her. I told her it was in keeping with our ethos to provide the best possible care with every attention to detail. It was another thing that aligned her with us.

More blue lights are flashing down the road. Two more police cars arrive and DCs Mearns and Stafford jump out of one of them. I feel a wash of relief. More officers run towards Leila's home and disappear around the back.

Neighbours are out on the street and a dog starts barking relentlessly. I want to drive away and never see a police car again. I want to erase the scene in Leila's home from my memory, but the horrors of what we found inside are going to be hard to forget.

In all the commotion going on around us, I hear Katie sniffing as tears roll down her cheeks. I hesitate for a moment, then reach out to hold her hand.

# Chapter Thirty-Seven

## Nicola

I lean over the bridge and watch the fast-flowing water. I get my old phone because that's the one I want them to find, with all the messages between Mark and me, so they know what he did. I dial 999 and wait.

'Emergency services. Which service do you require?'

I pause again. I want to make absolutely sure they have a location for the phone. I summon the whiney, horrid voices of all those girls who complained about their pregnancy and all the kids at school who had tantrums about watching TV.

'Police. I need the police,' I say breathlessly, making myself sound agitated.

'And can I take your name, please?'

I pause again. 'This is Nicola Green. The police have been looking for me. I'm sorry. Sorry for everything.' I try to do my best pathetic, small voice because I am not sorry at all. I look back at the car parked out of sight round a corner. A car passes and I walk a little to not arouse suspicion. The last thing I need now is a good Samaritan stepping in. I know the operator will patch through to the police and they will try to trace the call. 'There's no point trying to stop me. But I wanted you to know.'

I can hear the call handler breathing on the line. Then the line breaks and there is another voice. 'Nicola. Stay where you are. There's no need to do this. We understand. Just stay where you are, and we will come and get you.'

I pretend to sob, giving them time to triangulate the call. I did my homework. I am always one step ahead. 'I can't. I can't live with myself. It's too much. I'm sorry,' I say faintly, my voice barely above a whisper for maximum dramatic effect.

I don't end the call. Instead I throw my phone over the bridge. I watch it splash into the water. It's the last trace of Nicola Green and sinks below the surface of the water.

Already in my life, I have been so many people. I can't say I have loved every role I've had to play. But I have slipped in and out of them with ease. I could have been an actor in another life. I never meant for it to come to this, though. I drive away from the bridge, knowing that, now I've staged this little performance, the trail will go cold and I'll never be found. I drive along the straight road and see the blue lights in the distance, heading for Nicola's watery grave. They drive right past me: yet another moment where I've managed to hide in plain sight. Amelia gives a little whimper, and I laugh.

The Airbnb isn't far away. I like to tie up all loose ends, so I'd decided to go to the holiday home at which I'd planned to have a weekend away with Mark, a weekend that never happened. I can finally go and create some nice memories there. I park up and carry Amelia in her car seat, my travel bag slung on my shoulder. I won't need to unpack the rest. We won't be here long.

Once I've found the key and got settled inside, I feed Amelia. I wind her just like I used to practise with my dollies and pretty soon she's ready for a nap so I put her down. I fetch the hair dye from my travel bag. Going lighter is much more difficult than going darker. I didn't factor that in when I selected this one. It says on the box it takes about thirty minutes to develop, but I might leave it a bit longer.

I look at Amelia, lying there. My daughter. She is perfect. Amelia. Amelia Emma. Summers, of course, because that's who I am now. And with my new hair too, it's going to be my final transformation.

The old Leila will not make it out of my hiding place. I'd be surprised if she made it through the night after the complications during the delivery. I only realised at the last minute that I needed her non-pregnant weight to get the dose precisely correct. I didn't even have a recent weight for her. I'd deleted the records so they wouldn't be able to find her on the system and I didn't keep copies because why would I? But that meant I didn't know her weight or height.

I guessed. I am savvy enough to be able to estimate from all those women at the hospital. Some of them never came forward. I doubt they even knew what had happened to them. Twilight Sleep has a curious effect. The patient is there in the room, conscious, but sedated, and remembers nothing. Ingenious, and perfect for my plan. It was all good practice for this moment.

But, during the birth, Leila crashed in the middle of a contraction. She was unresponsive only for a minute. I brought her round with a shot of adrenaline and had to hope she would make it through to the delivery. She did, but she was in a bad way. The online information I read on Twilight Sleep never mentioned any reactions. I'm sure after all of that, plus the devastation of losing her baby, she's not going to have any fight left in her.

I've already packed up Leila's home as much as possible and made all the usual onward arrangements for her and her baby. They will all think she has gone away to make a new start. Except for the equipment, but hopefully the police will think Leila delivered the baby herself because Nicola ran. I should have cleaned up after myself, but no one's perfect, not even me. I'm glad that I can have something special for me and Amelia – I really deserve a break after the stress of the last few weeks, and it will be lovely to stay somewhere a lot nicer than Leila's fusty cottage.

I check myself in the mirror and it looks like the dye has taken. I rinse it with the shower over the unfamiliar bath. I apply a toner and sit on the toilet to wait the ten minutes.

I bought a burner phone and some internet minutes so I could see how things were progressing. I know it's not ideal to be constantly checking my phone while I am trying to look after Amelia, but I need to be aware of any issues in case there are any complications. It's only for the next few days until I can be sure we're both safe. Amelia is being such a good girl for Mummy. And I will be too from now on. I have responsibilities and I'm going to give her the best life.

I click on the news flash: 'Killer nurse in suicide bid'.

There is an old picture of me with my black hair and glasses. I look in the mirror. My face is much thinner now, and I have plucked my dark eyebrows into a thinner line and bleached them, too. My hair will be completely different. It's long now, but Leila had a shorter bob. I comb it straight and snip upwards, like all the hairdo videos on TikTok. Then I rinse out the toner as the newsreader reports:

*'Nicola Green, aged thirty, called police to tell them she was intending to jump. She was the woman the police were looking for in connection with the sample cases at Darkford General Hospital. DC Mearns from GMP gave a statement to the press earlier.'*

I glance at the screen as a tired-looking, middle-aged detective appears with an A4 piece of paper in his hand. If he's as useless as he looks, he shouldn't give me any problems.

*'Our officers have attended the scene at Stamford Bridge. We believe that a person jumped from the bridge earlier this afternoon. Personal articles belonging to this person were found at the scene. A body has not, I repeat, not been recovered at this time. We will update as soon as we have any further information.'*

I comb through my shorter, now blonde hair as the reporter reappears.

*'Police say they are not looking for anyone else in connection with this incident.'*

I lay out all Leila's documents in front of me. The photo ID is not as close a likeness as Erica Davies, but it will do. I won't be needing it for a while, in any case. Leila's passport is in date. Only six or so months to go. But no matter. I have her internet banking ID and passwords and her credit card. Everything I need to set up this new life for myself. Especially as, when I checked her bank account a couple of days ago, I discovered she has a surprising amount of money tucked away for a skank.

I am home and dry now that the police believe I jumped from that bridge. Me and my daughter will travel and start a new life. I have everything needed to register us both with a doctor and the hospital and, if my experiences are anything to go by, the proof increases with letters and util-ity bills. Just like Karen, people don't want to question you, so if anyone does think there's a problem, they won't bring it up.

I get my blow-dryer out to get rid of my natural curls. It suits me. Leila suits me. I'd never thought about going blonde before. I grab the story book from my bag and sit down to cuddle Amelia and read our first bedtime story together. The first day of our new life has gone even better than I could have hoped.

## Chapter Thirty-Eight

## Leila

I can see by the sunlight in the crack of the door that it must be morning. I've been lying here, almost too scared to move in case it takes any energy I have left. I've been dipping in and out of consciousness all night and the black numbness was punctuated by so many weird dreams that I couldn't tell what was real. I wish this was all a bad dream I could wake up from and find my baby hadn't been taken from me.

This place looks like someone has tried to live here years ago. There is an old Zed-bed with a striped mattress that has rotted in places. The workbench has a tea, coffee, and sugar set. There is a pile of tea towels stacked neatly, and six teacups and saucers just like the ones Erica served me poisoned tea in.

It would be so easy to give up. To lie here and accept the inevitable. I'm trapped. I've watched TV documentaries and wondered what I would do if I was ever in a situation like I now find myself in.

I can't believe everything my body has gone through in the last few days. I don't know how I even managed to survive the birth, but that all feels hazy and I can't remember everything. I can't believe Erica drugged me so much when she would know it couldn't be good for the baby she professes to love so much.

Heather Jane. After my mum. That's what my baby is called. Heather Jane Carson Summers. She might be able to take my baby girl, but she'll never really be hers. And Erica got me all wrong. I would have been a good mother. Katie was the one who helped me see that and I was going to make sure I gave Heather the best life.

I close my eyes and try to picture her pink pretty face when she was bundled up and the cute gurgle noises she made. If Erica has planned all this and bought those expensive baby clothes, I can only hope she's going to take good care of my baby and not let any harm come to her.

I have a sudden flashback of her leaning over me. Her worried expression and repeated words: 'Come on. Come on. Come on.' Over and over. Erica's cheeks red and her forehead sweaty. Her fingers on my neck, feeling for a pulse.

As quickly as the memory flashes into my head, it fades away again. It's so hard to make sense of everything because these flashes come and go, and I'm so light-headed and woozy I still don't feel as if I'm really here. Why did Erica save me? Why would she bring me round just to go through this? Did she mention something about deserving it? Being worthy?

Am I worthy? Maybe this is the way it has to be. I know that, although my body is telling me *no*, my mind is screaming *yes*. Yes to fighting. I don't want to die here. I'm not going to let it end this way. I don't want Erica to get away with my baby. I need to get out of here and find her before she's lost to me for good.

The ray of light grows brighter, and pinpricks of rust make it twinkle like stars. Nighttime in the day. Everything upside down. Then it strikes me. That's how she did it. Erica makes the truth into half lies and scares the living shit out of people. I was so terrified of Katie that I didn't even suspect Erica was up to something.

None of that matters now. I am counting the pinpricks and watching the light change. Listening to the birds sing and branches knock against the side of this steel structure. I figure it must be a shipping container. It has that look about it. It would have been airtight once, but now it is rotting away and that gives me hope because it's so old there must be a way out of here.

Something about rust from my chemistry lesson pops into my head and I picture myself covered in red dust or rust? Which one? I try to focus but my brain feels all woolly. I try hard to keep my eyes open, but I can feel them closing.

I spread out my palms and wiggle my fingers. Yes. Still here. I'm still here. I feel the soil underneath them, the dried leaves and sticks covering the container's metal floor. The dirt and the tiny stones. I dig through them with my finger-nails, making deep ruts in the dirt layer in case I completely disappear: at least I will have left my mark.

I wonder if anyone will miss me. Mum's already gone, so who will care? My friends might remember me as a harmless girl who was quiet. Ben might remember me as a fly buzzing around his head, nagging to marry him. But what will I leave, really? I haven't lived long enough. I need more time. When I get out of here, I'm going to appreciate life and make the most of it. Do nice things and create special memories with Heather.

*If* I get out… If I don't, I won't get to know Heather and she will be part of someone else's family. Erica's. Or, if she gets caught, some adopted family. I clutch at the dirt. Ashes to ashes. Dust to dust.

I shut my eyes. But then a feeling starts somewhere inside me. A fire igniting in me which won't let me give up. I'm not finished. I'm not. I can't be. I'm going to fight with every fibre of my being to make it out of here and find my girl. I clutch at the dirt and roll over. I hardly have any strength, but I make it onto my feet and towards the door. I drop down to my knees and feel the ground around it. I dig with my bare hands because this isn't what I thought it was. It isn't the scrape of a metal floor. It's dust and dirt, and below it is damp.

It's not a shipping container. It's another lie. Something pretending to be what it isn't. I scoop the earth, deeper and deeper, just in case I am wrong, and I am wasting my time. In case there is a steel base that I could never break through.

But there isn't. I dig and dig, scraping the earth behind me. It's getting hot in here, or perhaps I feel feverish from the shock my body is in, and I tuck my damp hair behind my ears and off my face. And then I see it. A strip of light underneath the door. The soil is harder and thicker, requiring much more effort as I get further down. But it isn't steel. And I must try. I must.

I crawl to the workbench. There are some knives and forks and spoons. I grab a knife. I hurry back to continue scooping the earth. If there is the slightest chance, I must try. No matter how tired I am, I must try.

I have to pull out two large rocks. I roll them to one side, and the soil collapses in on itself. My fingers are bleeding now, but I don't care and carry on scrabbling. And the light grows bigger. My eyes hurt and prick with dust and dirt. I've always hated that I was so petite, envying the tall girls who made a statement just with their presence. But now it might be the thing that helps me get out of here, that saves me.

I hear a noise outside. It sounds like a car. What if Erica has come back? What if she's outside, wanting to laugh at my pathetic little efforts before she finishes what she started? I dig faster. I can still make my mum proud. She is here with me, her patience and determination swirling around me.

I hear her voice. 'Come on, Leila. Come on.'

My first bike ride. My first time at bowling. My first sports day. *Come on, Leila*. She mouthed the words at school plays. She read books so she could help me with my homework. I can almost feel her pushing me, telling me I can do it.

The hole is bigger now. It will still be a squeeze, but I think I can do it. I can still hear a car. An engine running. Is she out there? Just waiting for me? I'm scared to go out but terrified of dying here alone. What have I got to lose? This is my chance. I have to take it.

I need to lower myself in and go out backwards. I still have a baby bump and I will need to squeeze through. It's only now I realise how weak I am. I am bloody and covered in red dirt. My hair is matted, my clothes soaked as the damp hole starts to fill with water.

But I pull myself through. I crawl along the ground and look around anxiously in case she is here waiting to strike. The sun breaks through the trees, and I lie there. No one is here. There is a rough pathway and the area around the steel structure is thick with old trees. I have no idea where I am. I feel stupid for a minute: as if someone was going to be here to rescue me. Getting out was only the first step and now I need to somehow get out of these woods to find help.

I can hear a car revving again, then more cars. There must be a road nearby. I try to get to my feet, but I am so weak. I am wet with sweat and my hair is sticky. I push myself into a sitting position. I don't know if it is the after-effects of giving birth, the drugs, or because Erica hauled me around when I was flat out, but every inch of me feels bruised.

Only the sounds of life in the distance spur me on. I roll to a tree and pull myself up. I am wobbly at first, but I put one foot in front of the other and soon I am moving forward, pushing myself from tree to tree to guide me along. I can feel a deep furrow of concentration form on my forehead. I can do this. I can. I move in the direction of the noise. My ears are somehow highly attuned to it, fear pressing in all around me.

The tree trunks are getting thinner and farther apart. I notice that the undergrowth is flattened in places where people have walked, and that gives me hope that I'm going in the right direction. Suddenly, I can see a building in the distance. I try to run, but my legs won't go that fast. *Come on, Leila. Come on.*

I reach a fence with a gate. I push against it, but it won't budge. I bang and bang and I hear a dog bark. Please be in. Please, someone be in. I hear footsteps. The gate opens and a woman with grey ringlets opens it. She looks scared and shocked. I push past her.

'Please. You've got to help me. Please,' I cry.

My knees buckle and she catches me. A man joins her, and they bring me into their house. She spreads a blanket on a sofa and locks the back door. They are shooting glances at each other, and I don't understand. I instinctively cover my stomach to protect the baby I've carried and I feel the bump that remains.

'I've… someone locked me in a container. I've…' I try to explain but it feels like I can't string a sentence together.

The woman disappears. The man stands by a doorway as if to guard it. He speaks slowly and gently. 'It's OK, love, you're OK. You just rest.'

I close my eyes. The room is warm and smells of fresh linen. I feel like I am floating. I don't know how long I drift off for but, when I wake up, I can hear someone in the background talking. A TV or a radio. I open my eyes.

'We understand that Nicola Green, the woman posing as a midwife, has been involved in a suicide attempt. Police released a statement earlier saying that some of her belongings have washed up along the river Medlock and some personal items have been found near a bridge. A police spokesperson said that no body had been recovered, and they are still searching the area. In the meantime, if you see Nicola Green, do not approach, but dial 999.'

I hear someone screaming. It's me. I am screaming that she has my baby. That she has killed my baby. I sense the man is no longer in the room, but I can barely move. I can't control my sobbing and then I hear voices.

Deep, male voices. I see the door open, and two police officers walk in. The man and woman stand in the background, holding each other. Somewhere in the room, someone is talking about climbing up the bank and surviving a jump. One of the police officers moves towards me and I sit up. *Thank God*. I've been found and everything is going to be OK. I hear my voice, barely audible, ask him where Heather is. Have they found her? I ask about Erica. Did they find her?

He stares at me but looks unmoved. His colleague comes over. I keep talking, asking them about my baby. But all he says is, 'Nicola Green. I am arresting you on suspicion of attempted murder and kidnapping.'

# Chapter Thirty-Nine

## Sue

'Thanks Karen, I'll see you next Monday then.' I let her say bye and then hang up. I'm going to have a meeting to discuss a back-to-work plan. I've said I'm not sure when I'll be ready to come back, some time in the future when I think 'things will be better', but Karen wants me to meet her in person so we can discuss everything and what a new role could look like for me. The way I feel right now, I'm not sure how things could ever get better.

I check the time and see that it's almost six o'clock. So Tom will be here any moment. I hear the car pull up and watch him walk up the pathway. The door opens and closes, and he comes through to the kitchen. I can see Katie in his car, looking straight ahead. Of course she came with him. Of course she did.

'Thanks for letting me have some time. I need to explain everything to the boys. I'll be the one to tell them and we'll do it just like we planned,' he says in a low voice. I nod in agreement before we walk through to the lounge. The boys stop whispering as soon as we walk in.

Tom sits down next to me. Two of our children stare at us expectantly. Dan looks out of the window, clearly not wanting to meet his Dad's eye. Liam frowns as if he already knows what's to come.

'There's no easy way to tell you this. Me and your mum love you very much and that will never change. But something will and, well, we're not going to be living together anymore. I won't be living here anymore.'

Liam raises his eyebrows. 'So, you're leaving,' he says matter-of-factly.

Tom stumbles on his words. 'No, not leaving as such, but…'

Liam snorts. 'What, then? As if Mum hasn't been through enough.'

Tom looks at me for help, but I shrug.

'We've all been through a lot. We've…' he protests.

Liam smirks. 'No. It was Mum who was wrongly accused. And arrested. And harassed. She stood in front of us. Stayed here, so the journos would stay here.' I hadn't realised how much he has grown up. We've been treating him with kid gloves, but Liam is a teenager now and clearly picks up on a lot more than we realise. 'The question is, Dad. Where were you? Why did you leave her to deal with all this?'

Three sets of eyes are on him, staring and waiting for an answer. Tom looks at the floor. Then he looks back up at me.

All through our marriage, I have saved him. Filled in for him and made everything run smoothly. Probably half of the time he never realised how much I did to make life easier for him. But this is one situation I'm not going to make easier for him. He did this, so he's going to have to explain it now. We sit in an uncomfortable silence as Tom decides what to say next.

'The thing is… right. I love you all and I love your mum. But I fell in love with someone else.'

Dan and David run over to me and give me a hug.

But Liam doesn't move. 'Who? Who is it?' he demands to know.

Tom bites his lip. 'It's Katie.'

Liam snorts and bangs his hand on the chair arm. 'Auntie Katie? Fuck. I did not see that coming. Fuck.'

Tom frowns. 'Don't use that language, Liam.'

I hold Dan and David tightly.

'You can't tell me what to do anymore. You're leaving. To live with your girlfriend,' Liam spits.

Tom runs his fingers through his hair. 'It's not like that. You're making it sound bad.'

I sniff. I can't stay silent. It's not easy but we must have an honest conversation about this. 'It might all be brilliant for you, Tom. You've fallen in love with someone else and got a ready-made house to move into. But you have to try and understand it from our point of view. The boys have grown up with us both here, and now that's changing.' I turn to my sons. 'It's going to be a big adjustment, but we'll find a way to get through it and, like your dad said, we do both still love you. That is the one thing that will never change.'

Tom nods. We took Liam to Cornwall when he was a tiny baby. We sat on the beach and Tom told me he would never leave me. And I believed him. Because when I say something, I mean it. That belief was the glue that held me in his life and made the bad times not so bad. He said he would stay, and I believed him.

Now he says hopefully, 'But I'll still be around. I want to be part of your life. I'm hoping that, when the dust settles, you can come and stay over.'

The boys run back over to Liam and all three of them whisper, discussing it.

Then Liam responds to his dad. 'You're kidding, aren't you? Stay at Auntie Katie's with you living there? What about Adam? Where's he? Is he just a throwaway, like us?'

Tom reddens.

Dan sobs. 'It will all get sorted out in the divorce. Some judge will tell us where we have to live.'

I hadn't even thought about getting to that point, but the boys are more pragmatic than I realised. 'That's not quite true. It's all decided outside court as much as possible. In mediation. And the kids get a say. We're going to figure this out together,' I promise them.

Liam remains defiant. 'Here's my say. I'm not staying anywhere except here. With Mum.'

Tom's expression darkens. 'But I'll still see you, won't I?'

I don't want Liam to tell Tom he never wants to see him again or say something he'll regret just because he's upset and angry. I look at him, pleading him to cool off. 'I know it's a lot to understand, and nobody needs to make their mind up about anything right now, OK?' I say, trying to be reasonable.

'We'll see.' He tuts.

Tom looks at me. 'I should probably go, but can I have a moment with the boys alone before I do?'

I nod and go back into the kitchen. After finding Leila's house empty, I didn't think things could get any worse. But this conversation has been one that no parent expects to have with their children, explaining their family is breaking up.

I check my phone to see if there's anything else in the news, any mention of Leila and her baby. I see a text from Katie:

> I know you need time and it will never be as it
> was but I hope when you've had your space we
> can meet up and talk properly. I want to
> explain everything and I also want to find a
> way to make sure the boys can come here and
> still see Tom.

My phone starts ringing – a police liaison number I was given. I go to shut the kitchen door and it sounds like Tom is still talking to the boys. I swipe to accept the call.

'Sue. It's Fliss Brown. We spoke earlier.'

'Yes, do you have any more updates?' I ask anxiously, hoping they'll have good news.

'We've found Leila Summers. She's in a bad way, but I know you were anxious about what might have happened to her.'

A wave of relief washes over me. 'What about her baby? Where is it? Is it safe?' I ask eagerly.

She hesitates and, in that moment, I know her baby is not safe. 'Has Nicola Green got Leila's baby?'

'We haven't found the baby yet and don't know for certain. Nicola could have taken her or Leila could have—'

'Oh, fuck off. Leila hasn't done anything to her own child. We saw the bed and the equipment. It's not fucking rocket science. This is what she planned all along, and now she's got away.' I calm a little. It isn't Fliss' fault. 'Sorry about that. It's been... anyway, sorry.'

Fliss speaks gently. 'I need to assure you we are looking for Nicola Green. We have put out media alerts to ask the public to report any sightings of a woman with a new-born baby. We now think she staged a suicide to throw us off her trail. But there are no guarantees. I need you to be vigilant too, in case she tries to approach you. I'll pop round one night next week to see how you are.'

I nod into the phone. 'Thank you. I will. See you next week.'

I end the call.

I hear myself screaming and shouting. I see twitching curtains and hear a door slam shut. Then I feel arms around me. Familiar arms. The smell of that shit perfume she loves so much that smells stronger when she is nervous. I drop the phone. She is crying too. We stand together on my front lawn swaying, the way we did when we lost a lady or a baby, or both. The way we did when it all went wrong, or someone shouted at us. The way we did when she had miscarriage after miscarriage. The way we did when my grandmother died. I pull her close because I share her pain.

She whispers into my cardigan. 'I spoke to Fliss. She took the baby. She took it. And Leila's in a bad way.' She wipes her nose on her sleeve. 'She was an easy target. The guy she was with was controlling and her mum had just died. I was round there a lot to protect her. He wasn't there for her, and someone had to be. But now…'

She is sobbing again. I pat her back. 'I'll give it to that fucking Erica, or whoever she is. She was clever. Had me fooled. But… that girl. In the flat. She killed her.'

She nods and sniffs. 'That could have been us. If we'd crossed her.'

I laugh through my tears. 'Well, she did nearly have you jailed for life. And she had a go with me too. None of this is funny. But we're going to have to find a level here. Because life has to go on.'

She says, 'I'll go if you want. None of this is right. I should never have…'

I snort. 'What, and he moves back in, and everything goes back to normal? Fuck off.'

She looks at the window. 'I know. It's a mess.'

I feel yet more tears. 'Not for you two. He told me. He told me he…'

She shushes me. 'He told me it was over between you. And you'd stopped talking about him. It was like he didn't exist for you.'

Was it? Was it over? Our family wasn't over. Not at all. But me and Tom? Was there a 'me and Tom' in between the online shopping and the working nights and him being away? Not for him. That's for sure.

I look at her. I missed her so much and now I need her to go. Again. 'None of it matters now. All that matters is our boys.' I want to underline that I mean *my* boys and Tom's boys, and I'm devastated that she will become their step mum, but I leave it in the air.

Tom appears. 'The boys said they'd come to the football with me on Saturday, if that's OK? Dan and Dave, anyway. Liam, well…'

'He'll come round,' I say.

And Tom finishes the sentence, the way we always have. 'Without water.'

I look into his teary eyes, and he tries to smile but fails. I walk him out and we plan to talk again in a few days to see if, when the boys have had chance to come to terms with things, they want to make more formal arrangements about the days they'll see Tom, to create a new routine.

'Dad's taking us to United. He's getting season tickets,' Dan says excitedly, his usual spark returned, as I go back into the lounge. Liam is staring at his phone while the TV blasts in the background.

I can't compete with taking the boys to the football but, if Tom wants to be as flash as the footballers the boys will cheer on during the game, then so be it. And that's when I think about the footballers and their families who all live in Alderley Edge. But not only footballers, it's a very well-to-do neighbourhood with great schools for rich families. And that's why Erica talked in a superior tone about her plans for the future and how she was going to live in Alderley Edge with her boyfriend Mark. It's all coming back to me. I remember her talking about an Airbnb they had stayed in there. How it was a perfect area for children to grow up in. How she had sent me and Katie pictures of it. She couldn't help showing off. I scroll back, back, back on my messages and there it is. Nine months ago. Right in the middle of nowhere.

She must have gone off with the baby somewhere and this could be as good a place to look as any. I feel my heart beat fast.

I call Fliss back. 'This might be nothing, but I think I know where she is.'

# Chapter Forty

## Nicola

The Airbnb is beautiful, and I wish we could stay. I've always wanted to live in this area. And Amelia is a very good baby. She sleeps and only cries for her bottle. It feels like it's always been the two of us and this is how it should always be. I wish I could stay here for a few more days and soak up the atmosphere, but something is telling me to go. I always listen to my instincts. I am usually right.

It really couldn't have worked out better to have this space together. This place is brilliant, but the internet is a bit patchy, although that's no matter as I don't need it now. In any case, I'll be ditching this phone and getting a new one as soon as I arrive at our forever home.

I can't stop looking at Amelia as she twitches. This is real love. I've been in love before, but never anything like this. I briefly wonder what it would have been like to give birth, to have the complete experience. Yet I know that's not always the way. Some parents choose to go through surrogacy or adoption, and it doesn't affect their bond with their baby. Plus, the way I see it, my time at the maternity hospital served this purpose. It was childbirth by proxy. I breathed and panted with them and felt the joy when baby arrived. I yearned for it to be my own, and now the final piece of the puzzle is in place.

I will register her when I get to Dorset. I know from the hospital administration that systems are not joined up. In fact, they are barely working at all. I have all Leila's documents, and her signature isn't difficult to forge. It's astounding how many people write down their pin number. Quite often they reverse it. Or use their birth date. Seriously. Leila had them all listed in the back of a little notebook she kept on the mantelpiece so she was asking for trouble really.

Of course, you wouldn't expect someone to be nosing around in your own home, but what if I was a burglar? It was careless and stupid of her. It was more proof to me that she wouldn't cut it as a mother: she was too sloppy.

But Leila is like most people. I learned that I was a very unusual and rare person from the psychometric tests I did. And Amelia deserves to have a special mummy. My one regret is that Amelia won't have a granny. My mum has deprived her of that by her bad behaviour.

In different circumstances, I still wouldn't have let her near her. I wouldn't let anyone harm a hair on her head. I am her mother, and I will protect her.

She's waking now. Her little fists are bunched and her nose scrunched. Now she is crying, surprisingly loud for such a small thing. She has hair already. Wispy tufts of blonde hair that I smooth down as I test the bottle on my arm. It is just right.

I lift her out of her travel crib and cradle her. She sucks on the teat of the warm bottle, and I search for the feeling of complete contentment that I have craved for so long. But it doesn't come. I stroke her hair and touch her warm skin, but I don't feel like she is mine and I don't know why.

A sense of despair threatens to take hold. The same feeling as when I was weaving a tapestry of what I would do to people, then, at home in the evening in my tiny flat, I would struggle to keep it alive. But I sweep up a sense of achievement at my plan coming to fruition.

It will all come when I am settled. When I'm settled in our new home, we will be introduced to people as Leila and Amelia Summers. A family. A spark lights up and I hold her tighter. I did it. Months and months of planning. Some errors, but nothing that could stop me. And the fact that I am here now, with my daughter, tells me that it is the right thing. I put myself out there and I was rewarded for my courage and determination. And not to forget my rationale. All I wanted was to make a positive difference to a child's life, so it wouldn't end up like me.

I knew what my mother was like. Before she met him, it was just me and her and lots of different random babysitters. I would be in my room, and they would watch TV downstairs. Then Mum would arrive home, all loud giggles and baby talk, with a man. Or men. I never saw them; at least she spared me that. But I would hear them in her room, deep voices and grunts. The banging of her head-board against the plasterboard wall between our rooms. Then two cups on the kitchen table and Mum smoking a cigarette with a glass of water and aspirin in front of her.

I didn't realise back then, because it was all I knew. I would climb onto a kitchen chair and stare at her, a broken version of the shiny Barbie doll who had left the previous evening. Smudged eyeliner and ragged hair. But her nails were always perfectly scarlet. She would have a manicure every Saturday while sometimes we would eat beans on toast all week.

As I got older, I realised it was wrong. I went to friends' houses and their parents were not drinking scotch with their dinner; there were no strange men wandering around. And my friends were not locked in their bedrooms. Yes, now I think of it, it had started even then. Before she met him.

I will not be like her. Leila would have been. She would have inevitably let that loser drag her down and this little mite would have ended up in a dank flat cared for by babysitters. I could see it a mile off. I have saved her from that. I have saved them both.

I try to get a signal on my phone, but it isn't happening. Amelia is sleeping again. I change her nappy gently and pull on her coat. She is a little doll. I touch her tiny finger-nails and pull on her hat. It's time to go and it can get chilly this time of year.

I gather up her things, neatly fold and pack them into the baby bag. It's a little sad we can't stay here forever.

Alderley Edge would have been my destination of choice, but sometimes plans change. In fact, I will never come up north again. It's best for me to go to a different part of the country and get as far away as possible from here. I have said my goodbyes. It is time for a new start.

I pick up the small leather case I have brought in with me. I don't want to leave this here, but I have to. I have to leave behind all the people I have been; all the people who have become part of me. The past is the past and I am Leila Summers now.

I pull out the reminders of everyone I have had to deal with and drop them into a Tesco bag. I place the Tesco bag in the bin inside the under-sink cupboard. They will stay, the ghosts of how I got here, and I will leave without them. Just me and Amelia. Then I think better of it. I am a mother now. I must be responsible. I pull it out and hook the bag over my arm.

I gently lift up Amelia, whose lips are pursed like little rosebuds, lost in a deep sleep. I hold her over my shoulder, carefully supporting her head. I have done this dozens of times on the ward, but this is my own precious cargo. I'll put her in the car first. I place her gently into the travel carrier and pull on my jacket. I stroke her cheek. I can't wait for when she can talk and to hear her call me Mummy for the first time. I pick her up, step into the tiled hallway and open the door.

I am blinded by a light.

'Armed police. Nicola Green. Please put the child down and step forward with your hands above your head.'

I step backwards. They've made a mistake. I'm Leila. Leila Summers. Someone is shouting loudly.

'Do not move. Lie on the floor. Hands above head.'

Amelia begins to cry, and I am starting to feel very cross at them distressing her like this. I squint and see there are six men gathered here.

'You're upsetting my baby. You've made a mistake. I'm Leila Summers.'

They don't respond, nor do they lower their weapons. I think about going in my bag to get my passport out but decide against it as these dumb units have guns and would shoot an innocent woman.

Instead, I try to reason with them. 'Look, this is silly. I've got my baby here. I was just…'

But a man screams at me, 'We are going to move in and collect the child. Please put the child on the ground and stand back.'

Two men come towards me. They are pointing guns at me. There is no way out of this, so I place Amelia on the ground, because the last thing I want is for her to get hurt. One of the men lowers his gun and grabs the carrier.

Something inside me snaps. I am angrier than I have ever been. Why are they taking her from me?

'If you hurt her, I'll kill you. You're making a mistake here. I'm Leila Summers. That's my baby.'

The other man grabs my arm. I try to shake free, but I am shoved to the ground. My face hits dirt and my arms are pulled behind my back. The man who is holding me pushes down on me and, from the corner of my eyes, I see

Amelia lifted from the carrier and given to a blonde woman who is sitting in the back of a police car.

Leila. I start to laugh, and I can't stop. The police officer is pushing me into the ground still and I am laughing.

'Give it up, love. Do yourself a favour and stop struggling. It's over.'

But it isn't. In so many ways, this has only just started.

## Chapter Forty-One

### One Year Later...
### Sue

I walk into the corridor at the court building. My last memory of being here was with Erica on the day I found out about Tom and Katie, and Katie was set free. It's been difficult coming back here and being called as a witness. Nicola Green pleaded not guilty and the trial has lasted seven weeks.

Leila was also called as a witness, and that's how I met her in the witness waiting room, both of us ushered in through a back door by the police family liaison officer. She sat with her daughter, Heather, rocking her backwards and forwards in a stroller. Heather is such a cute baby. She's walking now and Leila is great with her. Seeing them together, it seems even crueller that Erica nearly deprived her of the chance to become a mother.

Being a mum is something I've had to reconfigure over the past year too, with it being only me much of the week.

It's been hard at times juggling being back at work and trying to help the boys adjust. Liam has been enjoying college and is busy with the new friends he's made. Dan and David stay over on a Wednesday night with Tom and a weekend day too. It's been strange living in an empty house sometimes, but it's starting to feel better now.

I see Karen and Ian arrive together and say hello as they walk past me in the corridor. The maternity department feels very different these days. I am back on the ward, delivering babies and leading the team. The hospital has had new security doors fitted. Not that they would have stopped Erica. I still think of her as Erica. I can't help it. But I know from Fliss that she is still insisting she is Leila Summers.

I didn't come to the trial apart from my day in the witness box, but I'm back here today for the sentencing. This trial has been everywhere and hard to escape. Journalists reporting from outside the court on my TV. All over the newspapers and hundreds of articles posted online. Over the past few weeks, every tiny detail of Nicola Green's life has been presented to the court. She refused to submit to a psychiatric report and now everything she has done stands as evidence.

Attending court every day would have been too much, but I read every single word that was published about Nicola Green. I've gone over it all. It's the only way I could understand. I needed an answer. I needed something deeper than guilty or not guilty. I needed to try to understand why.

I see Leila accompanied by Fliss. She is hurrying towards me, looking anxious.

I kiss her cheek and hug her. 'Are you all right?'

She is flushed. Of course she isn't all right. But she forces a smile. 'Yeah. Fliss is taking Heather to the café across the road.'

Leila kisses the little girl and watches as Fliss wheels her away. I know she doesn't like to let her out of her sight, which is understandable after what happened. And she's become good at fending for herself after turning away her ex, who tried to come back. She feels she and Heather are better off without him. I link her arm. We've become close since the trial, having that shared trauma.

'We'll know the verdict today. Hopefully this will be the closure we need to help us get on with the rest of our lives.'

She nods. 'It's just… I don't know. That woman that died. The real Erica. It almost was me. That she…'

I hear the panic in her voice. She's been seeing a therapist to help her try to process everything that's happened to her, and likely will be for a while. She has put her mum's house up for sale and is moving to the city so she can get a job. I hope this will be the new beginning she needs, as that house must be full of painful memories.

'But it wasn't. And we are here. Your counsellor was right. Seeing this today will reassure you. She's going to be sent to prison and you're safe now. Don't worry.'

We go into the public gallery where the ghost of the end of my relationship still lingers. I see a vision of Tom, ignoring me, intently watching Katie in the dock. The wheel of life turns, sometimes faster than you think it will. I've thought a lot about what happened.

But I am still here. Changed by what's happened, but still here. The first time the boys went to stay with Tom and Katie, I sat alone in my home. The journalists were gone from outside my house and even the neighbours had gone out. It felt strange. I realised I was usually never alone. I always found some way to be around people whether that was in a lively house or on the ward. It's not been easy seeing Katie and Tom together when I've dropped the boys off or if they're in photos the boys show me on their phones after a visit. But I've tried to use this time to get to know myself, because I've perhaps lost myself along the way. I've learned put myself first instead of hiding behind duty and family. Thinking about Erica – Nicola – and how she took on people's identities made me wonder who *I* really was.

Mum, midwife, colleague, friend. Wife, or ex-wife now because the divorce is finalised. I went for one of those no-blame arrangements and he signed it the same day. All those identities were for others. So, what about me? I had nothing at all for myself. Not even love.

But, since then, I've realised I do have something. I have someone who understands a little of what I have gone through. One of the first things I did when the dust had settled was phone Adam. I'd thought about it before, but it didn't seem like the right time, and I'm sure he needed his space to come to terms with what had happened. But friends are important and that's what we'd always been.

He'd suffered like I had, and I didn't want him to think I'd forgotten about him. I wanted him to know that I cared.

I was surprised he hadn't changed his number. When I'd called him, he answered straight away.

'Sue?'

His voice sounded different. Softer, somehow.

'Yeah. I just wanted to... if it's convenient?'

He paused. 'Course it is, love. How are you?'

I told him I was all right, which is what I'd started to tell people when they asked me. I wasn't really, but I didn't want to get into it and end up being upset.

'You know how it is. I just wanted to touch base.'

I heard him sigh. 'I do know how it is. I'm still at my mum's. But I've put down a deposit on a rental place. It's time for a new start.'

I wanted to ask him what was going to happen to the house he'd shared with Katie. The house she now shares with my ex-husband. Ex. It still sounds strange.

'That's good. I'm still... the kids. I won't have to sell up until they are out of college. Or uni. Unless I decide to.'

In that moment, I realised a sense of my own freedom. *If I decide to.* It's as if I can finally climb out of that hole I fell into the day Katie was arrested.

Adam sounded awkward and stilted. 'I've met someone. It's early days. We're not moving in or anything. Just dating.'

I smiled, glad to hear he'd hopefully found someone who made him happy which is what he deserved.

'That is brilliant. I'm made up for you, love.' I swallow hard. 'I don't think I'm ready to start thinking about that yet. But maybe one day.'

He paused again and when he spoke, his voice broke. 'It seemed like the end of the world, didn't it? It did for me, anyway. But it's not. It's not, Sue. It feels like it's always going to be dark and cloudy, but then one day, glimmers of sunshine start shining through, finding a way through the clouds. Little pinpricks.'

He's right. Little pinpricks. My kids. Becoming friends with Leila. Getting back to work, which I've fallen back in love with. I nodded into my phone. 'They'll get brighter. They will. I'm glad you're...'

He finished the sentence for me. '... coping. Yes. Coping. Keep in touch, Sue. I might see you around the hospital if I'm bringing someone into maternity.'

I choked back tears. 'Bye, Adam.'

He ended the call. Knowing that he was coming out of the other side of this gave me hope that, in time, I would too.

We have a choice. Life can either make us or break us. And, from reading the reports about the case, it seems like for Erica it was her childhood, heartbreak over her ex and her miscarriage that made something inside her snap.

But, while there might be an element of truth in that, it's not the whole story. Lots of people could have reasons to snap. I've gone through a lot lately, too. But I haven't had any twisted ideas of revenge or worse. I haven't coldly decided to lock someone in a cupboard and leave them to die.

It was also reported that Erica has been causing problems in the high security prison where she's being held prior to sentencing. One of the inmates leaked information that Nicola Green is not scared of the usual criminal bullies and has them held under some kind of juju spell that they will 'get what they deserve'. It's apparently enough to make her untouchable. And, because she hasn't used physical violence, there's nothing the prison warders can do about it.

Leila grips my hand as Nicola Green appears in the dock where Katie once sat. Her hair has grown and is blonde at the ends while darker roots have emerged. She is expressionless as the judge asks her to state her name.

Then she looks up at us. A smirk appears on her lips. 'Leila Summers.'

The judge looks at her counsel, who shrugs. There is a huddle around the judges' bench. The lawyers retreat and the judge looks at her.

'As your legal name is Nicola Green, we will deliver your sentence to you as Nicola Green. We acknowledge that you wish to be known as Leila Summers, but that is not your legal name.'

Leila is trembling. I whisper to her. 'It's OK. You're doing well. It's all going to be over.'

She is strong, and this will make her feel safer. And that is what I have realised about myself. At first, I berated myself for being self-sacrificing and not seeing the wood for the trees. The guilt over not seeing what Erica had done to those women. And the shame of not noticing my husband was in love with my closest friend.

But when I searched deeper and sat alone, I realised that there was something underneath it all. Something precious that I am only starting to understand. Something straightforward and pure that doesn't need a complicated plan or manipulation. No revenge or hate. It's really simple. I am a good person. Like everyone, I have a temper and, at times, I curse like a trooper. I shout and scream and disagree and argue. But, at the end of it all, I would never harm anyone intentionally.

And that is the difference between me and Nicola Green.

The usher asks us to stand and I squeeze Leila's hand.

The judge clears his throat. 'Nicola Green. As you know, the jury has already delivered its verdict of guilty on all charges. This is a sentencing hearing. For the offence of attempted murder on ten sample cases, I sentence you to four years in prison. For the offence of kidnapping and attempted murder of Leila Summers, I sentence you to ten years in prison. For the attempted murder of Jack Soames and Mary Soames, I sentence you to four years for each offence. For the offence of kidnapping Heather Summers, I sentence you to four years in prison. And for the murder of Erica Davies, I sentence you to life imprisonment, with a recommendation that no parole be given. These sentences will run concurrently.'

Nicola Green doesn't move or speak. She is staring straight ahead. I turn around and smile at Mary and Jack who are sitting behind us. They have been amazing. She poisoned their milk. Mary nearly died. A living testament that Erica isn't as clever as she thought she was – thankfully she got the dosing wrong. I feel Leila exhale beside me, the heavy weight of the last few months lifted now she knows that Nicola is going to live the rest of her days behind bars.

The warders lead her away, but she glances over her shoulder to look back at us. There is not the slightest hint of remorse for her actions. She is a product of her life, like all of us, but what makes her bad is her refusal to accept responsibility for anything she has done. Her lack of empathy for anyone else at all. And most of all, her ability to harm others.

I look at Leila. 'Come on. Let's get a cup of tea so you can gather yourself before you get Heather,' I suggest.

As Nicola disappears through the doorway, I spot Katie on the other side of the public gallery. She nods at me. Because she now works in another hospital in the ante-natal clinic, and I always wait in the car when I drop the boys off, I never speak to her. That is one relationship beyond repair. No doubt we're both a little more damaged, a little more jaded. A little wiser to what this world is capable of.

But we will carry on caring for people, regardless. Because we took an oath as midwives, which I will always honour and feel even more strongly protective of now.

Do no harm.

## Acknowledgements

Writing this book was both a thrilling and unnerving experience. I set out to craft a psychological novel that would keep readers on the edge of their seats, while also reflecting the strength and solidarity women share. I hope I've achieved both.

Much of the research for this book came from delving into psychology textbooks and speaking with professionals about psychopathy. I remain both fascinated and horrified by the subject, and the stories of psychopathological women I encountered in my research will stay with me for a long time.

I want to extend my gratitude to the NHS for their incredible work, and to the midwives who graciously answered my many questions. My deepest thanks go to my brilliant editor, Daisy Watt, for her invaluable insight, and to the entire team at HarperNorth for their belief in this book. Meeting you all has been a true pleasure.

As always, I'm indebted to my agent, Judith Murray, for her wisdom and support. A huge thank you to my writing community – too many to name individually, but you know who you are – who have listened to me endlessly talk about my characters and their lives. Special thanks to Phaedra Patrick for our Tapas Tuesdays and endless encouragement, and to the incredible members of the London Writing Salon's Manchester Chapter for their constant support and talent. I'm also so grateful to Sue Lees for her laughter and company, and to Karen Schofield for being a constant source of joy in my life.

To my family, thank you for your patience throughout my writing process, especially during those long stretches when I'm entirely absorbed in my work and seem to disappear for weeks on end.

Lastly, I'm eternally grateful to the man who not only shares his time with me but also with my characters, and still manages to smile when I mention them – after all these years. Thank you, my love, for the endless cups of tea and words of encouragement. I couldn't have done this without you.

## About the Author

Anna Schofield is an Amazon Top 100 bestselling author and a short story and screenplay writer. From Ashton-Under-Lyne, she spent five years travelling and working in Greece, then returned home to work in healthcare, and runs online storytelling and change workshops.

She lives with her partner and their rescue dogs and enjoys cooking and walking when she isn't writing.